Readers love
RICK R. REED

I Heart Boston Terriers

"…this is a great short story, full of promise for the future, and it's sweet and light and a good mood-picker-upper."

—Hearts on Fire Reviews

M4M

"*M4M* is a poignant, thought provoking read…"

—Love Bytes

"As always, Reed combines story-telling with the human experience and I would highly recommend *M4M*."

—Joyfully Jay

The Perils of Intimacy

"I was rooting for these guys every step of the way. Another fantastic story from Rick Reed!"

—The Novel Approach

By RICK R. REED

Bashed
Big Love
Blink
Caregiver
Chaser • Raining Men
The Couple Next Door
A Dangerous Game
Dinner at Fiorello's
Dinner at Jack's
Dinner at Home
Dinner at the Blue Moon Café
With Vivien Dean: Family Obligations
Homecoming
Hungry for Love
Husband Hunters
I Heart Boston Terriers
Legally Wed
Lost and Found
M4M
An Open Window
The Perils of Intimacy
Simmer (Dreamspinner Anthology)
Sky Full of Mysteries
Tricks

DREAMSPUN DESIRES
With Vivien Dean: #15 – Stranded with Desire

Published by DREAMSPINNER PRESS
www.dreamspinnerpress.com

SKY FULL
OF
MYSTERIES
RICK R. REED

DREAMSPINNER
PRESS

Published by

DREAMSPINNER PRESS

5032 Capital Circle SW, Suite 2, PMB# 279, Tallahassee, FL 32305-7886 USA
www.dreamspinnerpress.com

Sky Full of Mysteries
© 2018 Rick R. Reed.

Cover Art
© 2018 Reese Dante.
http://www.reesedante.com
Cover content is for illustrative purposes only and any person depicted on the cover is a model.

Trade Paperback ISBN: 978-1-64108-113-9
Digital ISBN: 978-1-64080-158-5
Library of Congress Control Number: 2017915317
Trade Paperback published August 2018
v. 1.0

Printed in the United States of America

This paper meets the requirements of
ANSI/NISO Z39.48-1992 (Permanence of Paper).

For Lynn West, whose excitement about the concept for this story spurred me on. I hope the end result doesn't disappoint you!

The true mystery of the world is the visible, not the invisible.
—*Oscar Wilde*

Stars, too, were time travelers. How many of those ancient points of light were the last echoes of suns now dead? How many had been born but their light not yet come this far? If all the suns but ours collapsed tonight, how many lifetimes would it take us to realize we were alone? I had always known the sky was full of mysteries—but not until now had I realized how full of them the earth was.
—*Miss Peregrine's Home for Peculiar Children*

The presence of ghosts is only as close as your belief. The existence of aliens is only as far as your rejection.
—*Toba Beta, My Ancestor Was an Ancient Astronaut*

A philosopher once asked, "Are we human because we gaze at the stars, or do we gaze at them because we are human?" Pointless, really.
"Do the stars gaze back?" Now, that's a question.
—*Neil Gaiman, Stardust*

PART ONE
1997

CHAPTER 1

AFTER THEY made love, they were polar opposites in how they reacted.

Cole, barely minutes after coming, would be asleep, mouth open and snoring, body lax. A baby who'd just been fed. Rory looked down on him as he sat perched with his back against the headboard. Despite—or maybe because of—the spittle that ran out of one side of Cole's mouth, he felt a shock of warmth go through him as he gazed at Cole, wondering how he'd gotten so lucky. Although Rory was a few years younger, he was a nerd with glasses. He wasn't bad-looking; he just wasn't all that noticeable in a crowd. How had he snared a guy like Cole, with his perfect runner's build, his dark brown wavy hair, and the perpetual five-o'clock shadow that accentuated, rather than hid, the angular planes of his face and his sharp jawline. Rory snickered in the darkness at Cole as a snore erupted from him, almost loud enough to shake the glass in their bedroom window.

It was always like this—maniac in the sack until he came, and then it was lights out for Cole, as though he'd been drugged.

Rory, on the other hand, always felt energized, pumped up, alive, as if he should hop from the bed, go outside, and run a mile or three. Or make a meal. Or write the great American novel. Or catalog his collection of books alphabetically, and then by genre.

Tonight was no different. They'd just moved into the one-bedroom apartment in Chicago's Rogers Park neighborhood. The neighborhood, the Windy City's farthest east and north before heading into suburbia, afforded them a chance to live by Lake Michigan without the higher rents they'd encounter closer to downtown.

They were young and in love, and cohabitating was a first for both of them. Rory felt they were already having their happy-ever-after moment.

The apartment was a find—a vintage courtyard building east of Sheridan Road on Fargo Avenue. Their unit's bedroom faced Lake Michigan, which was only a few steps away from their front door. A lake view, high ceilings, crown molding, formal dining room with a built-in hutch, huge living room with working fireplace, and an original bathroom with an enormous claw-foot tub were just a few of the amenities they were delighted to find—all for the "steal" monthly rent of only five hundred dollars.

The apartment, which would eventually be filled to bursting with a hodgepodge of furniture and belongings, ranging from family antiques supplied by Cole to *Lost in Space* action figures from Rory, was now a scene of chaos with moving boxes everywhere, almost none of them unpacked.

They'd spent the whole day moving and were exhausted when they were finished. Even though it was August, by the time they were done dragging the boxes out of their U-Haul truck, through their building's courtyard, and then up to the tenth floor via the rickety but thank-heaven-reliable elevator, the skies above the lake had gone dark. They ordered stuffed spinach pizza from Giordano's, just south of them on Sheridan, and feasted on it, melted mozzarella on their chins, on a couple of beach towels they found at the top of one of the boxes.

And of course, Rory being twenty-three and Cole twenty-six, with their blossoming love all of six months old, they did find the time and the energy to make love, once on the beach towels and once in their bed. Rory knew there'd be more of the same come morning's first light.

Ah, sweet youth.

But getting back to postcoital bliss, Rory now found himself feeling restless as he lay beside the snoring Cole. The moon was nearly full and they'd yet to put up blinds, so it shone in the bedroom window, casting the room in a kind of silvery opalescence. Rory thought the boxes and the furniture—Cole's oak sleigh bed and Rory's pair of maple tallboy dressers, plus an overstuffed chair they'd found in an alley just before moving—all had a kind of grayish aspect to them, almost unreal, as if he were observing his own bedroom as a scene from a black-and-white movie. Maybe something noir… with Barbara Stanwyck and Fred MacMurray. Rory smiled and turned away from Cole. Just a half hour or so earlier, with the overhead light fixture shining down on them, Rory thought the movie would have been a porno, with himself cast as the insatiable bottom.

He chuckled to himself.

He tried to relax, doing an old exercise he'd learned from his mom. Starting with his feet, he'd wiggle, tense, and then allow that body part to go slack to relax. He worked his way up his whole body, wiggling, tensing, and relaxing as he went, until he reached his head.

And—sigh—he was still wide-awake.

Behind him, though, as if he had eyes in the back of his head, he noticed something odd.

It was like there was suddenly a waxing and waning of light.

Rory turned and looked toward the uncovered window. He couldn't quite see the moon, but it seemed like it was brightening and darkening, brightening, then darkening….

But the whole of this August day, it had been clear, with nary a cloud in the sky. Rory wondered if a cloud bank had moved in, obscuring the moon and then revealing it as the wind pushed it away. He could see this in his mind's eye but couldn't quite believe it.

The light was simply too brilliant. At its brightest, the whole room lit up, as though he'd switched on the overhead fixture. Rory was surprised Cole didn't awaken. Or maybe he wasn't so surprised after all. Rory had spent enough nights with his "great dark man" to know his slumber habits. When Cole drifted off, which he did effortlessly and with amazing speed, there was little that would wake him. Rory thought they could have a New Orleans jazz band march through their bedroom and all Cole would do, at most, was maybe turn over… or snort a little.

He lightly kissed Cole's cheek, undeterred by the scratch of Cole's scruff, and slid from the bed to peer out the window.

The lake was a great black expanse. The sky was only a few shades lighter than the water below it, with a slight yellowish tinge due to all the city lights. And the moon, just shy of full, shimmered, a lovely yellow-gold, completely unobscured by clouds. If Rory squinted just right, he thought he could just about make out a face in the surface of that moon….

The sky simply had no clouds to offer that night.

Rory stepped back from the window and glanced back at his slumbering man. *So why was the light getting brighter and then darker?* He turned to the window and peered outside again. If not for the city's light pollution, he was certain he'd see entire constellations of stars. He allowed his eyes to adjust a bit and saw more detail below, along Fargo beach. The water was not exactly black, after all. The waves, small and unimpressive due to the lack of wind, still managed to toss up a few whitecaps, especially near the shore, which looked grayer in the darkness. The beach, and the island of boulders just a few laps beyond it, took on more definition, enough that it made Rory come to a decision.

If he couldn't sleep, he might as well take the opportunity to go outside, enjoy the warm breezes and what appeared to be a deserted beachfront.

He dressed quickly and silently—even though he knew he needn't have bothered since Cole was beyond waking—in a pair of cutoffs and a Doctor Who T-shirt. He slid his feet into flip-flops, grabbed his keys off the dresser, and headed for the front door.

Other than the steady *whoosh* of traffic on Sheridan Road to the west, the night was quiet. Rory wished he'd checked the time before heading out, but judging from the silence all around him, he'd guess it was the wee small hours of the morning, maybe 2:00 or 3:00 a.m. This was Chicago, after all. There was usually someone stumbling around, even in blackest night.

But his street was empty. The tree branches and their leaves cast shadows on the silvery pavement beneath his feet because of the moon's brightness. His footsteps, even in flip-flops, sounded extra loud as he headed east, toward the beach.

At the end of the street, there was a cul-de-sac where cars could turn around, and beyond that, a set of stone steps that led down to the sand. Rory stood at the top of the steps, looking out at the sand and water, the pile of boulders just offshore that Cole promised he'd swim out to the next day with Rory. A white lifeguard chair, empty, sat crookedly in the sand, leaning as it sunk to the left. The moon shone brilliantly on the water, laying a swath of golden light upon its gently undulating surface. If Rory looked at this light just right, perhaps squinting a bit behind his glasses, he could almost imagine the light rising up, like an illuminated fountain, from the water's surface.

He took the steps quickly and was on the sand in seconds. He kicked off his flip-flops and sighed when he felt the cool sand squishing up between his toes. He looked around once more, paying particular attention to the concrete that bordered the beach, to assure himself he had the gift of a city beach all to himself.

And he did. He did!

He tore off his shirt, set it down, and then removed his glasses, placing them on top of the T-shirt. With a little cry, he dashed toward the water, a small laugh escaping his lips. He stopped briefly at its edge, gasping at the icy cold of the waves, even this late in the summer, as they ran up to meet him, lapping and biting at his toes. And then he took a deep breath, waded in up to his knees, and paused to consider if he really wanted to go whole hog.

What the hell.

He waded in a little farther, until the bottom dropped out from under him suddenly and instead of the water reaching to the top of his thighs, hit him just above his belly button. It was freezing! And Rory knew there was only one solution: get full immersion over as quickly as possible.

He raised his hands over his head and dove as a wave rolled in toward him. The world went silent as he went under, the murky depths of the water almost black. He held his breath as long as he could, swimming outward. His mother's voice erupted in his head, scolding, telling him to go back to shore because it was late and there was no one around. What if he, God forbid, got a cramp?

Rory shushed his mother and continued to swim toward Michigan or whatever was directly opposite, hundreds of miles away. He swam until he felt his lungs would burst.

And then he surfaced, shaking the water from his hair. The first thing he noticed was how full immersion had done the trick—he wasn't exactly warm, but the water temperature was at least bearable.

The second was the light on the water. It had changed to a strange pale radiance, a shifting, silvery opalescence that, in addition to his recent underwater swimming, left him nearly breathless.

He trod water and hazarded a glimpse up at the sky, expecting to see the moon and perhaps that bank of clouds that had managed to elude him earlier.

But the moon was gone. Or at least hidden.

Is this real?

Rory couldn't believe what he was seeing. He actually slipped under for a helpless moment because both his arms and feet stopped moving. He came back up quickly, sputtering and spitting out lake water, gaze fixed on the sky.

"What the fuck?" he whispered.

Was what he saw natural? Like, as in a natural phenomenon? What was above him appeared like some membrane, formed from smoky gray clouds, but alive. It rose up, mountainous, into the night sky. As he peered closer at the form, it seemed to almost breathe, to expand in and out. And within the gray smoke or fog, figures seemed to be spinning. They were black and amorphous, like shadows brought to life. The fact that the cloud—or whatever it was—cast an otherworldly silvery light from below didn't make the figures any more distinctive.

This can't be real. I'm back at the apartment right now, sound asleep next to Cole. That pizza really did a number on me. Rory knew his notions were simply wishful thinking.

The membrane or cloud or whatever one wanted to call it was as real as the moon had been above him.

The black figures, spinning, began, one by one, to drop. They were too far distant for Rory to hear any splashes, but he could plainly see that some of them were disconnecting from the membrane or cloud or whatever one wanted to call it and plopping down into the placid surface of Lake Michigan.

Because of its immensity, Rory was unable to determine if the thing above him was close by or distant. It could have been hovering directly overhead. Or it might have been as far away as downtown or even the western edge of Indiana. Perhaps it was some industrial disaster thrown up by the city of Gary? Perhaps it was a military experiment, a new kind of aircraft?

And of course Rory, ever the science fiction geek, came to the last supposition almost reluctantly, because it terrified him—perhaps it was some sort of alien vessel, a UFO in everyday parlance. The kind of thing Rory had both dreaded and hoped to bear witness to almost all of his young life.

He stared at it in wonder, lost for a moment in time. He hoped he'd gain more clarity on what the thing was, but the longer he stared, the more confusing it became. Was it some freak of nature? Some hitherto unseen cloud formation? Was it really a spaceship beyond his or anyone's wildest imagination?

Whatever it was, he was certain it was warming the water around him, which led him to the conclusion that it must have some powerful energy to heat up a body of water as large as Lake Michigan. What had been cold, now felt almost as warm as bathwater.

And that scared Rory just as much as this monstrously huge thing in the sky above him. What if the water continued to heat up? What if it reached the boiling point and he was poached alive in it?

What if the black, shadowy beings he witnessed spinning within the mist meant him harm as they dropped from the cloud? What if they were, right now, swimming toward him, all bulbous heads and soulless gray eyes?

He shuddered in spite of the warmth of the water around him. He leveled himself out, lowered his face to the water, and began the fastest crawl he could manage toward shore, which suddenly seemed impossibly far away.

And a new fear seized him as he paddled, panting, through the dark water—what if something as prosaic as drowning claimed him? Would they ever find him?

What would Cole do when he woke at last, to find himself in bed and alone? What would he do as the sun rose, lighting up their little love nest, and there was no Rory?

Rory didn't want to see the thing anymore. Just looking at it induced in him a feeling of dread so powerful, it nauseated him. So he kept his face in the water, only turning his head to the side every few strokes to grab a breath of air, until he neared the shore. He squatted low, panting hard, in the shallows and at last hazarded a glance up at the sky.

It was empty.

Save for a muted orange glow from light pollution and the moon, now distant, there was nothing in the sky. Rory crawled from the water and plopped down on the damp sand at the lake's edge.

Had it simply been a hallucination? Or maybe there *had* been a cloud bank, a thunderhead maybe, and his sci-fi geek's mind had transformed it into something much more wondrous? And much more threatening?

He shivered and rubbed his hands up and down his bare arms to warm himself. After a while, when he felt he was ready, he stood on shaky legs, the comparison to a newly born colt not lost on him, and staggered over to where he'd left his T-shirt and glasses. He yanked the tee over his head and put the glasses—chunky horn-rims—onto his face. He'd been wearing glasses since he was five years old. It felt more natural with them on than without.

It crossed his mind for half a second that his blurry vision had been a contributor to what he'd seen—or not seen; he was already doubting himself—but even with the glasses restoring his vision to twenty-twenty, the view of the sky above remained placid, dark, unremarkable.

He scanned the horizon for a while, still looking for something he'd lost, but saw nothing new other than an industrial ship way out there, at the very edge of what Rory imagined was the world.

Perhaps the ship would topple off the edge and into the mouth of a waiting giant membrane that looked something like a cloud with lights and spinning figures inside?

Rory thought he should laugh at the notion but couldn't quite bring himself to. He walked slowly across the sand. It wasn't until he got halfway up the steps to the street that he realized he'd left his flip-flops on the beach.

He hurried back to claim them. As he was stooping over to grab them, he noticed a dog running toward him. It was a black Labrador, or something like it, because it appeared as if it was some kind of charging shadow.

It rushed by him without slowing to sniff or in any way regard him. "Hey!" Rory called after the animal, which ignored him. Rory looked around to see if there was a frazzled owner, leash in hand, running after the dog, but the beach was empty.

When he looked back, the dog was gone.

Could it have been one of the dark figures that dropped from the cloud?

Rory froze at the middle of the stairs. The thought chilled him. The whole idea of his sanity suddenly came into question.

He hurried up the rest of the stairs and headed back toward his apartment. He hoped Cole hadn't awakened and gone looking for him.

As he neared the courtyard of the building, he decided, unless he couldn't avoid it, he would keep this whole weird episode to himself.

As he headed for his front door, he thought things would look better, more rational, in the light of day.

Right?

Chapter 2

And they did—look better. Or at least things looked more like a dream, something weird that could only happen alone very late at night, having none of the earmarks of reality.

Not really.

When Rory got back to the apartment, he undressed quickly and slid into bed beside Cole, who was snoring like a truck driver after a long haul. His snores were almost musical, rhythmic, punctuated every so often by a gasp. As Rory slid into bed beside him, Cole mumbled something in his sleep that sounded like "What's the frequency?" but Rory knew that couldn't have been what he said. Rory's mind was playing weird tricks on him.

He lay still for a long while, knowing he wouldn't sleep. Gray light started to seep into the room, and the sounds outside—birds singing, more traffic on Sheridan—also began to filter in.

Rory thought he could never fall back asleep, not after what happened at the beach, but he did.

When he awoke, bright sunlight streamed into the room, making dust motes dance in the beams. He looked over to see Cole, on one elbow, staring down at him. "We have to get something to throw over that window, or else we'll never be able to sleep in on the weekends."

"What?" Rory rubbed his eyes, got up on his own elbows.

"Curtains, blinds, a sheet, *something*. It's only a little after six, for Christ's sake." Cole lay back down, huffing. "I'm still tired, but I feel like I'm being interrogated or something." He laughed, but there was a sense of bitterness behind it.

"Want me to do something?" Rory cast his gaze around the bedroom. The beach towels they'd picnicked on the night before were in a ball in a corner of the room. Maybe he could jury-rig a way to cover the window with them?

"Yeah. Take care of this." And Cole flung back the sheet to reveal his erection standing proudly, a steel girder pointing up at his belly button.

The sight, with the butter-yellow sunlight streaming in on it, made Rory gasp with delight. He'd never seen anything more beautiful. He got immediately to his knees, positioning his lips just above Cole's dick and went down on him.

Cole groaned, and Rory stopped for a moment to look up and ask, "Better?"

"Well, it doesn't do anything about the sun, but it does tend to make one forget it." He thrust into Rory's mouth while at the same time gathering up a handful of Rory's hair. It wasn't long before Rory was enjoying his first protein-packed smoothie of the day.

It went a long way toward making him forget the weirdness of the night before.

After they'd both come, and in spite of the bright sunlight, they fell asleep again in each other's arms, come on Rory's chest sealing them together.

Rory didn't wake until well after noon. He was alone in bed but smiled anyway. The smells of coffee and frying bacon wafted in from the kitchen. Were there two more heavenly morning smells?

How had he gotten so lucky? Not only had Cole obviously begun unpacking the kitchen, he was cooking, something he did very, very well. At the start of their relationship, Cole had told him he could be good in either one room or the other—the kitchen or the bedroom. But not both.

Rory was torn and had never voiced a preference. He didn't have to. His man was equally good in each. How could Rory *not* love him like there was no tomorrow?

He sat up, back against the headboard, and peered out at the glaring brilliance of the sun. It looked like they were in for another day of blue skies and high temperatures. "Hot enough to fry an egg on the sidewalk" was what his grandma used to say.

A perfect day for the beach.

The last thought chilled him as an image of the cloud thing popped into his imagination, unbidden.

Cole must have pulled out his portable radio from one of the boxes, because suddenly the Spice Girls started singing, "2 Become 1." It was kind of sweet—and timely. Rory lay back a bit on the pillows, throwing the sheet off him. At least it wasn't Will Smith's "Men in Black," which seemed to be playing everywhere this summer. That would just be too weird.

He yawned and got up. He slid into his shorts from the previous night, knowing they'd continue to get sand everywhere, and padded toward the kitchen, making a brief detour at the bathroom to relieve himself.

When he got to the kitchen, he paused at the sight of chaos and loveliness that greeted him. Boxes were open everywhere on the small kitchen's black-and-white tile floor. Strewn about that same floor and crowding the countertops were a toaster, measuring cups, mixing bowls, tea towels, an apron proclaiming "Kiss the Cock," and, weirdly, Rory's black interview suit, thrown over the back of a chair.

The window over the sink was open, and the smell of lake-scented air, with a slight fishy tang, wafted in, beneath the more wonderful smells of Cole's cooking.

Cole himself was at the stove, totally unaware of being watched. He wore only a pair of tighty-whities. His broad well-muscled back, dusted with brown freckles at the shoulders, and his powerful legs were causing Rory's mouth to water as much as the bacon and coffee.

"When did you find the time to do all this?" Rory asked, by way of announcing his presence.

Cole jumped a little and turned to him, fork in hand. "You were out, buddy. Like a log!" He chuckled. "I was hungry when I woke up, so thought there was no time like the present to do a little unpacking." He turned back to the stove, and Rory could discern from his movements he was flipping the sizzling bacon. Over his shoulder Cole asked, "How do you want your eggs? Scrambled would be easiest. But I can do anything at all for you, my love. Even over easy if I'm in the right mood."

Rory snickered. "I have a funny feeling you're not talking about eggs."

"Ah, you're just saying that to get in my shorts."

"Nah, I don't have to work that hard. Scrambled it is. You make the best."

Rory laughed as Cole moved to the refrigerator and pulled out a carton of eggs, along with a pitcher of orange juice. "Wow," Rory marveled. "You *have* been busy. Go to the store too?"

"Yeah, there's a little convenience store around the corner on Sheridan. Prices are outrageous, but it'll come in handy, I'm sure. You know, when we have midnight Brown Sugar Cinnamon Pop-Tarts attacks."

"Right." Rory plucked his suit off the back of one of the two ladder-back chairs and took it into the bedroom, where he hung it in the closet. When he returned, he sat down on the same chair as Cole whisked.

"I was hoping they'd have some chives or something, but no such luck," Cole said.

"Oh, don't worry about it. This is way more than I expected anyway. I'm surprised I didn't wake up with all you had going on."

"As I said, you were *zonked*."

Just as Rory spied a loaf of wheat bread on the counter, Cole asked if he wanted toast. "Sure. Can I do anything?"

"You can just stay put and keep me company. We have a lot to do today, mister! You're gonna need your energy. Besides, I want to squeeze in at least a little time to get out to the beach."

Mention of the beach sent a little chill through Rory, despite the heat of the kitchen. The morning routine seemed so normal, it had almost made him forget what occurred out there the night before.

He wondered if he ever could forget it.

A COUPLE of weeks passed. It was still hot, and the promise of autumn, right then, anyway, appeared to be much the same as a promise a crooked politician would make—sounding good, sounding possible, but never to be delivered on.

Rory had just come in from his job downtown, where he worked in the IT department of a large insurance company. The work was mind-numbingly boring, involving installing and maintaining software on the company's hundreds of computers. There was no challenge and no excitement. Still, the job had good benefits, paid him a decent salary, and he never had to work overtime. And he was right in the heart of the Loop, on Wabash, and his "L" train commute was easy.

Someday he'd find something more interesting. But right then, life at home with Cole was all he needed.

He threw down his messenger bag by the secretary desk at the front door and surveyed their home. Rory's almost obsessive-compulsive personality had ensured the place was now completely unpacked and truly looking as though the two of them had lived there for two years instead of a mere two weeks.

Rugs were laid. Pictures were hung. Books and CDs were shelved and, at least for the moment, alphabetized. The television and stereo system were all set up, the audio patched in by Rory to the TV so they had stereo sound. In the kitchen, everything was in its place.

Place mats on the dining room table. Cole's mom's good china in the built-in hutch. In the bedroom, the dark blue comforter was a nice contrast to the quilted gold throw at the foot of the bed. Cole's boyhood stuffed monkey, Charlie, even lounged among the throw pillows at the head of the bed.

There was really nothing for Rory to do until Cole got home.

Well, that wasn't quite true. Guiltily, he thought he *could* go into the kitchen and rattle some pots and pans, at least make an effort to come up with something edible for dinner, but he sorely lacked any talents in that department.

He scolded himself and knew he was just making excuses. Cole always told him there was nothing to cooking, not if you kept it simple, and that people who said they were hopeless at it, like Rory, simply didn't like doing it.

He did make a quick tour of their small kitchen, opening and closing the fridge, peering into the pantry and a couple of cupboards, before deciding he had no idea what he could manage to make out of what they had on hand.

He ignored the voice that told him there were dozens of possibilities— spaghetti and meatballs, roast chicken, pork chops, a big salad, even a frozen pizza from Jewel—so he could do what he really wanted: sit down at the dining room table, where their desktop computer was set up, and pick up on his game of *Warcraft*. He could get lost in it, which was exactly what he wanted—it made the time pass so much more quickly while he waited for Cole to come home from his job in the suburb just north of them, Evanston, where he worked at the Pier One store downtown as a clerk. Rory tried not to think what he always did about Cole and suitable employment—that he could do better.

Rory lost himself in his game, and before he knew it, two hours had gone by. He leaned back in his chair so he could see the wall clock on the soffit above the kitchen sink and saw that it was already six thirty. It was Monday, so that meant Cole would work until seven. Maybe Rory should show the guy some mercy and at least order a pizza—for the second night in a row.

He shook his head and went back to his game, lost once more until the wall phone in the kitchen rang. He paused the game and hurried to answer.

"Hey." It was Cole.

"Hey. Everything okay? I was just thinking about ordering some pizza, or maybe Italian from Leona's?"

Cole sighed. "Do whatever you want for dinner."

"Oh?"

"Yeah. I forgot they want me to stay late for inventory tonight."

"I don't even know what that means," Rory, who'd never worked retail, said.

"And you don't want to." Cole said nothing for a minute and then, "So I probably won't be getting home until after ten, maybe not even until eleven. So feel free to order in, play your games, watch something on TV I wouldn't like, like *Doctor Who*...." He trailed off as he laughed. When it came to entertainment, Cole was an out-and-proud chick-flick movie lover—he'd never met a romantic comedy he didn't like and could tear up at the drop of a hat.

"I'll miss you," Rory said. And he really would. They were still so new to one another that time apart truly was agony. The prospect of spending the evening alone wasn't a welcome one. Maybe he should pay a long overdue visit to his mom and dad in Wilmette tonight? He shrugged. At least they'd feed him and he wouldn't be by himself.

"I'll miss you too, buddy. But it won't be long and I'll be sliding under the sheets next to you." He whispered the word "naked," and Rory immediately got hard.

"Okay, okay. I guess I have that to look forward to. I might hop on the train and go see Mom and Dad. They've been bugging me to visit. I think the last time I saw them was when we went to their house for that Fourth of July cookout. My mom's going through withdrawal." Rory laughed.

"That sounds like a good idea. Give me a buzz when you leave there. Maybe you can meet me on the platform at Davis Street and we can ride home together."

"That would be great. If I go, I'll definitely do that."

"Listen, they're calling me, so I gotta cut this short. I'll see you in a little while. Try not to miss me too much."

"Impossible." Rory wanted to tell Cole that he loved him, but he'd already hung up.

While he had the phone in his hand, Rory punched in the number he knew by heart—that of his parents.

His mom answered on the second ring.

"Hey, Mom!"

"Um, who is this?"

"Oh, cut it out," Rory said. His mother had the worst cornball sense of humor ever. "What are you and Dad up to?"

"Right now?"

"No, in the year 2016."

"Oh, sweetie, we'll probably both be dead by then. Cancer. It's all the rage."

"You're not gonna get cancer," Rory chided. "So, are you guys doing anything special tonight? Cole has to work overtime at the store, and I thought I might come up and pay the parental units a visit."

"You mean see if you could cadge a free meal?"

"Well, yeah, that too. Especially if you're making your famous meatloaf." Rory wasn't kidding. His mom made the best meatloaf in the world—she said the secret was in the finely chopped mushrooms she used.

"Oh, honey, I hate to say this, but your father and I won't be here tonight."

"Come on! It's a Monday night. Where would you be?" Rory laughed. Sometimes his mom's sense of humor didn't even make sense.

"You know, we do have a life…."

"Since when?"

"Rory, my dear, you're bordering on the disrespectful."

This time Rory was smart enough to know his mom wasn't kidding around, and it was true—he had crossed a line. "Sorry, Mom. What are you guys up to?"

As if to prove the truth, his dad called in the background for her to "Get a move on."

"Your father and I have a little date night on Mondays. We've been doing it for a while, which you'd know if you were ever around anymore. Tonight we're going to dinner in Evanston at the Lucky Platter and then going to see *The Full Monty*."

Rory had to laugh, and then grimace at the thought of his mother seeing such a film. He knew at heart he was a worse prude than his own parents. "You know what the full monty is, don't you, Mom?"

"Not sure, but I'm looking forward to finding out!" She giggled and sounded a lot younger than her years. Rory was certain she knew exactly what it was and shuddered to think maybe his dad was taking her to see the full monty in a movie theater so he could show her his own when they got home. "I need to go, sweetie. Maybe you could come by tomorrow night?"

Rory couldn't help but feel disappointed. Tomorrow was Cole's night off, and they'd planned their own date night—at home, just the way Rory liked it. "I'll talk to Cole. He's off tomorrow."

He wished he hadn't admitted that.

"Well then, perfect!" his mother chirped. "I'll expect you two at six. And yes, I will make my meatloaf, with mashed potatoes and creamed corn."

Rory pictured himself at the parental table, wearing a bib.

"Okay, can we bring anything?"

His mother thought for a moment and then said, "See if you can get Cole to make us a batch of his chocolate chip cookies. You know how much your father loves them. I do too!"

His father yelled, "Greta!"

"I've got to go." And without even a goodbye, his mom hung up.

Rory sat down on the little stepstool they'd positioned under the kitchen wall phone and wondered what to do with himself for the night. He knew he could easily play *Warcraft* until the wee hours of the morning. Cole was amazed at how Rory lost himself in what he referred to as a "stupid video game."

In a way, he knew Cole was right. His gaming *could* sometimes border on the obsessive-compulsive.

Maybe see what was on TV? He went into the living room, grabbed the remote off the coffee table. Sprawled on the couch, he aimed it at the TV and powered it up. He sighed. *America's Funniest Home Videos* (lame), *Suddenly Susan* (lamer), or *Melrose Place* (Cole loved it; he should tape it for him). He switched the TV off within minutes of looking at the onscreen cable guide. He could pull out one of their videos and watch something. But he shook his head. He didn't really feel like being so passive—and he knew it.

He got up from the couch and looked out the window. The sky was getting darker, a mix of smoky gray and violet at the moment. He knew other gay men his age would probably use this free time as an opportunity to go out, to head down to the bars on Halsted, even if it were just to innocently watch videos at Sidetrack. And he knew Cole wouldn't mind if he did that, but Rory had never had much interest in bars. He'd met Cole at the gym. And Rory didn't much like the taste of alcohol anyway. Cole called him a lightweight. And Cole was right.

Rory preferred his own company. Whenever he was dragged to a gay bar, he felt like he didn't fit in, as though it were peopled with exclusive club members who all knew some secret word he wasn't privy to. Despite sharing the same sexual orientation, Rory could never be one of them.

Alone was good. He really didn't mind it. Really.

So solitude would be just what he would treat himself to for the night.

He'd take a walk along the lakefront, appreciating the relatively clean air and the soothing sound of the waves, and head south—see where it brought him. When the mood struck, probably somewhere around the Edgewater neighborhood, he'd head west, find a place to eat dinner on Clark or Broadway. Rory had never minded eating alone, especially if he had a book.

Which reminded him. He got up and went into the bedroom, where he snatched his current read, Stephen King's *Desperation*, off the nightstand. He was finally getting around to reading it.

After checking his back pocket for his wallet and his front pocket for his keys, Rory headed out for his own little night on the town. Maybe there'd be cheeseburgers involved. Moody's Pub on Broadway?

Once outside, Rory headed toward the beach. The nice thing about where they lived was that he could walk practically all the way downtown if he chose to without ever losing sight of the changing waters of Lake Michigan.

Sheridan Road, behind him, was still alive with late rush-hour traffic. Buses spewed exhaust into the air, the hiss of their pneumatic doors a constant. Horns blared. A siren did its Doppler thing as it raced north or south on the busy thoroughfare. Distant conversations rose up as pedestrians made their way home from work.

Rory felt grateful he was headed toward the lakefront. He felt a sense of liberation. As he descended the steps down to the beach, he noticed an immediate lowering of the urban soundtrack just a couple of blocks west of him. Here, on the sand, it was quieter, peaceful. Lazily, the surf rushed to shore.

Rory sat down on the bottom step and watched as the last of dusk's tepid light faded into complete darkness. Tonight there was no moon. There were a few clouds in the sky—cirrus, stretched out like long strands of cotton candy, gray against the inky dark of the sky.

He remembered what he'd borne witness to here a couple of weeks ago. He kicked at some sand. Had he really seen anything? Wasn't it just a bank of clouds his overactive imagination had transformed into something more? Rory shrugged, looking south as the sound of laughter came from that direction. There was a young couple, a boy and a girl, kicking their way through the water at the shore's edge, holding hands.

His imagination played tricks—that's what he told himself—and he'd told himself enough times that at this point he pretty much believed his own self-delusion. Except not really. In his mind, maybe, he could fall for the lie. But in his heart, he knew he'd seen something strange and otherworldly.

He got up and began walking south, a part of him on the lookout for the thing he'd seen in the sky that night. But all he saw were fellow travelers on the lakefront paths—people with dogs, people running, guys rollerblading despite the dark, a group of high-school-age kids smoking a joint on some boulders and giggling as Rory passed by. Somewhere distant, perhaps out of someone's open apartment window, the sound of Oscar Peterson's piano.

As he entered the campus of Loyola University, he started to feel a couple of things. The first was simple—he was hungry. All he'd had for lunch was what he'd brought: a tuna salad sandwich Cole had made for him and an apple, which had been a little too soft. He hadn't finished it.

The second thing was that he felt oddly alone—and maybe just a tad lonely. As comfortable as he imagined himself in his own skin, Rory realized he longed for Cole's company or, if he couldn't have that, the company of his parents.

Someone. Anyone.

He walked south until he came to Thorndale and then headed west over to Broadway and made his way to Moody's Pub. The place had been there forever. Rory could remember his parents taking him there as a kid for their most excellent cheeseburgers. Which was exactly what he craved right now.

It was Monday night, so the place wasn't busy, and Rory had his choice of tables outside on the patio. His waitress was a woman about his own age, with long blonde hair parted in the middle. She had a very 1960s vibe, right down to her peasant blouse and cutoff jean shorts. He supposed if he were wired differently, he might have found her attractive.

He ordered a bleu cheese burger and a Diet Coke.

"Aw, come on, man!" his waitress, whose name tag read Dora, exclaimed, laughing. "You got to have a beer with that."

Rory almost never drank. But he thought maybe a beer or two tonight might give him a little oblivion, cast away that slight blue feeling he had about being alone. He shrugged and told her to bring him a Bud Light.

"Atta boy!" Dora hurried away.

Rory ended up staying at Moody's far longer than he'd intended. The warm air, the beers (he'd ended up having three—a lot for him), the heaviness of the burger and the hand-cut fries relaxed him and made sitting outside very pleasant. Even the traffic rushing by just beyond the fence on Broadway began to sound more liquid, like the sound of the lake lapping at the shore. That was, until some dick blew his horn and sent the fantasy into the garbage. Fortunately there weren't many horn blowers out that night.

Rory pressed the little button on the side of his digital watch to illuminate it and was surprised to see it was already 9:40. He knew Cole had said he might be home as early as ten, but Rory figured he was simply softening the bad news of actually being home later.

Still, he didn't want Cole to come home to an empty apartment, and he certainly didn't want him slipping *naked* into an empty bed. So he looked around for Dora and realized he was all alone on the patio.

When had that happened? The patio had been about half-full when he sat down. Between eating, downing beers, and squinting through a few pages of *Desperation*, Rory hadn't noticed his fellow diners leaving.

He stood, wobbled, and grabbed the edge of the table, letting out a little snort of laughter. He plopped back down, too hard, onto his plastic chair. That almost made him laugh some more.

"Whoa there, party animal!" Dora emerged out of the shadows. "You okay?"

Rory snickered. "Great. I'm great. Just a tiny little inner ear problem. Can I get my check?"

"Coming right up." She opened a little leatherette folder, licked her fingers, and paged through a few different checks. There must have been other customers in the dark-wooded interior of the bar. "Here we go." She set his check down in front of him, then snatched it back up, grinning. "Unless you want another Bud Light for the road?"

That struck Rory as very funny, and he roared with laughter, slapping his hand so hard on the plastic table one of his empties toppled over, rolled, and crashed to the cement below, where it shattered.

He looked helplessly at Dora. "As my mom would tell you, I need another beer like I need a hole in the head."

Dora nodded. "Don't worry about the broken glass. I'm on it."

Rory peered at his check, decided it must be somewhere in the vicinity of twelve bucks, and handed Dora a twenty from his wallet.

"I'll be right back with your change."

He waved her away. "Don't worry about it. Keep it."

"Really? Okay. Thanks!" She hurried away so fast Rory thought maybe she feared he'd change his mind.

Outside, he wished he hadn't been such a generous tipper, because all he had left in his wallet was a lonely one dollar bill. Not enough for a cab home, not even enough for the "L" over on Thorndale. He really didn't relish the idea of walking all the way home now.

What was wrong with him?

Still, even if he staggered home slowly, most likely he'd beat Cole to their bed. And that was all that mattered.

He headed east, for the lakefront.

But before he got there, the beer began doing its work. Rory thought he could ignore the urge to pee and wait until he got home. He quickened his pace, trying to think of anything other than the fierce-and-getting-fiercer urge to urinate. He tried to map out his agenda for his workday tomorrow. He wondered how the characters in *Desperation* would get out of their jailhouse predicament. He tried to figure out just how one went about doing an inventory in a retail store.

None of it helped. At the end of every thought, his physical need was there, like some sort of punctuation, reminding him in a needling way that attempts to divert the urge, to bury it under thought, would only cause the need to redouble its efforts, making it even stronger.

He looked around for someplace that might have a men's room. This was Chicago, after all. Certainly there should be a gas station, a bar, a restaurant. Hey, maybe even one of the academic buildings on the Loyola campus. But all he found to his dismay and aching bladder were businesses that had closed up shop for the day, signs in windows that warned Restrooms for Customers Only, and when he finally got to Loyola, that all the campus buildings were either locked or required key cards.

He was through the campus and back on the path that bordered the beach and the lake when he decided he'd just be a guy and relieve himself outside somewhere. This was not the way Rory usually behaved, and certainly not how he was raised, but when one's bladder was threatening to explode, well, it called for desperate measures.

Rory made his way a little to the west and found the perfect alley. The streetlight had burned out, and there was a large dumpster for additional cover. High-rise apartment buildings rose up all around him for protective cover. Hand on his fly, Rory wanted to laugh with relief. The quiet and dark little spot appeared as an oasis, the perfect solution to an embarrassing problem.

Rory stood next to the dumpster, unzipped his fly, and then, hand on the brick wall and leaning his weight into it, let go.

The relief caused a deep sigh to issue from his lips. The release was so pleasurable it was a slice of heaven. His sigh approached a growl of contentment, almost sexual. He closed his eyes with delight.

And then, from even the cover of his closed eyelids, he saw it.

Bright light.

Shit was the first thought that sprang to mind. *The cops* was the second. Rory opened his eyes, trying to make his stream go faster, to finish up, because there was no way he could stop himself now. He wanted to bark out some giddy, hysterical laughter, even as he imagined calling Cole from a police precinct to bail him out on a charge of indecent exposure.

All this went through Rory's head in a millisecond. When he finished—because he had to finish, it didn't matter who was watching—he looked around.

Sigh. There was no police car at the mouth of the alley, no beat cop shining a flashlight on him in all his unzipped glory.

No, the light, Rory realized, was coming from above. He quickly shook off and stuffed his dick back in his shorts. He raised his head, shielding his eyes from the brilliant light and squinting into it at the same time, but even those measures were feeble against the blinding illumination. The light was so bright it ignited a shooting pain in his head, made him fear scorching his retinas.

There was a grinding sound too. It took him a moment to notice that, because he was so stunned by the hovering light of a thousand suns above him. It was like the mechanical drumbeat of machinery going about its business. *Boom, boom. Boom, boom*—like the beating of a clockwork heart.

Rory was too stunned to be afraid. He turned and leaned back against the wall, a little breathless, and closed his eyes to witness myriad suns, orange and red, pulsating on his inner eyelids.

When he opened his eyes again, careful to keep them cast down on the bricks of the alley, he noticed how the shining illuminated everything at his feet—the crushed Old Style beer can, the used condom, the coffee grounds, and the oil stains. He took this in dully, like he was observing these mundane castoffs as someone who was studying them, but for whom they were foreign. Like an archeologist peering down at relics from an ancient civilization.

For a jarring moment, he couldn't, for the life of him, recall where he was.

Maybe this way of occupying his mind was a defense, he realized at last. A defense against horror and recognition.

Because, with a certainty that approached 100 percent, Rory knew what was issuing the bright light above him, knew without having to go to the trouble to peer into its blinding white light once more. The realization made him shiver, despite his racing heart and the light sheen of sweat that covered his face.

It was *it*. The membrane, the cloud, the ship. It was not in the distance, as before, but directly above.

The cold seized his limbs, paralyzing, like the very blood in his veins was slowing, freezing.

And then he felt nothing at all, save for a few vague physical sensations—a pulling at the top of his head, so hard he could feel his hair rise, strand by strand, then faster, until all of it stood straight up. His limbs followed, arms stretching up above his head, but not of their own accord.

And then, with a terror so acute it made him not scream but laugh hysterically, his feet lost contact with the ground as he rose slowly into the light.

CHAPTER 3

COLE DIDN'T get off work until almost eleven thirty. He'd given up any hope of meeting Rory at the Davis "L" stop. He was certain Rory would be home and in bed by then, but hopefully he wouldn't be asleep yet. Even though Cole was bone-tired, so exhausted he could barely see straight, he still longed for the moment when he would slide into bed beside his Rory. He relished that future moment when he would caress Rory's smooth body, tracing every freckle and mole on that alabaster skin. Just the thought gave Cole a second wind, a little more spring in his step.

This late, the streets of Evanston were quiet. Cole ran across a Northwestern student or two, hurrying back to an apartment or dorm, but otherwise he found the streets deserted. There was a slight breeze that made the shadows of leaves dance on the pavement at his feet. He could smell the lake a few blocks to the east.

Cole made his way rapidly to the "L" station and took the stairs up to the platform two at a time. His timing was spot-on—a train was just pulling into the station.

"Lucky me," Cole whispered and hopped onto the closest car. The doors hissed closed, and the train was in motion again seconds later. Cole plopped down in one of the seats near the door and looked around. He was one of only three people in his particular car. There was a middle-aged woman in a black Joy Division T-shirt and black jeans. She had dyed black hair, wore lots of mascara, and stared resolutely out the window at the backs of storefront and apartment buildings as the train trundled past. There was someone Cole assumed to be homeless. It made Cole sad because he appeared to be about Cole's age, with stringy blond hair and a beard grown not out of fashion but necessity. His clothes, a flannel shirt and a pair of Carhartt pants, were grimy, the pants rolled up because they were far too long. His left shoe had a hole in it. Besides being filthy, the clothes were much too hot for the temperature outside, which hovered around seventy. He had a bunch of plastic Jewel bags piled up beside him. Cole's heart went out to him, and as he always did when he saw a street person, he thought how easily it could be him riding the "L" through the night, just as a way to be off the streets. Cole made himself look away.

The only other person in the car was an older guy with a buzz cut and a Loyola sweatshirt. He had white earbuds in his ears and was nodding to the beat of a different drummer, Cole thought, one only he could hear. His eyes were closed, and Cole thought he was probably the most oblivious traveler that night.

Good for him.

Cole leaned back and closed his eyes for what he thought would only be a minute, but before he knew it, he woke with a snort to the announcement that they were pulling into Howard Street station, the northernmost "L" stop in the city of Chicago. Everyone would have to get off the train and switch to another line. Except for Cole, of course, who could walk home from the station.

A little disoriented and wondering how he'd managed to miss all the Evanston stops, Cole rubbed his eyes and looked around. The train was empty. Whether his fellow travelers had disembarked in Evanston or right here at Howard, he would never know. He'd also never know if other people had gotten on the train while he slept.

He patted his back pocket, making sure his wallet was still there. He hoisted himself up from his seat and left the train's air-conditioning for the humid night. There were several trains in the station, all huffing and puffing as they idled, reminding Cole of dragons. Even this late, there were still people hurrying to and fro on the platform.

Cole headed for the stairs and hurried down. Home was only a ten-minute walk from the station, and Cole was now actually grateful for the nap. *If that boy's not up when I get home*, he thought with a grin, *I'll just have to poke him awake.*

Cole was certain Rory wouldn't mind.

When he reached the courtyard of their building, the exhaustion Cole had felt on leaving work entirely vanished. He was ready to howl at the moon. He wished only he'd thought to stop off at a convenience store or something so he could have brought Rory a little surprise, maybe a box of Swedish Fish or a roll of SweeTarts. He'd have to find other ways, he supposed, to thrill his sugar-loving man. He'd give him some sugar, all right.

Cole unlocked the front vestibule door and headed into the cool tile lobby of their building. He loved the 1920s vibe of the lobby and the building in general, glad no one in all the ensuing decades since it had been built had decided the gem of a vintage building needed updating. He loved the mica-colored wall sconces and the Mediterranean floor tile. He even loved the battered brass mailboxes along one wall.

He stopped to check the mail, found the box empty, and headed for the elevator.

Out front, Cole hoped Rory had left the door unlocked for him. No such luck. He fished his keys from his pocket and quelled his first impulse, which was to shout, "Honey, I'm home!" at the top of his lungs. If the poor guy was asleep, Cole reasoned, let him sleep. There were subtler and much more pleasurable ways to wake him.

As he made his way through the living room and toward the bedroom, he dropped clothing as he went. He also shut off the lights Rory had thoughtfully left on for him. By the time he reached the closed bedroom door, he was smiling and sporting an erection.

He opened the door slowly. It took his eyes a moment to adjust. They had, in fact, thumb-tacked a sheet over the sole window, so the room stayed pretty dark.

Cole groped his way to the bed, suppressing a giggle.

But when he got there, the giggle died on his lips. He felt around the surface, up, down, left, right, as though his own hands deceived him. He frowned and then turned to the light switch on the wall and flicked it. The room filled with warm yellow light. No Rory. Cole hadn't expected that, and he cocked his head. Absurdly, he looked around the room, thinking maybe he'd find Rory sitting on the chair they used to pile their clothes on before hopping into bed for the night. Maybe he'd rolled out and was fast asleep on the braided rug they'd positioned beneath it.

But the room was empty. Unusually neat—the bed made and no clothes lying on the chair in the corner. Cole crossed the room and opened the door to the single closet. Maybe Rory was hiding from him? One of the things they both loved about the apartment was the size of the bedroom closet. It was walk-in, with rods on either side, shelving above, and even a window that looked outside. Rory could be weird. Maybe he lay within, naked and waiting, ready to pull out all the stops on yet another fantasy.

But the empty closet mocked him.

Where was he?

Cole retreated from the bedroom. "Rory? Babe?" Cole made a quick tour of the small apartment, knowing as he did it that the search would be wasted effort. And it was. Rory wasn't in the living room, the dining room, kitchen, or bathroom.

Cole returned to the bedroom and ran his hands along the top of the dresser. Rory usually left his wallet and keys on top of it. But just like the rest of his search, this maneuver was only an empty gesture. Rory's keys and wallet were gone, indicating he was still out there somewhere.

That was odd. Cole glanced at the alarm clock on the nightstand and saw it was approaching twelve thirty. Cole knew Rory had to be up early for work in the morning—he had flex hours at his job and liked to work the earlier spectrum—usually seven thirty to four. And Rory loved his sleep! Sometimes he dragged Cole to bed as early as nine o'clock. Cole never complained.

So what was he doing out so late on a school night?

Cole plopped down on the bed, head in his hands. *Don't panic. Don't even worry. It's most likely nothing at all. Maybe he got over his aversion to gay bars and is down on Halsted Street, living it up, downing shots backed up by beers.* The thought made him chuckle, as that scenario was about as likely as Cole being on a jet bound for Paris, France. Still, in spite of its improbability, the notion did cause a stab of jealousy to jab at Cole—right in his solar plexus. Sure, Rory might be one of the few gay men their age Cole knew who actually didn't like to go out to bars, but he still could have. It was *possible*, as he might say if queried on a witness stand in some court of law. Cole felt sick to his stomach as he allowed himself to think what was lurking at the back of his mind, like some black shadow. It was also *possible* that Rory had gone out and hooked up with someone and lost track of time.

Cole licked his lips, mouth suddenly dry. He had a lot of gay male friends and acquaintances and knew fidelity was a fairly rare thing, even among the ones who claimed to be in committed, monogamous relationships. Why, some of those fellas had even come on to Cole when the boyfriend was out of town or just out of the picture.

Maybe their relationship wasn't as solid as Cole thought? Rory could have been tempted. It was possible. He was a cute guy who didn't know it, which made him even cuter. He could see him being hit on—and maybe if he was lonely or bored, he might have given in? *Are any of us truly immune to temptation?*

No. Not Rory. Cole knew in his heart of hearts that Rory would never cheat. He just didn't have it in him, literally or figuratively.

So where are you? Cole stood and began pacing. He pulled aside the sheet tacked up over the window to look outside, hoping against hope he'd see Rory down there on the beach. He did see someone, a guy, sitting on the sand at the edge of the beach, his feet pushed into the waves. But even from up there, Cole could tell the guy had at least fifty pounds on Rory, if not more. And he was smoking....

A woman walked by. A big dog, maybe a pit bull, dashed ahead of her, splashing at the edge of the surf. Cole could see the leash in her hand. She called the dog back, and it sounded to Cole like its name was Pashmina.

There was no one else on the beach this late.

He turned away from the window. The bedroom's emptiness made him feel even sicker, bad enough that he veered toward the bathroom, afraid what little he'd eaten that night might come up.

Now you're just being silly. Whatever's going on, there's a logical explanation. And Rory would probably be home any minute now to tell Cole what it was.

Cole left the bedroom and went into the living room. He turned on the TV and then flicked it off again. He sat down on the couch and smacked himself in the head. Of course!—Rory had told him he was going to visit his mom and dad up in Wilmette. He'd probably just lingered after dinner. Rory's family loved playing cards, especially hearts and canasta, and sometimes their games could get contentious—and go on for hours.

Sure, Rory had just lost track of time. He snagged the cordless off the end table and punched in Rory's parents' phone number and listened to the ringing.

His mom sounded sleepy when she answered. Not a good sign.

"Hi, Greta. I hope I didn't wake you up." Cole continued to pace, the phone pressed too hard against his ear. Rory's family, he knew, were not his biggest fans. Although they were never anything but completely nice to him, he had the impression—and this was probably more a result of his own self-questioning coming to the fore—that they thought he wasn't quite good enough for their only son.

"Cole?"

"Oh yeah," Cole laughed uncomfortably. "Yeah, yeah, it's me. I should have said so."

Greta sounded a little more awake. "It's okay, honey. Is everything all right?" Gently chiding, "It *is* kind of late, you know."

"I know, and I apologize. But, uh, I had to work late at the store tonight, you know? And, um, I didn't get home until around midnight, and, um, well, Rory wasn't here. *Isn't* here. He told me he was coming up to see you guys since I was working tonight—"

Greta cut him off. "He's not there?" There was the subtlest hint of alarm in her voice. Was she about to tell him Rory left their house hours ago? All the horrible things that might have befallen Rory in those intervening hours came crashing into Cole's consciousness, causing his already upset stomach to churn even more.

"No." Cole moved to the window and looked outside at the black night. *Where are you?* "Can you tell me when he left?"

"When he left?"

"Yeah."

"Honey, he was never here. Mr. S. and I were out this evening. We went to dinner in Evanston and to see a movie. We didn't get home ourselves until about an hour and a half ago." A nervous giggle escaped her. "Now you've got me worried."

"Me too!" Cole said, pushing down the lump that formed in his throat. "The only thing he told me earlier was that he thought he might come up and see you guys tonight, since I was working so late."

She explained that Rory did call, but that she'd turned him down since they'd already had plans. In the end, she sighed and said, "I'm sure things are okay." She didn't sound convinced. There was a quivery edge to her voice. To Cole, her certainty about things being okay seemed designed more to calm her than him.

"You're probably right," Cole said, even though at the moment he was the one lying. He looked over at the clock on the VCR to find it was after 1:00 a.m. He gnawed at a hangnail that had sprouted out of his thumb.

A voice grumbled in the background, and Greta whispered "Hang on" to Rory's dad. "Listen, Cole, you call me when he gets home, okay? No matter how late it is. And if he doesn't get home in the next hour or so, call me, okay?"

"That's not gonna happen," Cole said. "I'll let you know when he gets in." He repeated that he was sure there was nothing to be alarmed about and said goodbye.

His mouth felt dry. He felt restless and couldn't imagine sitting down. Continuing to walk in an endless loop around their apartment, he pondered his next move.

Should he start calling area hospitals? Maybe Rory had fallen, been hit by a car, mugged. Things like that happened every day, probably every hour in a city as big as Chicago. But where to begin? And did he really want to hear bad news if one of them had some on Rory? Yes, yes, of course he did. Anything was better than not knowing. Well, maybe one thing wouldn't be better. But maybe if he'd gotten hurt, they were fixing him up and he'd head home soon.

Okay. But why wouldn't he call? Or have someone call for him?

Should he phone the police? Rory was a grown man, and Cole had always heard the old saw about the police not filing missing person's reports until at least twenty-four hours had passed. Or was it forty-eight? Cole shrugged. It didn't matter. Unless there was some evidence of foul play, he was sure the cops wouldn't be interested in his missing *grown man* boyfriend who was out past his bedtime—and didn't leave a note.

Should he go outside and look for him? *What? Search Chicago? Yeah, good luck with that.*

Finally Cole flung himself down on the couch and simply shut his mind off. If he kept up with his worry, he was going to be physically sick. He threw his head back on the edge of the couch and forced himself to close his eyes. But when he did, images of Rory rose up—of him lying in the street, or next to a dumpster somewhere, or with a gunshot wound to his forehead, or worst of all, in bed with some muscly guy sporting a dick twice as big as Cole's. Cole's eyes shot open. He certainly hoped he didn't suppose the last image was the worst. What kind of person would find that the *worst* possibility? But in his own heart of hearts, the thought of Rory in bed with some other guy *did* make him feel the queasiest, because Cole knew it was the most commonplace, and therefore the most likely, explanation.

The clock now told him it was going on 2:00 a.m. It was too late to call his big sister, Elaine, even though Cole knew she might still be up. Her insomnia was a constant complaint whenever he saw her. But it would be just Cole's luck to wake her from a rare good night's sleep.

At a little after two, Cole jumped and gave out a little scream when the phone rang. He snatched it up, hoping against hope it was Rory. It had to be Rory. Now, whatever had happened, things could start to get back to normal.

It wasn't Rory.

"Cole? It's Greta, Rory's mom." As if she had to make it clear. Cole shook his head but hoped she had some news.

"Have you heard something?"

"No, honey, I wish I had. I'm guessing you haven't either. Mr. S. and I are worried sick over here. Tell me Rory's there, sweetheart, and you just forgot to call me." She sounded on the verge of tears, and that made tears well up in Cole's eyes as well. If Rory's absence wasn't so damn out of character, Cole imagined he wouldn't be this upset.

"Ah, I wish I could. But I haven't heard a thing." He stood and looked out the window to the courtyard, praying he'd spy Rory coming in through the gate. But the courtyard was empty. "He's not home either."

"Cole, you can tell me. Is this like him at all? Does he go out sometimes, like to those gay bars? I mean, I know kids don't tell their parents everything. And if he does, I mean, it's okay."

"I wish I could tell you I thought he was at a bar. But Rory's never been too keen on the places. He'd rather go out to dinner with some of our friends, or go see a movie, or do a museum—almost anything over a bar."

"That's what I thought," Greta said. "Um, one other thing crossed my mind."

"Okay."

"Uh, I don't mean to pry into you guys's business, but has there been any trouble lately? Maybe a little lover's spat?"

Cole wanted to sob. "The truth is—really—Rory and I have never fought, Greta."

"Really?"

"Really. Oh, we might have a disagreement over what to have for dinner or what to watch on TV, but fights? No. And certainly there was nothing wrong earlier when I talked to him on the phone. We were looking forward to seeing each other when I got off from work."

Greta fell silent, and Cole didn't know what to say next. He knew that to admit to a big fight would have been reassuring to Rory's mother, for obvious reasons. It would make his absence a lot less mysterious.

Finally Greta said, "Well, again, please call when he comes home or if you hear from him." She sounded defeated, and that caused a hole to open in Cole's heart. "Don't worry about what time it is. We'll be up."

This isn't good. It can't be.

Cole hung up the phone and sat very still on the living room couch, his hands in his lap, staring straight ahead. He was not sleepy. He was not hungry.

He was numb.

He sat unmoving on the couch until the gray light of dawn began to illuminate the room. Cole sighed. He couldn't just sit there any longer. When morning came in full, he'd call Elaine—he could always rely on her for her common sense. He'd call Rory's parents again.

But right then he had to do something, worthless as that something might be.

He wandered into the kitchen, where they had a small legal pad and a pen for jotting down items they were out of so they'd know to get them on their next grocery store run. He wrote:

Hey, honey… I don't know where you are, and I'm worried. I'm going to take a walk around the neighborhood just to keep myself busy, I guess. Maybe you're out there somewhere? Anyway, if you're reading this, it means you're home now. Two things: Stay put. Call your mom and dad. And just wait—I'll be home soon.

Cole signed the note with a row of *x*'s and *o*'s and took it into the living room, where he left it out on the coffee table, where he hoped Rory would immediately see it upon opening the door. Cole prayed he would. Cole prayed for stupidity—for failing to see a logical reason for all this, something that was staring him in the face the whole time but he just didn't get it.

And then he grabbed his keys out of the bowl on the table by the front door, put them in his pocket, and headed outside.

Dusk. Quiet. Cole walked first along usually busy Sheridan Road, which was remarkably still that early, just a few lonely cars heading north and south with lots of space between them. A city bus, nearly empty, headed for Lake Shore Drive.

The air had a cool dampness. Tendrils of fog hung low to the ground, stirred up when a vehicle did pass on the road. Rogers Park had the feel of a party that had either just happened or was about to occur. Cole thought a little of each was true.

He walked a couple of blocks to where the apartment buildings along the lakefront opened up at Touhy to reveal a green park, a playground, a broad expanse of beach, and the lake. There was a band of orange light just over the water, and Cole would have thought it beautiful under different circumstances. Waves were a little bigger today, and their crash against the shore and, a little farther south, the breakwater sounded paradoxically angry and comforting.

Cole cast his eyes both left and right as he walked slowly south, thinking maybe, just maybe, he'd see, if not Rory, a clue. Maybe his wallet lying on the ground. *Hell no, that would be really ominous.*

He had to be honest with himself—he wasn't going to find Rory out there, at a convenience store, buying a Payday, his favorite candy bar, or strolling along the beach. He thought how walking south could be all wrong. He should be walking north. Or west. Or east. Or he should be pacing up and down Chicago's ubiquitous alleys. Or at home, waiting for the phone to ring….

He wanted to kick something, he felt so frustrated.

He turned toward the walkway that went through the park at Touhy and headed down to one of the benches facing the water. He passed two that were already occupied, both by sleeping homeless people.

He sat heavily when he found an empty bench. He stared out at the pewter-colored water for a long time, letting his mind go blank. Because to think meant imagining things too horrible to contemplate.

When he did permit his mind to function again, a sliver of sun was emerging just above the water, and Cole allowed memory to take over. Just something sweet, something he could think about as a diversion—a way to escape the dread and fear that was eating into him.

The first time he saw Rory was at their gym.

They both belonged to the Bally's in the Century City mall. It was a cruisy gym, and Cole ruefully thought of all the hookups he'd had as a result of being a member, one memorable one in the showers.

But when he'd been sitting on the abs machine that day not so long ago and spied Rory walking by on his way to one of the elliptical machines, very curiously, he didn't feel lust. Not exactly.

Rory was almost comical. His shoes were all wrong. (Who wore an old pair of Sketchers leather bowling-style shoes to the gym?) He had on a pair of khaki Bermuda shorts and a *Star Trek* T-shirt. His reddish-brown hair was an unkempt mop, and his glasses screamed *geek.*

It was because Rory was so precisely the opposite of all the other pumped-up gym bunnies running around in their spandex and clinging nylon that he caught Cole's eye. Some might say he looked pathetic, and

Cole would have been inclined to agree. He'd also agree with those who might claim this doofus had never seen the inside of a gym, not only because of the ridiculously inappropriate attire, but also because of that skinny Ichabod Crane build. Behind the thick lenses of his glasses, Cole thought, was someone who looked completely lost.

But the urge Cole had upon seeing this stranger took him completely by surprise. He didn't want to suppress a chuckle. He didn't want to roll his eyes, as he saw a couple of other guys doing in the heavily gay club. He didn't even want to maybe clue the guy in on a good pair of cross-trainers, Nike, maybe. Reebok?

No. He wanted to kiss him. Passionately. There was something so vulnerable and sweet about Rory that Cole simply wanted to press his lips against Rory's slightly puffy ones. He could imagine nothing more satisfying—not even sex.

He just wanted to kiss him. *A kiss is never just a kiss.*

Cole got up and followed him over to the elliptical, where he watched as Rory awkwardly mounted the machine and pondered its screen as though the words on it were written in code.

"Just press any one of the buttons to get the thing started." Cole walked up beside Rory, heart hammering away, feeling a little flushed. He never felt this way when cruising other guys, not even when they were naked in the shower. He was always confident.

Maybe it was because he wanted to meet—no, kiss—this new guy so much that he was all flummoxed. Bamboozled. Atwitter. Maybe because these first few words were so important, determining, as they might, their whole future.

Rory regarded him, and Cole got his first look at that impish smile.

And he was in love. Right then. Right there.

"What would I do without you?" Rory asked.

They ran into each other just outside the gym in Century City's multileveled mall space, and since it was almost lunchtime, Cole invited him to ruin the effort of burning all those calories with a slice or two of pizza.

And Rory had said yes. He said yes after lunch when Cole asked him on a proper first date. He said yes when Cole asked if he could kiss him, right there on busy Clark Street. And he also eventually said yes to spending the night… again and again and again… until they put an end to the ruse of maintaining separate apartments and moved in together.

Now Cole stared out at the water, a horrible thought springing to mind. *Are you in that water, Rory? Are its currents tossing you to and fro? Is your hair floating in its blue-green cold?*

Cole shivered and stood up, banishing the thought from his mind. It was too horrible to contemplate.

The sun was full up above the lake now. It was time to go home and make some calls.

CHAPTER 4

DORA REYNOLDS was too tired to do anything other than sprawl on the couch in front of the TV, a bowl of Lay's sour cream and onion potato chips at her side and a glass of Diet Coke on the coffee table before her. Yesterday she'd worked a double shift at Moody's Pub, where she'd been a server for the last four years, because that imbecile cokehead Travis had called in sick *yet again* and she had to cover for him *yet again*.

Dora was only twenty-four, but she felt more like fifty-four or even sixty-four today. Her very bones ached. Breathing was a task that very nearly seemed beyond her energy to achieve. Anything she'd do in a normal morning—cleaning out the litter box, emptying the sink of dirty dishes, calling her mom out in Des Plaines, reading a few pages of the book that had been on her nightstand for six months, *Neverwhere*, taking a walk, for heaven's sake—she put on hold, laying down these daily tasks as a kind of tribute to the great god Fatigue.

Today she'd be a blob, remote in hand, and passively watch whatever she could find on offer to stare at while she drank soda and ate junk food. She deserved the indulgence and promised herself she wouldn't feel one whit of guilt about it. Her cat, Paula, a smoky gray domestic shorthair, snuggled against her side, completely in favor of Dora's agenda, since it aligned so perfectly with her own feline one.

Outside, rain lashed against the windows. Good thing. Dora didn't have to feel guilty about not going outside and doing something crazy, like a bike ride or a run along the beach, just because the sky was blue and the temperature was in the eighties.

When the local news came on at noon, Dora wasn't really watching until an image popped up during the drone of new stories that grabbed her attention. She set down her Coke and sat up straighter on the couch.

"That guy looks familiar," she said softly to the cat.

Indeed, the young man with reddish-brown hair and black horn-rims nudged something in Dora's memory. She told Paula, "I've seen that guy before. But where?" The cat chirped as though telling Dora to shut up and listen to the news story.

A blonde reporter stood outside an older apartment building, informing her audience that Rory Schneidmiller, age twenty-three, of Rogers Park, was missing. He was last seen a little over a week ago on Monday night at his place of employment, an insurance company in the Loop.

"Who *is* he?" she reiterated to the cat.

And then it came to her. Sure, she'd waited on him at the restaurant last Monday night. He wasn't "last seen" at work; he was, maybe, "last seen" by her. She tuned in more to the story, learning that the guy disappeared on Monday night, leaving no trace of his whereabouts. A tingle went through Dora at the reporter's words. He'd seemed like a nice guy, a little lonely, eating by himself and reading a Stephen King book. She'd wanted to ask him how he liked it because she was a fan and hadn't gotten around to reading it yet, but just ran out of time.

She remembered it all clearly now. How he'd broken a beer bottle on the pavement outside. How he was a little tipsy, not in an obnoxious way, but in a way that had been kind of cute.

Had he met with something bad on his way home from Moody's? She shook her head, feeling a sudden and powerful welling up of sympathy for a young guy who was, really, little more than a stranger. She could see him now clearly in her mind's eye, a little unsteady on his feet as he headed out.

Dora, no longer tired, watched as Rory Schneidmiller's mother appeared on the screen. She had the same reddish-brown hair as her son and similar glasses. The worry on her careworn features was obvious as she implored anyone in the viewing audience to contact the Chicago Police Department if they'd seen Rory or had any news at all of him.

At least she held up better than the next person interviewed, a very handsome young man described as Rory's "roommate." Dora raised her eyebrows. She had a lot of friends with "roommates." The cute guy with the pale eyes, dark hair, and way-past-five-o'clock shadow was barely holding it together as he spoke. His eyes were filled with tears, and he had to pause a couple of times to prevent breaking down in sobs on camera. He reached out much the same way the mother had—desperate for any information regarding the young man's mysterious disappearance. The title on the screen said the guy's name was Cole Weston.

Dora leaned forward to snatch the folded-up section of yesterday's *Tribune* she'd left lying on the coffee table. She'd discarded it earlier after failing to complete the crossword puzzle. With the pencil she'd been using for the puzzle, she jotted down the name Cole Weston in the paper's margin. She added Rory Schneidmiller next to it. She wasn't quite sure why.

The news faded to a commercial, and Dora picked up the remote to mute the sound. She leaned back on the couch and called out, "Hey, Tommy! You up?"

Her roommate (which was *not* a euphemism for any other label), Tommy D'Amico, wandered in from the bathroom, clad only in a white towel. With another white towel, he rubbed at his head of bright red hair.

"Hon, I've been up since six, studying. This torts course is killing me." Tommy was in law school at Loyola downtown. "What's up?"

"I just saw the weirdest thing on TV." Dora wished she had the power to rewind the TV, as she could do with a videotape.

Tommy plopped down beside her, smelling of sandalwood from his shower gel. Part of her wanted to lean over and nuzzle her nose in his neck so she could get a big whiff, but that would be crossing a boundary line.

"Oh yeah?" he asked, setting aside the towel he'd used to dry his hair. Paula immediately rushed over to it, thinking, obviously, that this new piece of fabric would make a great bed, once she kneaded and rearranged it to her liking.

"Last Monday night, I waited on this guy who came in to eat alone on the patio."

"Earth-shattering."

"Would you let me finish?" Dora shook her head. "Anyway, I just saw on the news he went missing last Monday night." She turned to Tommy and met his green-eyed gaze. "Missing without a trace." Dora rubbed up and down her arms. "It gives me chills to think I might have been the last person to see him. They said on the news no one had seen him since that day at his job downtown, so chances are I *was* the last to see him."

"See him alive," Tommy mumbled.

She punched his arm. "Don't say that! He's missing, not dead."

"Well, come on, a young guy goes missing without a trace and still hasn't turned up over a week later? He's dead." Tommy crossed his arms across his bare chest.

"You're heartless." Dora reached over Tommy to grab the cat off the towel and set her down on her own lap, where she could stroke her. Paula purred. "Do you think I should call the police?"

"Do you know anything about what he had planned after he left Moody's?"

"No, but, I don't know, maybe it would help them to have another piece of the puzzle."

"I don't see how. Don't get involved." Tommy picked up the remote and began scanning through the channels.

"Give me that!" She grabbed the remote out of his hands and returned to the news. Tommy's words ignited a stubborn—and nurturing—streak within her. She had to help, even if her help was little aid at all.

"Well, I think I should call. Who knows? It might help, even though we don't know how. I won't know unless I try."

Tommy stood. He was a fine-looking man, a perfectly proportioned and muscled body dusted with freckles and light reddish-brown hair.

Too bad he was gay. Or maybe it wasn't, since they lived under the same roof. And Lord knew he could get on her nerves.

She didn't feel quite as tired as before as she went looking for the cordless between the couch cushions. At least now she had a plan.

IT WAS evening before Dora found herself back on the couch, Paula keeping watch at her side. The report of the missing young man had unnerved her, and she knew why. When she was eight years old, just a little girl growing up in the small town of Aliquippa, Pennsylvania, her father had vanished without a trace. She'd recalled how people wanted to surmise that he'd run away from taking care of a too-large family—Dora had three brothers and four sisters—on his decent but hard-to-stretch steelworker's pay. The talk around town was that he'd simply taken off to escape the shackles of matrimony and parenthood. But her mother, her siblings, and Dora herself knew that would have never been the case. Not with *her* dad. He loved his wife and kids with a fierce devotion. No, much like what she'd learned in the intervening hours since she first saw the news story, her father's disappearance so long ago was very similar to Rory Schneidmiller's. Both men had simply vanished without a trace one night. They both left—or were taken—without any of their personal belongings and without a word to a single soul of any plan of leaving. There were no signs of foul play, no telltale evidence that would at least provide some clue to the mystery of their disappearances.

Dora shook her head, pointing the remote control at the TV to turn it on. Tonight *Mad About You* and *Frasier* were both on, two of her favorites. But it was hard not to be distracted.

Earlier, she'd called the Chicago Police Department and had been lucky enough to catch the detective who was looking into Rory Schneidmiller's disappearance in her office and willing to talk to her. The detective's name was Jordyn Adkins, and she listened as Dora unspooled her story about waiting on Schneidmiller the previous Monday and how, when he left, he'd been a little under the influence. Detective Adkins asked all the right questions—Did he mention any plans for after he left the restaurant? Had she seen him speaking to anyone else? Did he seem troubled? And Dora had tried to paint a picture of a young man who, she thought, simply didn't want to cook and had gone out for a quick burger and a few beers with the company of the book he was reading, a Stephen King potboiler called *Desperation*. It had surprised Dora that she'd recalled the actual title of the book because it hadn't come to her until her phone call to the police.

In the end, though, she knew what she'd provided wasn't of much use, other than narrowing the timeline for Rory Schneidmiller's disappearance just a bit. If she had seen him talking to someone or if he had revealed something about his mental state to her or a plan for where he was off to next, then maybe her intervention might have helped. But Dora had been busy, mostly inside the restaurant, waiting on a rowdy bunch of Loyola University frat boys. She'd almost forgotten the young guy sitting outside.

Yet his face continued to haunt her. He'd been cute. Not in a way that was necessarily attractive or sexy or anything like that, but in a way that brought out her nurturing side, even though they were about the same age. His being slightly tipsy she saw not as a sign of trouble, but as someone who obviously didn't drink much and couldn't handle his liquor. She did remember he'd only had three beers, not exactly enough for most people to get as smashed as Rory appeared.

Maybe, drunk, he'd wandered down the wrong alley? Maybe a mugging had gotten out of hand? Maybe he'd fallen into the lake, hit his head on a boulder? Drowned? Who knew?

The thing that bugged her, that made her want to help in some way, was that she didn't want Rory's mother and roommate to go through the same agony her family did when her father had vanished. All her family thought there was no ache worse than simply *not knowing*. Death—as horrible as that would have been—would have brought a tiny bit of relief because it would also bring closure. But as long as a loved one was missing, whether it was days, weeks, months, or yes, even years, there was always, somewhere in the back of one's mind, a tiny flame of hope that refused to be extinguished.

It was impossible to truly move on, whatever that meant.

She picked up the cordless and punched in 411. "Do you have a number for Cole Weston in Chicago?" Dora asked when the operator answered.

And there was only one, on Fargo Avenue. Dora thought that had to be the same guy she'd seen on the news and jotted down the number.

She wasn't sure yet what she'd do with it.

CHAPTER 5

"I'VE DONE everything I can think of." Cole sat across from his sister, Elaine, at a diner a couple of blocks away from his apartment. The diner was on Sheridan Road; they'd done more watching the traffic go by than talking to each other. That traffic was also fascinating enough to make both of them pretty much ignore the breakfasts laid out in front of them on red Formica. The only thing Cole had partaken of, like his sister, was lots and lots of black coffee. Together, they must have drunk about a pot of the stuff.

Maybe that was why they were out of sorts, jumpy.

Maybe that's why Elaine snapped, "Everything? Surely there must be something you haven't thought of."

It was now over two weeks since Rory had gone missing. In that time, not one clue about his whereabouts had emerged. Cole still woke up some mornings expecting to hear Rory in the shower, humming some bad eighties tune.

Cole put his head in his hands, staring down at the table, breathing hard. He didn't want to blow up at Elaine, who was only trying to be helpful. She'd stopped by the apartment this September Saturday morning specifically to take her little brother out to breakfast because the whole family was worried about him, worried about the changes they'd seen over such a short period. Because when Rory vanished, so, in a way, had Cole. While Cole was still present physically, almost every other aspect of his personality had gone into hiding the night he came home to an empty apartment. Cole was once quick to laugh, lighthearted, carefree, never worrying about the serious parts of life, like work and education. He lived for pleasure but wasn't hedonistic—his joy was not satisfied until everyone around him was as happy as he was.

That person had vanished. Since Rory's disappearance, Cole was often morose, moving slowly and rarely smiling. And no one could blame him for his sense of loss, his sadness, his confusion, his lack of interest in life. He looked like he'd lost at least ten pounds.

"I'm sorry," Elaine said softly. She took a bite of toast.

Cole looked across the table at his sister and wiped the tears out of his eyes. "I know. You didn't mean to say that. You know better than anyone else I've done just about every possible thing I could." He reiterated all he'd done over the past trying weeks—the appearances on local TV and even radio, the tacking up of hundreds of signs around the north side of the city, the long hours spent with detectives at the Chicago Police Department trying to come up with something, *one tiny little thing*, for Christ's sake, that would explain why a perfectly happy, healthy, gainfully employed, and in love (or so Cole thought) twenty-three-year-old man would simply disappear off the face of the planet. He'd even seen to it that Rory was registered in the database of missing persons. Detective Adkins and everyone who worked with her took the case seriously.

But there was simply nothing to go on.

Sure, a woman had come forward a few days ago, saying she'd waited on Rory at some burger joint on Broadway the night he vanished. And Cole supposed she had, but he couldn't help but harbor a little bit of doubt in the back of his mind about her story. She said Rory was "tipsy," which Cole found hard to believe. Rory hardly ever touched alcohol, despite Cole pushing it on him all the time.

But why would that waitress lie? Maybe to grab her fifteen minutes of fame? That would be stupid, right? But who knew what motivated people these days?

Yet in the end, whether she was being truthful or not didn't matter because her seeing Rory that night was just another dead end. Another thing to be frustrated about. Whether he was at Moody's or not, tipsy or not, simply didn't matter, because the information led them nowhere.

"You about ready to go?" Cole asked.

"But you haven't touched your breakfast," Elaine complained. Cole glanced down at his nearly full plate of pancakes and bacon. Once upon a time, such a plate would have been cleared in about five minutes flat. Pancakes were Cole's favorite food.

Now they only looked unappetizing, as though they'd not nourish him but lay heavy in his gut, making him even more tired than he always seemed to feel these days.

His sister had been nice enough to come around and offer to treat him to breakfast. She even said he could pick a movie out for a matinee later on that afternoon. He hated to hurt her feelings, but he didn't think he could swallow even one more bite of the pancakes.

He tried to smile. "I'll have them wrap it up. I can eat it for dinner later."

Elaine's eyes were full of concern. She put her hand over his and gave a little squeeze. "Sure." She looked around for their waitress. As she was signaling to the heavyset, older gray-haired woman who'd waited on them, Cole sat up straighter as he saw another waitress enter the diner, obviously not one that worked here.

"Wait a minute," Cole said. "Isn't that the woman from Moody's?"

Elaine swiveled to peer over the top of the booth.

Cole and Elaine had been at the police precinct when she'd come in to tell her tale of having served Rory the night of his disappearance. They'd even had a chance to talk with her a bit themselves. She seemed nice enough, even if Cole had doubts about her.

Elaine turned back to Cole and nodded. "Yeah, I think that *is* her. Kind of a coincidence, don't you think?"

"Why? She has to eat breakfast too."

"What was her name again? Dora?"

"Dora, Dora Reynolds."

"Like Debbie Reynolds?"

"Yeah."

Elaine asked, "Should we say something to her?"

Cole shook his head. The woman was with a guy—an olive-skinned redhead with a big nose and broad shoulders. He was leading her toward an empty booth two over from theirs.

But whether Cole wanted to say anything to her or not was out of his hands because Dora spotted him and made eye contact. She gave him a small and sympathetic smile and waved.

"Here she comes," he said under his breath to Elaine.

He watched as Dora headed their way, her boyfriend trailing behind.

"Good morning, you guys," Dora said. As she stood by their table, it was obvious she was uncomfortable, demonstrated by the fact that she kept restlessly shifting her weight from one foot to the other.

Cole barely managed a smile and a nod. Elaine spoke up quickly. "Hey, Dora. We were just finishing up here. Good to see you." Elaine grabbed her big red leather purse off the seat beside her to prove her point. She dug around in it.

"I was just wondering if you'd heard anything. I hope your friend's come home." There was such a sincere, concerned look on the young woman's face that Cole felt bad for not speaking and, indeed, ignoring her.

So he answered, "We still haven't heard a thing." Cole stared down at the table for a moment, then lifted his gaze again to meet Dora's. "But we're not giving up hope."

"Oh, I'm sure something will give soon." She must have realized the dark import of her words because she quickly amended them with "I mean, I'm sure he'll come home."

"I hope you're right," Cole said.

"Well, we were just getting ready to go. We're going to catch an early matinee." Elaine gathered up the check and a credit card in one hand. This was the kind of place where you paid at the cash register on your way out.

The four of them, two standing and two sitting, were silent for several awkward moments. Finally Cole couldn't help asking, "Have you thought of anything new, Dora? About that night? Maybe you remembered something he said about where he was going? Or if maybe he met someone outside the restaurant?"

Dora shook her head, and Cole didn't know how long he could abide the pity he read plainly in her eyes. "No," she said softly. "I've been over it in my head a dozen times. I really think I told you—and that Detective Adkins—everything I recall. I'm really sorry I can't be more helpful." She stepped back and away from the table, bumping into the man she was with. "Oh!" she gasped, startled, as though she'd forgotten he was with her. "This is my roommate, Tommy D'Amico."

They exchanged pleasantries and names, and when Tommy offered his hand to Cole, Cole found the presence of mind to shake it, although he didn't meet the guy's eyes.

"We need to get going." Cole stood. "Don't we, sis?"

"Right." Elaine stood too. "Enjoy your breakfasts."

"The pancakes are great," Cole said. He looked down at his almost full plate and felt stupid. "I need to tell our waitress to wrap mine up."

Elaine steered him away. Cole could feel their eyes on him.

"That was weird," Elaine said.

"It was nice of her to stop and ask about Rory," Cole responded.

"I suppose so." Elaine paid, and the two of them exited. Cole didn't care about the pancakes he'd left and was glad his sister didn't remember his plan to get a doggy bag.

Once they were back on the street, Elaine commented on how she could really feel the fast-approaching autumn in the air. And indeed, even though it was warm, in the upper seventies, there was a cool undercurrent, a harbinger of the season bearing down on them. She asked what he wanted to go see at the movies that day.

"We could see *Mimic*. I hear that's really spooky and good. Great special effects."

"I don't want anything spooky. My life is spooky enough." Besides, Cole thought, *Mimic* was exactly the sort of movie Rory would have loved. He didn't know if he needed the reminder.

They began walking north on Sheridan. As usual, Cole couldn't keep himself from eyeing all the faces of strangers on the street and even driving by in cars. Maybe one of them would be Rory. It was weird, because suddenly he was seeing guys who looked like Rory almost everywhere.

Elaine said, "I thought a little escapism might do you good." They continued on in silence, with Cole forcing himself to stare down at the sidewalk. He suddenly wished Elaine, with all her good intentions and her need to cheer him up, would just go away. The realization took him by surprise. Cole was nothing if not an extrovert; he usually couldn't abide being alone. He thought people who went to see movies by themselves or even ate out alone were strange. Could one change from being an extrovert to an introvert? It didn't matter anyway. Cole knew he simply wanted to be alone.

They waited for the Walk light to illuminate at Sherwin, and when it did, continued on their way. Elaine sighed. "I've been wanting to see *G.I. Jane*. How about that?"

Cole stopped in the middle of the street. A guy on rollerblades veered sharply around them. "Then why don't *you* go see it?"

"What do you mean?"

Cole hated seeing the hurt in his sister's dark eyes, but he didn't think he could abide one more minute with her. The need to go off and shut himself up in an apartment that used to be *theirs* but now was *his* pressed in. He wasn't sure why. All he knew he'd accomplish would be to make himself even more miserable than he already was. But maybe he needed that misery. In some ways it was becoming like an old, reliable friend, one that knew him better than anyone else.

"I mean I don't know if I feel up for a movie."

"Okay," Elaine said.

They turned the corner at Fargo, Cole's street. His building was just ahead.

Elaine offered, "We can just hang out. It's cool if you don't want to go anywhere else today. We'll just check out what's on TV. Or I could run over to Blockbuster and get us a couple videos. Maybe later, we could order in Thai. There's that new place over on Clark."

Cole closed his eyes and forced himself to take a deep breath. His sister's kindness was almost painful. He didn't know why and he didn't understand it, but there it was. He needed her gone.

"Don't you get it? I need to be by myself," he snapped.

Elaine's face crumpled. He'd hurt her.

Cole reached out a hand, then dropped it before making contact. "Look. I'm sorry. I'm just not dealing with this. I still need—" Cole's voice trailed off. What did he need? He wished he knew. So he simply told his sister he needed space.

"Why won't you let me help you?" Tears stood in Elaine's eyes.

"I will," Cole said. "You can. But I just need a little time. Okay?" He reached out and at last touched a fingertip to her cheek. "I know I'm being an asshole. But can you understand?"

Elaine said nothing. She simply pulled him into a fierce embrace, so hard Cole had to gasp for air. He knew she was crying—and wished he could cry too. But all he felt at the moment, other than his desperate need for solitude, was numbness. It was as though all the emotions had slowly drained out of him with each passing day with no word from Rory.

How would life ever get back to normal?

Elaine held on to him for a long time, until Cole finally had to gently extricate himself. He tried to mollify her with "Look, give me a few hours. Then, if you're not busy tonight, come on over and we'll order in. You can sleep over. You can even have my bed." It wasn't much of an offer—he hadn't slept in their bed since the night Rory vanished. "I'll just take the couch."

Elaine smiled and wiped a tear away. "Really?"

Cole felt guilty for how hopeful she looked. "Sure. And ordering in Thai sounds great." Even though it didn't. "We'll find some stupid comedy to watch. We can mix up a pitcher of margaritas." Cole already dreaded the evening.

"Okay." Elaine turned back to head toward her car, which was parked in the lot at the end of Touhy Avenue. "I'll swing by around six? Seven?"

"Make it seven."

She opened her mouth, and he knew she was going to encourage him to go for a run or take a bike ride or simply *do something*, even if it wasn't with her. And even though he had no intention of taking out his Asics or his bike, he was ready to tell her he'd think about it.

But all she said was "Good." And then she hurried away.

Cole stood watching until she turned the corner.

He walked slowly back to the apartment, and when he got to the courtyard entrance, he simply stopped and stared up at the gothic building. It was a pale salmon color, with terra-cotta embellishments. The courtyard's grass was still green, and there were mums and asters planted in the pots at each corner of the yard in readiness for fall.

With a lump in his throat, he remembered the day he and Rory had first looked at the place. They'd gone to some apartment-finder service on Broadway that Saturday morning in June. It had been a gorgeous day, sunny, with a few big, puffy clouds riding high. Their agent had been a fellow gay man, not much older than themselves, and Cole could tell he was new to the job and a bit nervous as he drove them around the north side of the city to view a few places in their price range.

The agent, whose name was Neil, was hunting for parking as Rory and Cole stood in front of the building.

"It's kind of like that movie," Rory said, snapping his fingers as he tried to remember. "You know the one? With the witches!"

Cole shook his head. "Sorry."

"*Rosemary's Baby!*" Rory yelled as it came to him.

"Never heard of it," Cole said.

"Oh, come on! Really? We have to rent it ASAP. Anyway, this couple goes and lives in this old building in New York. This place makes me think of it. It's not as foreboding, but just the age. Maybe it was built around the same time as the place they used in the movie."

Cole shook his head. "Is something bad gonna happen to us if we move in here?"

The memory today made him shiver despite the warm lake-scented air. He went back into the memory.

"Like what? In the movie Satan rapes her and she gives birth to the anti-Christ. I don't think we have anything like that to worry about. Although it might be fun to have you dress up like the devil and try to impregnate me. I'm always up for that!" Rory laughed.

Cole snickered, shaking his head. "But this looks really nice."

"It's gorgeous. You can tell they keep it up." Rory swiveled and pointed to the steps and turnaround at the end of the street and the big ocean-like expanse of Lake Michigan beyond. "And we can just hop on down to the beach whenever we want."

Cole smirked. "It's probably way over our budget."

"Well, let's just see." Rory turned as Neil came up to them with keys jangling.

Surprisingly, the apartment *was* in their price range, and—when they'd signed the lease later that afternoon under Neil's watchful eye— they'd both been overjoyed. So lucky....

Cole sighed. How could he have known, back then, how short-lived their stay in paradise was to be?

He headed in through the gate into the courtyard, ignoring the flowers, and barely nodded when an old lady who'd probably been a tenant since the building opened said hello.

Head down, he scurried to his little warren, his sanctuary.

Once inside, after closing and locking the door behind him, he leaned against it, feeling a sense of relief as he shut out the world. The more he missed Rory and worried about what had happened to him, the more this apartment seemed like a safe harbor, a place to hide. Where he could, even in his lowest moments, pretend Rory was coming home soon. Sometimes he'd even swear to himself he heard keys in the front door dead bolt.

One thing he had accomplished since Rory had gone missing was installing blinds on all the windows, and now he went about closing them all, shutting out the day's brilliant light. Somehow he felt better, safer, in the muted semidarkness.

After that task was done, Cole stood in their—his—bedroom, hands at his sides, wondering what he should do with himself. He'd been sleeping so much more lately, so different from the self he used to know who'd rather do almost anything than the time-wasting act of slumber. But now the bed called to him, the bed he'd refused to sleep in. It told him to simply lie down and pull the covers over his head. He could escape into oblivion, where there was no pain of loss and where sometimes Rory appeared to him in dreams.

Wasn't that preferable to reality?

He shook his head. "You're pathetic." And even though he'd just labeled himself pathetic, he turned to the closet opposite him and went to it to do something he'd done before, something even more pathetic. He flung open the door and stared inside at Rory's clothes on hangers, at his sweaters on the shelf above, folded neatly, waiting for a cold season that might now never come for Rory. Cole took in the sneakers and the dress shoes, the hiking boots. He allowed himself, almost entranced, to go slowly inside.

And then he began, article by article of Rory's clothing, to caress each T-shirt, each pair of jeans, each sweatshirt, to rub the fabric between his fingers. And last, he did as he always did and lifted the fabric to his nose, desperate for a whiff of what he could only describe as Rory's unique smell, something clean, manly.

Then he sat on the floor with Rory's clothes piled all around him and wept.

CHAPTER 6

COLE AWAKENED to brilliant sun streaming in through the slats of his bedroom miniblinds. He squinted at the butter-yellow illumination, noticing how it made the dust motes dance in the air. There were lots of dust motes. Cole realized he needed to clean. The place hadn't been dusted—or anything else—since they'd moved in.

It was his day off. He *could* give the place a proper going-over—mop the hardwood floors, dust, throw away the pizza boxes and beer bottles littering the living room—that would be a start. Maybe carry that overflowing basket of laundry downstairs to the machines in the basement?

He moved to the window and cautiously opened the blinds' slats a bit so he could look out at the lake.

It shimmered as though diamonds had been cast upon its aquamarine surface. It looked summery out there, nearly tropical. Cole could almost make himself believe he was someplace like the Bahamas or Jamaica.

It was late September, a Tuesday, and Cole's day off from the store. Cleaning the place would be something practical *and* a distraction from thinking about Rory, who'd now been gone for well over a month. Cole was trying to come to terms with the fact that it was most likely he'd never see him again, yet his dreams every night brought back Rory's face, his arms, the startling paleness of his body, peppered with freckles. And he'd wake, just as he had today, with those dream images taunting him, giving him hope he knew *in his head* was useless, but not in his heart.

He continued to peer out at the day, one his mom would have called Indian summer. She would have insisted he take advantage of it. And Cole knew she was right. Autumn had already been settling in, like a guest that planned to stick around for a while, just long enough for one to get comfortable before the horror of winter arrived to take its place. Winter always seemed to settle in the longest, even though each Chicago season was, in reality, about three months. Winter, with its seemingly endless darkness, bitter cold, and heaps of grimy snow, always seemed as though it would last forever when in the grips of its icy fingers.

So today he should get outside—head downstairs to the basement and pull his Trek hybrid out of the storage locker. It had lain idle there since they moved in back at the beginning of August. Cole had never had the inclination or even the energy to want to ride the blue-and-silver bike lately, even though when he'd moved in, with the long lakefront trail so close by, he'd intended to ride almost every day.

He could pump up the bike's tires, grease its chain, and take it out for a spin. There was the path along the lake, which he could easily follow south all the way down to Hyde Park, or north through Evanston and the Northwestern University campus. If he went that way, he could cut across Evanston to the west and hook up with the Green Bay Trail, which ran parallel to the Metra train tracks. The trail was a beautiful paved path, most of it under a canopy of trees whose leaves were just now beginning to change.

And a bike ride, with the sun on his back and the wind in his hair, would also be a distraction, a much more pleasing one than cleaning. Anyway, if he cleaned today, he'd just need to do it again, so... why bother? He smiled and realized he hadn't done so in a long time. He felt a little guilty for feeling this small twinge of happiness and freedom when Rory was God knows where.

Cole stared down at the dusty hardwood floor. He *knew* where, or if not where exactly, what. Alone in his own space, Cole could allow the thought that was always behind the others to peek its ugly monster face out—Rory was, most likely, no longer even alive.

It was the explanation that made the most sense.

Cole sprawled back on the bed, tempted to just pull the covers up over his head and spend the day there, hiding. Hiding from truths too terrible to contemplate for long.

No. He would get out. He would do his best to enjoy this day. Who knew what it would bring?

AFTER A shower and a breakfast of cold pizza from two nights ago, Cole went down to the basement and pulled his battered Trek from the storage locker. He had to move aside some boxes, and in the process almost talked himself out of going. The boxes were mostly Rory's stuff, filled with things like Star Wars action figures and drafts of science fiction short stories he'd written in college.

But gamely he soldiered on and extricated his bike from the cluttered and crowded locker. He grabbed his pump and helmet from a shelf. The bike looked ready to go, except the tires were soft when he squeezed them.

It took only a few moments to pump them up. Cole donned his yellow Giro helmet and hoisted the bike up on his shoulder to carry it upstairs and outside.

The basement door slammed behind him, and Cole squinted against the bright sun. It was the tail end of the morning and relatively quiet. Rush hour was over, and Cole found himself actually looking forward to the ride, to stretching muscles, to feeling the breeze against his face. Because it was a weekday, he expected to find the trail relatively free of other bikers, runners, and walkers. He'd appreciate the solitude.

He hopped on the bike and headed out to Sheridan. He'd hook up with the lakefront just south of the Evanston border. The sun warmed his arms and shoulders, even though there was a little nip in the air. The temperature hovered in the midsixties. Perfect.

He rode north, letting his mind go blank, centering himself in his body and feeling its reactions. He found himself smiling again as he headed toward Evanston, and the lake, bordered by boulders, stretched out on his right in all its azure glory, the sun glinting off its ever-moving surface. To his left was Calvary Cemetery, and Cole made a mental note to stop in on his way back. He'd always found cemeteries to be places of peace.

Rory loved cemeteries too.

It was something we had in common. Our second date was at Graceland. We had a picnic among the tombstones, and the quiet and peace in the middle of the city was something I won't forget. You taught me that, Rory. You showed me the beauty of a cemetery.

As he turned onto the trail bordering South Boulevard Beach, Cole shoved aside the memory. He was glad he'd made himself get out of the house for something other than work. For once he found it easy to be in the moment, to put his concerns and thoughts at bay as he pedaled along, paying attention to the pleasant ache of calf muscles and his heavier but regular breathing. He even pondered stopping at a café in Evanston on the way back for lunch. There was a Chinese joint downtown, the Pine Yard, that he really liked.

Cole was surprised at the miles he accumulated so quickly, keeping his mind free of the worries that normally pressed in on him. He allowed himself, for perhaps the first time since that awful night, to simply relax and enjoy the world around him a bit. It wasn't that difficult with the scenery he had to view. Not only was Lake Michigan, in its ever-changing motion and colors, a constant to his right as he pedaled north, but there were also dozens of other things to look at, like old historic mansions in Evanston and Wilmette, the grassy parkland that bordered the lake, even the occasional shirtless runner on the trail. This last surprised him and made him feel a little guilty, as though any attraction should have been wiped out by his situation.

He was only human, after all.

He headed west to the Green Bay Trail, enjoying the canopy of trees over his head and how the leaves were beginning to light up in hues of orange, yellow, and red. Away from the lakefront, it was quieter, save for the passage of an occasional Metra train, headed south into the city or north, up to Kenosha, Wisconsin.

Cole rode all the way north to Highland Park, nearing the gates of Ravinia, the outdoor music venue, before turning around.

Coming home, the temperature rose, the clouds cleared, and the sun upped its intensity. It almost felt like summer. It must have gotten at least ten degrees warmer. He found himself hungry, and a big plate of spaghetti with a giant meatball in its center sounded like the perfect way to replenish his energy.

Visions of pasta danced in his head as he raced south on Sheridan Road in Evanston, near Lighthouse Beach. He could just about smell the aroma of simmering tomatoes, basil, and garlic. His mouth watered. He pedaled faster, legs a blur.

And then it happened.

A runner, looking southward, darted out from a side street right in front of Cole. Cole had time only to gasp and slam on his hand brakes as hard as he could. The action did indeed bring him to a sudden and complete halt. Well, at least it brought the bike to a halt. Cole didn't have mental time to even react to the terror of suddenly being airborne as he hurtled over his handlebars.

His impact with the pavement was hard, knocking the wind out of him. He groaned as his head bounced off the concrete.

The runner, a guy about his own age wearing a tank and nylon running shorts, stooped down beside him. Cole stared at his red-and-white nylon shoes. Asics. His gaze shifted up—the guy was saying something.

"Shit!" He lifted a shaking hand to his mouth. "I'm so sorry! I should have looked where I was going. I'm an idiot." He reached a hand out to Cole, who, dazed, managed to get up to a sitting position on the sidewalk. He placed a hand to his forehead. It came away bloody.

"Oh shit, you're bleeding." The guy's green eyes were alive with concern. "You should maybe go to the ER, get checked out." He paused for a moment, thinking. "My car's parked over in a lot on campus. I can take you. We'll throw your bike in my hatch. Okay?"

Cole wondered suddenly who this man was and why he'd taken such an interest in him. He glanced down at the blood on his hand and laughed. He showed it to the man. "Where did this come from?"

"Yeah, we need to get you to a hospital."

"Why?" Cole asked.

The guy cocked his head. "Um, you just flew over your handlebars."

"I did?"

"Yes, yes. Don't you remember?"

Cole racked his brain. All he could recall was speeding along the Green Bay Trail and the autumn colors. Did he have an accident? When? He looked at the bicycle lying on the ground beside him. Whose was it?

He tapped the runner. "Is that your bike?"

"No, it's yours. Look, I think your tumble shook you up. You might be in shock. If I leave you here, will you stay? It'll take me, like, five minutes to run to my car and five minutes to get back. We'll take you down to Saint Francis, have 'em check you over. You might have a concussion." He nodded and smiled sympathetically at Cole. Cole noticed he had a really nice smile, very white and even teeth. But there was a little gap between the two front ones, not too big, but just enough of a flaw to make him human. And kind of sexy....

"Okay?"

Cole smiled again. "Okay what?" He laughed.

The guy bit his lower lip and looked out at the street. A fair amount of traffic was rushing by in both directions. "I'm gonna take you to the hospital, bud. You might need stitches in that eyebrow. It's bleeding pretty bad."

Cole reached up and touched his split-open forehead. It stung, and seeing the blood, and for the first time noticing it dripping down the side of his face, made him shudder. "I'm Cole," he said, extending his hand.

"Okay." The guy smiled. "Tommy. Tommy D'Amico." Cole watched as the guy stood, took in his lean runner's build, how his calves looked like someone had secreted a couple of oranges beneath the skin. Tommy's gaze, though, was trained northward. There was a woman with short gray hair walking a standard-size poodle down the street. The poodle was black, which contrasted wonderfully with its bright fuchsia leash. And were those rhinestones in its collar? How fabulous!

Cole sat calmly and listened as Tommy introduced himself to the woman. "My friend here took a tumble off his bike and is kind of shaken up. Would you be able to do me a huge favor?"

"What's that?" The woman smiled and reached down to pull her dog away from Tommy's crotch, which Cole thought was hilarious. The dog wasn't stupid!

"I don't want to leave him here by himself while I run over to the campus to get my car so I can take him down to Saint Francis. It's dangerous." Tommy looked pointedly at the busy road, only a few feet away. "He's not, uh, thinking right."

What did Tommy think? That he'd dash into traffic? Sheesh, he wasn't three years old.

"Would you mind?" Tommy asked. "I don't know what else to do. I'll hurry and—"

She cut him off with an upturned palm. "It's no problem. Go. I'll stay here with—" She glanced down at Cole, her eyebrows coming together quizzically.

"Cole." Cole smiled and held out his hand and then withdrew it quickly as he realized it was covered with someone's blood. He reminded himself—*your blood*. He didn't know why everyone seemed in such a panic. Other than the blood, he felt pretty good, albeit a little confused. He knew he must have had an accident, but for the life of him couldn't remember what the hell had happened.

"Babs and I will stay here with Cole." She sat down on the grass beside him. She wore jeans and a red Bulls T-shirt, sandals. Her gray hair made her appear, from a distance, much older than she was. There were no lines under her warm dark eyes. The dog sniffed Cole and began licking away the blood on his face.

"Babs!" the woman cried, yanking the dog away by her leash.

"I'm so sorry," she said to Cole.

"It's okay. Dogs love blood. She's being herself."

Tommy spoke up. "Okay, I'm gonna go. I'll be right back. Ten minutes or less, I promise."

"Just be careful," the woman said. "We'll be here."

They both watched as Tommy took off as though he were racing toward the finish line of some imaginary race. And maybe he was.

The woman turned to him. "I'm Mary Ellen. What happened to you?"

Cole removed his helmet to scratch his head. "I'm not really sure. Everyone seems to think I had some kind of accident on my bike, but I can't remember it for the life of me." He chuckled. "And I suppose that's my bike there. I mean, common sense would indicate that, but I don't recognize it."

Mary Ellen rummaged around in the small backpack she'd taken from her shoulders when she sat down next to him. She pulled out a wad of Kleenex and held it out to Cole. "Here, hold this against that cut on your head. Apply good pressure—or I can do it if you want me to." Cole took the wad of tissue from her and held it to his head.

"It's okay," he said. "I've got it."

Mary Ellen eyed him. "All I can say is it's a good thing you were wearing a helmet." She shook her head. "I'm actually a nurse practitioner, so you're in good hands. My diagnosis? You're in a little shock, and you probably have a concussion. You might have cracked a rib or two as well." She turned his head with her hand and with her other hand, pulled the wad of tissues away for a moment, then put it back. "And that will definitely need stitches. You might have a scar, but that could be kind of sexy, right?" She smiled.

Cole liked this woman. "Yeah, tough guy."

"You just need to stay still right here with me and relax until your friend comes back."

"Oh, he's not my friend. He's my lover." Cole laughed.

Mary Ellen said, "*Okay*. Just chill until he gets here to take you to the hospital."

Cole nodded. "I'm not going anywhere. It just feels really strange, almost like I'm dreaming."

The poodle chose that moment to bark at a squirrel running nearby, straining at her leash. "Babs! Cool it!" The woman placed a hand on Babs's hindquarters, forcing her to sit.

"Is she named after Streisand?" Cole asked.

"God, no! A lot of people ask that. But I just liked the name. And I love giving human names to pets. It suits her, don't you think?"

Cole nodded. "It's nice of you to stay here with me. I'm sure you have better stuff to do." He drew in a deep breath. "As time goes on, I'm starting to feel a little more in touch with myself. Things are starting to hurt—like when I take a breath, *ouch!* And I feel a headache coming on."

Mary Ellen nodded.

"You can probably go. I promise I won't run into traffic, no matter how tempted I am." He smiled, and she gave him a grin back, her dark eyes twinkling.

"It's okay. I'm in for the long haul," she said.

It was only a couple more minutes before a rusting red hatchback in need of a new muffler made a U-turn on Sheridan, narrowly avoiding an accident. Drivers, both northbound and southbound, sounded their displeasure with their horns.

Tommy whipped the car over to the curb and cranked down the window. "Your chariot awaits," he called out.

"Can you get up okay?" Mary Ellen asked.

"Yeah," Cole said. "My legs are fine." Belying this, he stumbled a bit when he stood, but that was due to the dizziness he felt, not from any pain in his legs.

Mary Ellen put a hand on his shoulder. "Do you want me to come with?"

"Oh, that's sweet of you, but you have Babs, and I need to get my bike in the back. You've really earned your Good Samaritan gold star for today." Cole glanced at his bike, lying on the cement like a fallen soldier. "But maybe you could help me get my bike in the car?"

"Sure." Mary Ellen turned to Babs and told her to sit and stay. She motioned Cole out of the way before hoisting the bike off the ground. Cole was surprised to see it didn't look damaged in the least.

Tommy hopped out of the car to help Mary Ellen load it inside. He looked over at Cole. "At least your Trek escaped without a scratch."

"I'll say a little prayer of gratitude just as soon as we get to the hospital." Cole hopped into the passenger seat. Tommy joined him in the car.

As Mary Ellen backed away, hands in her pockets, Cole called out, "You're really kind! Thank you so much for staying with me."

She smiled and waved, and then walked rapidly away because Babs was tugging hard. She'd seen another squirrel.

TOMMY PULLED up to the emergency room doors of Saint Francis Hospital in south Evanston. "You okay to go inside on your own? I need to find a place to park this piece of shit."

Cole eyed him. "You're not gonna ride away with my bike never to be seen again, are you?"

"I'm not gonna do that." He pulled out his wallet and withdrew a DePaul University student ID. "Here, hang on to this. That way, you'll know where to find me if I try to abscond with your wheels. I can understand why you think I might be tempted after riding in this jalopy." He grinned.

Cole glanced down at Tommy's student photo, in which he wore a blue-and-green rugby shirt that contrasted beautifully with his red hair and green eyes. "Okay. So, you'll come back? And wait for me?"

"Of course. It's the least I can do. Again, I'm really sorry."

Cole shrugged. "It was an accident. That's all."

"Still. I should maybe have had the music in my ears at a lower volume and been looking where I was going."

Cole hesitated. He didn't know if he was supposed to absolve the guy any further or what.

Tommy nudged him. "You should go. Unless you need me to help you get in there?" He nodded toward the emergency room entrance.

"I'm a big boy. I think I can manage." Cole hopped out of the car and started up to the sliding doors, weaving around an ambulance that had just pulled up, red lights whirling.

He let the EMTs go in first with their gurney. An old woman wearing an oxygen mask lay upon it in a floral-print housedress. Her rheumy gray eyes looked terrified, and Cole's heart went out to her.

When their gazes met, he mouthed the words, "You're gonna be okay."

He turned to see Tommy's car round the corner at the end of the street. Would he ever see him again? Cole was already pretty sure he was a good guy, so he didn't think he had much, if anything, to worry about.

What a strange way to meet a guy. I wonder if he's gay. I wonder if he's single.

What's wrong with me?

Cole headed inside, gaze trained on the admission desk.

LATER, COLE lay on a bed in the large ward of the emergency room. A nurse had earlier pulled the curtains on either side of him closed so he'd have some privacy. He wished Tommy was there and wondered if he'd truly be waiting when he was done.

A very young doctor pushed one of the curtains aside and stood next to Cole's bed, smiling down at him. He looked like he was still a teenager, with pale brown hair, freckles, and nerdy glasses that Cole ached to make fun of.

"I understand you took a bad tumble off your bike."

"Who are you? Doogie Howser?" Cole asked, referring to the old Neil Patrick Harris sitcom he'd only seen in reruns.

The doctor laughed. "Believe it or not, you are not the first person to have said that. Just to reassure you, young man, I was thirty-two on my last birthday and am a fully licensed MD. In spite of my appearance, I know a lot, particularly about head injuries." Without pause, he took a small flashlight from his lab coat and peered into Cole's eyes, holding the lids open as he did so.

"Can you tell me what happened to you?"

Cole was surprised. He remembered the details of his accident. Just like that, at the prompt, the memory appeared—Tommy running out in front of him unexpectedly, the bright clean white of his tank top against his olive skin, the very, very brief nylon running shorts. The back of his head as he looked south, seeing whatever the hell was going on down that way and completely missing a bicyclist hurtling toward him at high speed. Tommy was lucky he'd made it out of their first encounter unscathed. He had Cole's quick reflexes to thank for that! He gave the doctor a quick summary of what happened.

"And what day is it?"

"Tuesday, silly." Cole grinned. "It's my day off."

The doctor smirked. "Great way to spend it. Can't say I'm glad you came to see us here."

The doctor asked a bunch of other obvious questions like where they were, who the president was, and how many fingers he was holding up.

"I don't think we need to do any X-rays at this point," he said. "But if you find yourself getting a really *bad* headache, or vomiting, I want you to come back in. You *can* sleep, but I'd like it if you have a friend or something stay with you just to make sure you wake up normally. Cool?"

Cole didn't know who could stay with him. His sister, maybe? He shook his head. Elaine was in New York this week with her job. Whatever. "Cool," he told the doctor.

"We'll just get you stitched up and on your way. I want you to take it very easy for the next couple of days. Nurse told me you most likely have a cracked rib too."

"Aren't you gonna do something for that?" At the mention of his rib, Cole's side started to ache with a dull throb.

"Nothing much we can. It'll heal, buddy." The doctor pulled a tray toward the bed. Cole looked over to see all the supplies the doctor would need to stitch the gash in his eyebrow closed.

"Gonna need to clean that up first. Here comes the water." He squeezed cold water on Cole's forehead and wiped it away before it could reach his eyes. He then grabbed a needle from the tray. "Gonna numb you up a bit before I start sewing." He held the needle up to the light and squeezed the plunger. The needle squirted a little clear fluid into the air. Cole shuddered.

"Ready?"

Cole shut his eyes.

DRESSED, AND with a *Frankenstein*-esque lateral row of black stitches cutting through his left eyebrow, Cole emerged into the waiting room. He glanced in a mirror over the magazine rack and was horrified. He looked like he'd been in a fight. No, he looked like he'd been in a fight and *lost*.

The room, with its rows of oak-and-blue-vinyl chairs, magazine racks, and posters reminding people to wash their hands and get vaccinations, was filled with coughing, unsettled, and generally unhappy-looking people.

Save for one.

Tommy hadn't noticed him come in yet. He sat in a corner, legs crossed, thumbing through an issue of *People*. Cole got it just then— the guy was Italian. Cole didn't usually associate redheads with Italian heritage, but everything else about Tommy, including, duh, his last name and nose, spoke of a Mediterranean heritage.

And then his rapidly returning memory sent him a download—he knew this Tommy D'Amico. Well, to use the term "knew" was a stretch, but he'd met him before. He flashed back to a few weeks ago when he was having breakfast with Elaine at a neighborhood diner and Tommy walked in, trailed by—oh my God—the woman who'd last seen Rory on the night he disappeared. Or at least the last they knew of.

Too weird. He stared at Tommy, asking himself if he was sure this was the same guy. But it was. His mind said he *might* be wrong, but his gut was certain. And if Cole had learned one thing in his young life, it was that he could trust his gut. When he did, it never steered him wrong.

He shook his head. *What're the odds?*

Gone was the numbness Cole had felt initially after the accident. Now he was just kind of wiped out and weak. There was a little guy with a tiny ice pick chipping away at his brain, right behind his eyes. Even though it was daylight out, he wanted nothing more than to just go home, pull a blanket over his head, and sleep for hours.

And this new association? It just made him want to get away from Tommy, really. The guy, of course, had done nothing wrong, but just the taint of what had occurred hung over him, and for that, Cole didn't know if he could stand to look at him. It was strange. It wasn't fair. But it was the truth.

He suddenly recalled the doctor's advice that he should have someone with him to make sure he woke up okay. He'd kind of thought of asking Tommy to sleep over—in a platonic, safeguard kind of way. But now? Forget it. He supposed he didn't have to follow the doctor's advice to the letter. He'd just call Elaine and have her give him a wake-up call. If he didn't answer, she could call his mom or 911.

Cole thought it was kind of sad to realize he didn't really have anyone who could come to stay with him. In the wake of Rory's disappearance, he knew he'd shoved most everyone he cared about away so he could be alone, lick his wounds in private. He stopped near where Tommy was sitting, suddenly wishing he'd just left his bicycle and headed home.

Tommy finally looked up from the magazine, and their eyes met. Tommy smiled. Yet Cole couldn't find it in himself to return it. Tommy hopped out of his seat and gestured for Cole to sit, since every other chair was occupied.

Cole sat.

"How you doin'?" Tommy asked. His gaze drifted up to Cole's stitches. The doctor had told him they'd look a lot less frightening after a day or two, when the redness and swelling went down. He could get them out in about a week. "You looked wiped, man."

"Yeah. I do feel really tired. Headachy."

"I would too. Again, I'm so, so—"

Cole cut him off with an upturned hand. "Please don't apologize again. As I said, it was an accident. I don't blame you for it. I'm not mad. I'm not gonna sue. So calm the fuck down." Cole smiled.

"Well, I do feel bad. You ready to go home?"

Cole sat up a little straighter. "You don't have to do any more. I'll just have them call me a cab, after I get things squared away with the billing folks." As he uttered the word, Cole felt a chill go through him. How would he pay for this? When you worked less than full-time at a retail store, you didn't get niceties like health insurance. Up until today, his young and fit self thought he really had no need for insurance. But wasn't that how everyone thought? Until they needed it? He put a hand to his forehead. "God. I don't have insurance." He dropped the hand. "My parents will help me out, I'm sure."

Tommy *stared down* at him. "One, you are not calling a cab. Why do you think I waited for you? I'll see that you get home. *And* I'll unload your bike and bring it in for you too. It's the least I can do. It would make me happy.

"Two. Don't worry about billing. I already took care of it."

"You did?" Cole asked.

"Hey, I'm prelaw. I worry about things like lawsuits, so I was proactive and took care of things while you were getting yourself stitched up. *And* I'm a good guy. Yes, it was an accident, of course it was. But that still doesn't change the fact that it was my fault. And I should pay for that. Not you."

"Can you afford it?" Cole blurted.

Tommy laughed. "Let me worry about that."

Cole stared at the tile floor, feeling unaccountably depressed. Here was this handsome guy, hot body, sweet face, and he was really compassionate and kind to boot. A really good guy, it seemed. And yet he still wanted nothing to do with him.

"Okay? Cole?"

Cole looked up. Tommy was staring down at him, concern obvious in his eyes. Cole had to admit Tommy had a point. He was in no shape to get his bike out of Tommy's car, load it into a cab, and then lug it down to the storage locker in the basement. For practical reasons alone, he should try to swallow his pride and allow Tommy to take him home.

Allow him? Come on! Be grateful. "You sure you have time to do this?"

"What if I said I didn't?" Tommy put his hands on his hips.

"Then I'd have one of those nice nurses over there call me a cab."

"You're being stupid. Come on, let's go."

And Cole stood to follow him out of the waiting room. He felt a nauseating paradox as he stared at Tommy's back. One part was queasiness at the association he'd just remembered linked Tommy with his own personal tragedy, and the other was that he found, even in his current state, he was unable to keep his eyes off the rise and fall of the man's ass.

"THE PARKING gods are with me," Tommy said as he pulled into a spot just a car length to the east of the entrance to Cole's building. He turned to Cole. "Aren't we lucky?"

They were. Parking on Cole's street was notoriously difficult, almost impossible. The fact that Tommy drove up and parked right outside the building was something to be appreciated only by a true city dweller. It was a small miracle.

"Let's get you in and settled."

"Okay," Cole said softly. The fatigue he'd felt since the accident was now a wave crashing over him. He felt he could barely move. Getting out of the car, he realized why his grandpa, with his arthritis, groaned whenever he emerged from a vehicle. He felt like groaning too, but would not make himself a victim. He was certain if he voiced the pain he felt, Tommy would run around the car and help him emerge. That would just be too much and too embarrassing for words.

He stood on the sidewalk, watching as Tommy unloaded the bike from his car. He smiled at Cole. "Where to?"

Cole waved him away. "I can get it inside." He knew he was letting his pride and his unreasonable distaste for this guy and his association hurt him. But he didn't care. Once more, he just wanted to be alone. When had he gone from being a man who loved having people around him at all times to one who always wanted to be by himself? *Oh, that's right. The night the love of my life vanished into thin air....*

"I'm not gonna let you do that, buddy."

"But—"

"No buts! Do you keep it in your apartment, or do you have storage somewhere? Or is there a rack? Maybe in the back?"

Cole felt he had no choice. He simply groped in his pockets for his keys, pulled them out, and said, "This way."

AFTER THEY'D locked the bike up and headed back upstairs to the building's courtyard, Cole said, "Well, thanks again. You really went above and beyond, and I appreciate it." He tried to smile and thought he succeeded pretty well.

"Ah, I did what anyone would do in my shoes." Tommy looked around. It was late in the afternoon, and the air had turned chilly again. The sky had grown cloudier while Cole was in the ER. He could smell rain coming.

"You're a hard man to thank."

"Well, I should thank you for helping alleviate my guilt."

"Oh, please!" That statement actually elicited a laugh from Cole. "Do you have any bad traits at all?"

"Running out in front of bicyclists?" It was Tommy's turn to laugh. "And that's just for starters." Tommy toed the grass with the tip of his shoe and then looked into Cole's eyes. Just that gaze, held for a little longer than what might be considered normal, answered Cole's earlier question about whether Tommy was gay.

Tommy asked, "Do you need anything else? Can I, uh, make sure you get in okay?"

"You're being really nice, and I appreciate it. But the building has an elevator. I think I'll be okay." Cole sighed. "I just want to sleep."

"Is that all right? I mean, didn't you say in the car they said you had a mild concussion?"

"Yeah."

"Well, isn't it dangerous to go to sleep?"

"No. It's dangerous not to wake up."

Tommy looked hopeful. "You live alone?"

Cole realized then that, while he knew who Tommy was, Tommy really had no recollection of their prior meeting. Cole almost blurted out that he lived with his boyfriend. But it had been over a month now, and the truth lay somewhere in a gray area, even though there were still two names on the lease.

"Yes, I'm alone." Cole thought he knew what Tommy was getting at—concern over his waking up normally in the morning. Or was it something else? He told him, "I'm gonna give my sister, Elaine, a call. She's in New York this week with her work, but she can give me a wake-up call and check up on me in the a.m."

"I could do that too. Just give me your number."

"I don't have anything to write with or on," Cole said. "And I doubt you do either, not with those shorts."

A blush rose to Tommy's cheeks. "Just tell me. I'll remember."

"Really?"

"Yeah, you'd be surprised at what I can remember." He tapped his forehead. "Photographic."

Too tired to stand anymore, Cole plopped down in the grass. "Seriously? Then I'm surprised you haven't mentioned anything about us meeting before."

Tommy joined him on the grass. "We did?"

"Yeah. You met my sister, Elaine, too."

Tommy stared at him for a minute, and then Cole could see the tumblers suddenly click into place. "I thought you looked familiar!" Tommy exclaimed. "I just put it down to some actor I'd seen in the movies or on TV. You're cute enough."

Yup, he's gay.

"So you remember now?" Cole asked.

"I just needed the prompt." Tommy frowned. "Your boyfriend...."

"He's still missing."

"God. I'm sorry. That sucks." Tommy stared off, maybe looking at the sky, which was growing darker and cloudier by the minute. "Give me your number, Cole. I want to check on you in the morning. It'll bug me if I don't."

Cole let out a sigh and then recited his number. He didn't really believe Tommy would remember it.

They sat on the grass for a while in silence until a big, fat raindrop landed on Cole's head, quickly followed by another, then another. Cole and Tommy hopped up off the grass at the same moment.

"I better get inside," Cole said.

There was a flash of lightning, and then, a few seconds later, a long drumroll of thunder. Cole started toward the front door. But his conscience wouldn't allow him to just leave Tommy out there in the rain, not when he'd been so nice to him. Yet he *really* wanted to be by himself. All he needed was a glass of water and a soft place to lie down.

Cole forced himself to say, "You want to come up? Wait out the shower?"

A bolt of lightning hit close, right on the pavement outside the building's courtyard. Cole's eyes widened. He could have sworn he smelled ozone. The peal of thunder that quickly followed was so loud it drowned out Tommy's answer.

Whatever it was, Cole grabbed Tommy's arm and pulled him toward the front door. Once they were in the vestibule, Cole laughed. "Jesus, we were out there in that for, like, what, ten seconds? And we're soaked!"

"I would have been okay running in the rain," Tommy said. "It's just to my car."

"Cut it out. Your application for sainthood is hereby denied." Cole pressed the Up button to call the elevator.

"Seriously, I actually like it."

Cole nodded. "You like getting struck by lightning too?"

"You sound like my dad."

The elevator doors rolled open.

UPSTAIRS, COLE went into the bathroom and dried himself off. He caught a glimpse of himself in the medicine-cabinet mirror and was stunned all over again at his reflection. He'd definitely have a scar. He didn't know how he felt about that, especially since it would be in such an obvious place.

He headed toward the bedroom and threw a clean towel at Tommy as he went. "There you go. I'll be right out."

In the bedroom, he changed into jeans and a T-shirt. He grabbed a pair of sweats out of the closet and another T-shirt from Rory's shelf, feeling a hot twinge of guilt as he did so. But the truth was, Tommy was smaller than Cole and much closer to Rory in size. He heard his sister, Elaine, in his head: *Rory's not coming back for his T-shirts, sweetie.* Cole shut his eyes. The thought pained him as much, if not more, than the throbbing ache at his temple.

When he returned to the living room, Tommy had just finished drying off. He held the towel out to Cole. "Thanks, man." He moved to the window and looked out. "It looks like it's slowed down out there. Just a drizzle now. I can probably get home okay." He turned around and looked at Cole with hope in those amazing green eyes. "Unless you want me to stay? I could fix you some supper while you take a nap?"

Cole exchanged the towel Tommy held out for the clothes he held in the other hand. "That's too kind of you. I'll be okay. Got some leftover Giordano's in the fridge." He chuckled. "I live off that stuff."

"It is good pizza," Tommy said. "But I think I could make you something healthier." He pulled his tank over his head and had his fingers in the waistband of his running shorts when Cole stopped him.

"Dude, the bathroom's down the hall." He jerked a directional thumb over his shoulder.

Cole was shocked. Under other circumstances, this might be the onset of an erotic encounter. But today was definitely *not* the day. He frowned and wondered if the day would ever come again. Since Rory's disappearance, Cole's libido had also taken a powder.

Tommy blushed. "Sorry!" He hurried into the bathroom. Cole turned to look. Tommy hadn't bothered shutting the door. Cole couldn't help it—he stared as Tommy finished undressing. He could see him in the medicine-cabinet mirror, and it was obvious the man didn't eat much pizza. In fact, he must subsist on things like skinless chicken breasts, fruit, nuts, and salad. There was hardly an ounce of fat on his body. Unless you counted that beer can dick....

Cole forced himself to turn away and move toward the window. The rain had all but stopped. He could see from the sway of the trees outside that it had gotten windy. He was hard, and that felt like a betrayal.

"Cole?"

When Cole turned around, for just a moment, it wasn't Tommy D'Amico he saw standing there, but Rory. He shook his head and the image dispersed. "Black looks good on you," Cole said.

"Thanks." He held up his wet clothes. "You wouldn't have a plastic grocery bag or something for these?"

"Sure." Cole went and fished out a Jewel bag from under the sink and returned to the living room with it. He handed it to Tommy.

Tommy took it and stuffed his wet clothes inside. He looked up at Cole and smiled. "Dora—my roommate—is gonna be worried. I went

out for a run about—what—six hours ago? She'll think I was abducted."
A look of concern wrinkled Tommy's eyebrows, or maybe Cole should
say *eyebrow*, because he appeared to have only one. "God, I'm stupid.
Sorry I said that."

Cole didn't even realize what Tommy had said that was worthy of
apology. Then it dawned on him—Rory, gone. "It's cool. Tell Dora I said
hi." Cole could vaguely remember a blonde woman, sort of a grown-up
Jan Brady in his mind.

Tommy laughed. "I will." He started toward the door. "I'll call you
in the morning."

Cole walked with him to the door. "Sure you will." He tested him:
"What's my number?"

Without a pause, Tommy rattled off the phone number.

"Wow. You weren't kidding."

Tommy headed out into the hallway. "You get some rest. Take care
of yourself. And if you need anything…." He waltzed back inside, moved
to the coffee table, and sat down on the couch. He pulled a pizza box over
to him, grabbed a pen, and wrote his number on the grease-stained inner
top. He stood and wiped his hands on the sweats. "If you need anything,
seriously, don't think twice about calling. No matter the time."

And with a smile and a little salute, Tommy D'Amico was gone.
Cole closed the door, then leaned against it. He shut his eyes, disturbed
by what he felt.

All he kept telling himself over and over was that it was too soon,
too soon.

CHAPTER 7

"WHERE HAVE you been? I've been frantic!" Dora was up in Tommy's face the minute he opened the door to their apartment in Edgewater. She even gave him a little shove.

A jolt of guilt ran through Tommy, almost like something physical. He gave her what he knew had to be a half-assed smile, one a writer would call "sheepish."

Heat rose to his cheeks, and he laughed uncomfortably. "Sorry."

Dora shook her head and sat back down on the couch. The apartment was silent—no TV or radio going. Tommy could just imagine her sitting there in silence, stewing and worrying over his whereabouts.

The only sound was the patter of rain against the window. "Where were you?" Dora repeated, staring out the window. The question was more of an accusation.

Tommy knew he could get all self-righteous and tell her they were roommates, not lovers, and that, as an adult, he had a right to keep his own hours. But he was touched by Dora's concern, actually grateful that he had someone in his life who cared about him enough to worry. He also knew that part of her concern was motivated by her recent experience with the missing man, Rory Schneidmiller. Dora cared too much about people—it was hard to state that as a flaw, but it hurt her at times. He knew she obsessed endlessly over her brief encounter with the missing guy, searching desperately for a clue as to what had happened to him. Why she took this responsibility on herself was not evidence of masochism, but of kindness. Of a fierce desire to help. Compassion. Tommy knew she'd be an overprotective, but great, mom someday.

Tommy sat down with her on the couch. He leaned over and gave her a little kiss, from which she flinched, but she grinned anyway. "You won't believe it," he said.

She looked over at him, mock anger creasing her features. "What? Another hookup? Yet another sleazy sexual encounter?" She laughed. "Someone see you in that running getup and—" She stopped herself. "Hey, where are your clothes?" She slapped her forehead. "*Of course* it was a hookup. It always is. You *guys*." She continued shaking her head.

In her mind, gay men, the young ones especially, lived for little more than the pursuit of the next hookup. Tommy had to admit to himself he'd probably fed into the idea. He was not exactly Mary Poppins. More like a Mary Magdalene....

"It wasn't a hookup." Tommy picked up the remote control, then set it back down. "Although that would have been nice."

"So? What *did* happen?"

He told her about the bike accident and what he'd done to cause it—and the subsequent trip to the ER.

When he was finished, Dora looked a little more forgiving. Actually, she was smiling. She touched his arm. "You're such a good guy. But I still don't get why you have different clothes on."

"Well, after the ER, we hooked up. Naturally. It's what us gays do. We don't let things like concussions and cracked ribs stop us—no sirree! Since he tore my clothes off, ripped them to shreds, really, he had no choice but to give me these." He grinned.

She punched his arm—hard.

He yanked it away, rubbing his bicep. From looking at her, one might not guess how hard the girl could throw a punch. "Ow."

"Really?" she asked.

"No. Not really. I drove him home, helped him get his bike inside. We got caught in the rain, and he gave me these clothes. Which I will need to return, which is also the perfect excuse to see him again."

Dora said, "I knew there was something more going on than being a Good Samaritan."

"What? You think I'm not capable of a simple act of kindness?"

"I didn't say that. But you do like the pretty boys." She leered at him. "Was he pretty?"

Tommy closed his eyes. "Oh yes, the stitches in his forehead made him even sexier."

"And he's a friend of Dorothy's? You checked—or got some gaydar, I assume?"

And this was the part where Tommy felt motivated to tell Dora the whole story. He hesitated, though, because it was just too weird. One of those truths that was stranger than fiction.

"Oh, he was gay," Tommy said.

"What, did you make googly eyes across the emergency room?"

Tommy laughed. "Not exactly. I'd met him before."

"Oh?"

"Yeah." Tommy got up and went into the kitchen. "Have you eaten yet?"

"No."

"I was thinking of making a big salad. You want I should make enough for two?"

Dora came into the kitchen. "Sure, but what I really want is for you to tell me where you met this guy before."

Tommy rummaged around in the fridge, gathering up romaine, spinach, marinated artichoke hearts, celery, red onion, cucumber, and some deli turkey.

He set them on the counter and then turned to Dora and smiled. "You met him too."

Dora cocked her head. "Me? I don't get it."

"You won't believe this." Tommy pulled out a cutting board and began chopping up the romaine. Dora stepped up to him and grabbed his hand to stop him. He looked at her. "You do realize I'm holding a knife in this hand?"

"I do realize you're avoiding the question."

Tommy blurted out, "He's the boyfriend of Rory Schneidmiller."

Dora stepped back, as though jolted. "No."

"Yes." Tommy went back to prepping veggies for salad. "It's too much of a coincidence."

"It is!" Dora said.

"But it happened."

Dora stepped close again. "Did Rory come back? Please tell me he's back and that he's okay."

Tommy set down his knife. "No. There's still no clue about what happened to him."

Dora frowned, and Tommy noticed a new brightness in her eyes, which she tried to minimize by making herself smile. "I wish there was some good news. I can't get that guy out of my head. I dream about him."

"You do?" Tommy asked. Dora had never mentioned this.

"Almost every night. It's always the same." She turned away and went back into the living room. The TV clicked on, then canned laughter.

He stood in the archway between kitchen and living room. "Are you going to tell me?"

"It's stupid." Dora shrugged, staring at the screen. There was an old rerun of *Gilligan's Island* on. She muted the sound and turned to him. "I always see him on a beach, probably Lake Michigan, but I suppose it could be anywhere."

Tommy sat down beside her. She was staring ahead as though she could see the dream in her head right at that very moment. She drew in a breath. "He's just standing there. It's night. There's no moon. The scene is kind of peaceful. But then there's this weird *thing* that moves into place."

"Like an animal?"

"No, no. It's in the sky. Kind of like a big cloud, but almost like it's alive, like some kind of mass. And I can see dark figures, like people, moving inside it. There are bright lights shining down on the water from the very bottom of the thing." Dora stopped, breathing just a little harder.

"And then, and then Rory is being pulled up into it." She stopped suddenly and didn't say anything for a minute. "That's when I wake up. And I'm always in a sweat. Heart racing. I'm terrified." She turned to him. "What do you think it means?"

"I have no idea," Tommy said. "It's probably just your subconscious preying on you. You know, because you've been so concerned about this guy."

"I know," Dora said softly. "I've been trying to let it go. I mean, what's the point? I've done all I can to help, which isn't much, but still. Just when I stop thinking about him for a while, the dream comes back."

"I don't know how to explain it."

Dora touched Tommy's shoulder. "And I don't know how to explain that, of all the millions of people in the Chicagoland area, the one *you* choose to run out in front of and cause an accident is this guy's boyfriend."

Tommy felt a little chill. "Strange but true." His voice was barely above a whisper.

They were quiet for a long time, listening to the rain, watching Ginger in an evening gown move across the TV screen. Dora looked at him. "You like this guy, don't you?"

"I think I do," Tommy confessed.

"Lord help us." Dora picked up the remote and unmuted the TV. A burst of laughter followed her pronouncement.

THE NEXT morning, Tommy woke early with Cole on his mind. There were scattered images of him remaining from dreams, which might explain the tent in Tommy's boxers, although truth be told, he woke up like that almost every single day.

He lay in bed for a moment, thinking of the darkness of Cole's hair, the way the stubble highlighted the angular planes of his face, his beefy body. He glanced over at the clock and saw it was only a little after six.

He had his first class at DePaul in a couple of hours. Every single class, *every single one of them*, bored him to tears. Why was he wasting his life this way? His father, in Long Island, was an attorney… family law. And *his* father before him? An immigrant, he came over on a boat to Ellis Island from Sicily. Tommy's own dad had grown up the son of the owner of a shoe repair shop. His dad always said his family didn't have much, but they'd always had enough.

Despite that, his dad had wanted more for himself. He worked construction all through college and then law school, just to pay his own way. He was fond of saying, and it was true, that he was a self-made man. He wanted more for his only son, Tommy.

And Tommy hated to break his father's heart. But this life wasn't for him. With each class, each test, each paper, that fact became more and more apparent. What *was* for him was his passion for stories. He'd always loved to read. And he'd written several short stories, all hidden away in a box under the very bed in which he now slept. How could he disappoint his father? Especially when the man had spent most of the family's savings and even gone into debt to put him through DePaul.

Thinking of Cole helped put those worries aside for the moment. Thinking of Cole made Tommy happy, especially if he chose to forget, as he did right now, that Cole was in a kind of tragic and mysterious situation that would make him unsuited to forming any kind of attachment, let alone relationship, with Tommy.

Maybe they could be friends?

Tommy shrugged, turning over in bed to look out the window. From his perspective, all he could see was sky, and that sky was gray, flat. He knew, even though he barely *knew* Cole, that being friends would only be frustrating.

He picked up the cordless on his nightstand and punched in Cole's number. It rang four times, and each time it rang, Tommy wondered if he'd misremembered the number. The answering machine clicked in, and Tommy's heart broke.

"Hey, it's Cole," Cole said.

And then, "And Rory."

Together: "And we're not home right now. You know what to do and when to do it." The beep cut off their laughter.

Tommy pressed the button to end the call. Cole hadn't changed the message? How sad. And how hopeful. Obviously he held out some hope the guy was coming back.

Of course he does. He wouldn't be human if he didn't. Tommy thought his feelings were a true paradox. He wanted Cole to be free, unencumbered by memories of his missing boyfriend so Tommy could put a few of his expert moves on him. Yet he also wanted Cole to be a kind man. Because there was nothing sexier, no matter what they looked like, to Tommy's head and heart than a kind man....

It worried Tommy that Cole had not answered. And that worry was all about his head injury, an injury Tommy felt responsible for. He pictured Cole lying comatose in his bed, the phone ringing right beside his ear.

Tommy called back. This time he left a message. "Hey, Cole, it's your buddy Tommy. Just calling to see if you're feeling okay this morning. Maybe you're sleeping in? Call me when you get this, all right?" He was about to add that he was concerned, but that sounded too much like a worrying mom, so he hung up.

He got up and took the phone into the bathroom in case Cole should call him back. But the phone remained disappointingly silent all through his shaving, tooth brushing, and showering.

After he was dressed in jeans and a Blue Demons hoodie, he padded barefoot into the kitchen. Dora sat at the table in her quilted bathrobe, a towel wrapped turban style around her head, with a mug of steaming coffee before her. There was also a plate with remnants of scrambled eggs, which Dora liked with ketchup. Her preference grossed Tommy out. He was glad she was done eating.

"Good morning, starshine," she said.

"Morning." Tommy poured himself a mug from the Mr. Coffee on the counter.

"You want some eggs?"

"I can get it if I do. Coffee for right now." He took a sip. He liked it black. He glanced into the refrigerator, eyed the eggs, the milk, the juice, and then shut the door without taking anything out. He wasn't hungry. Tommy usually ate like a truck driver. It wasn't uncommon for him to down three eggs and four pieces of toast in the morning, or to devour three or four bowls of Apple Cinnamon Cheerios, his favorite.

He went back into his bedroom and tried Cole again. Still no answer.

What if he wasn't waking up? Wasn't that why Tommy had always heard you should have someone with you when you sleep if you've had a concussion?

He eyed the clock on the nightstand again. Did he have time? It didn't matter. He wouldn't hear a word his professor said if all he could do was worry about Cole.

He slid into a pair of socks and his running shoes and returned to the kitchen. "I'm heading out."

"You don't usually have class this early." Dora was scraping her plate into the waste can.

"I'm not going to class." He debated whether he should tell her his destination or just say he was headed to the library to get in a little last-minute studying before his first class. She'd accept that story without question, but it just didn't seem right.

"I'm going over to Cole's."

"Really?" Dora rinsed her plate and set it in the sink. "What for?"

"I'm worried. He didn't pick up when I called." He reminded her about Cole's concussion.

"Well, if he's not waking up, what good will it do to go over there? He's not gonna answer the door either."

She had a point. But he had to do something. "I don't know. I just have to go. Otherwise I won't be able to do anything other than worry. You know how I am. I'll figure something out." He had a thought. "He lives in a big building. They probably have a janitor who lives on the premises. If Cole doesn't answer the intercom, I'll try him."

Dora walked with him to the front door. She opened it for him, frowning. "Why are you doing this? I mean, I know a pretty face turns your head, and always does, but this feels different."

"It is," Tommy confessed. "And I'm as surprised and puzzled by it as you are. But there's something about the guy. I just can't seem to get him out of my head."

Dora chuckled. "Sounds like you've got a bad case of love at first sight."

"Don't be ridiculous." Even as Tommy said the words, he realized she wasn't being ridiculous at all.

He opened the door, and as he was about to say goodbye, Dora put a hand on his shoulder. He eyed her.

"Be careful, okay?"

Tommy cocked his head. "What do you mean?"

"You know those dreams I told you about?"

Tommy nodded.

"There's more. I kind of—" She looked away. "*Feel* him. Rory. The guy who disappeared."

"You *feel* him? I don't understand."

"I don't know how to explain it. But I just feel like he's alive. He may not be okay, but he's *not* out of the picture. Not the big picture, anyway." She pushed him through the open door. "Go. I'm just being stupid. I hope everything's okay."

Tommy thought he was inclined to agree with her stupidity assessment. He mumbled, "See you later" and headed out.

CHAPTER 8

COLE ENTERED the courtyard to see Tommy D'Amico outside his front door, pressing what was presumably Cole's buzzer on the intercom. He'd press it, wait a second, tapping his toe, then press it again. Cole recognized impatience when he saw it.

Cole had just been down to the beach, where he'd sat in the damp sand—his ass was still wet—for a long time, simply staring out at the very still water. Today it was pewter gray, a reflection of the foreboding sky above. Cole woke early, no worries about his concussion, feeling restless. He thought it might calm him to go out and simply sit on the beach, try not to think of much of anything, and let the chilly air and relative peace of the beach calm him.

And it had. Until he saw Tommy.

What's he doing here? I know he said he'd call, but I took that as a gesture, something you say. I didn't really think he would. And I certainly didn't think he'd show up here. Cole knew Tommy was interested in him, in a physical or maybe even romantic way. It wasn't vanity, Cole told himself, but there was no mistaking the way Tommy looked at him, even with his stitched-up forehead. Like a heroin addict eyes a syringe or, to put it more innocently, the way his sister Elaine might eye a box of dark chocolate, her favorite.

But the last thing in the world Cole wanted was a man in his life. Not now. Not with Rory gone for over a month but still fresh in his mind and especially in his heart. The idea of another guy, dating, or even a quick down-and-dirty sexual encounter with someone was anathema to him. His main objectives in life these days were getting through the tiresome and boring hours at work, eating, and sleeping. And of course, licking his wounds and pining for Rory. Oh, he could pine with the best of them! He marveled that he didn't bay at the moon. Sometimes, although he felt horrible guilt and shame for thinking it, he wondered if things wouldn't be easier if Rory had been found dead somewhere instead of this awful limbo of not knowing. It was cruel to keep him in a state of despair married to hope.

He debated whether he should turn around and slip quietly back to the beach, or maybe head over to the little café on Jarvis and buy himself a cup of coffee.

But that wouldn't be right, would it? Tommy was here, in his courtyard, because he was obviously concerned. At the very least, Cole should let the guy know he was awake and okay, his worst physical complaint a general soreness around his midsection.

He opened the gate and went into the courtyard. The clang of the wrought iron gate swinging shut behind him alerted Tommy to his presence, because he jumped a little at the sound of it and then turned. When he saw Cole, the relief on his face was apparent, even from a hundred feet or so away. A smile lit up Tommy's features. That lopsided grin forced Cole to concede that Tommy *was* cute. Adorable, really. Under different circumstances, Tommy would have been just his type. But he was Cole's type because he was a lot like Rory—the same slight but tight build, the same expression of openness on his face that expected every encounter to be delightful. And, although Tommy was a true ginger, his red hair reminded him of Rory too, even though Rory's unkempt mop was more reddish-brown.

It was precisely Tommy's similarities to Rory that both attracted and repelled Cole.

He'd have to ponder stuff like that later, because right now Tommy was rushing toward him, grinning from ear to ear. Cole wouldn't have been surprised if he outstretched his arms as he ran, if a swell of violin music rose and their movements shifted into slow motion. The notion made him laugh.

"I was just ringing your janitor's buzzer." Tommy stood close. "I was picturing you lying comatose in your apartment. I was going to tell him to bust down your door or at least call 911."

"You're not much of a drama queen, are you?"

Tommy laughed. "Who are you calling a queen?" Tommy stuck his nose in the air and crossed his arms, indignant.

Maybe Cole's gaydar had been wrong? "I'm sorry. I just assumed."

"You assumed right," Tommy said, raising one eyebrow. "Dora says I'm as gay as a picnic basket."

"Well, I wouldn't go that far." Cole shifted his weight from one foot to the other. He wanted to get inside, not only to get away from Tommy, but because he had to pee.

"Gosh," Tommy gushed. "I'm so relieved to see that you're *not* comatose!"

"Yeah, ain't that a blessing?" Cole laughed. "But not comatose at all. My only complaints are a little sand in the shorts, *and* I have to piss with a vengeance." Cole pulled his keys out from his cargo shorts and edged by Tommy. "Do you mind?"

"Of course not," Tommy said, following Cole into the vestibule. He walked with Cole to the elevator, smiling. The look reminded Cole of a puppy.

Cole turned. "Look, I'm sorry I worried you. If you tried to phone and I didn't answer, that was my bad. I really didn't think you'd call, but maybe I should have waited around on the off chance that you're a man of his word." Cole forced himself to smile. "So, I do appreciate you coming all the way over here to check on me, if that's what you're doing. But as I said, I need to get upstairs before I bust a kidney."

The smile vanished from Tommy's face. "Okay," he said softly.

Am I being an ass? Cole asked himself and then answered, *Yes, you are.* He relented. "Do you want to come up?"

"Oh, would you mind?" Tommy's smile returned like sunshine emerging from behind a dark cloud.

Hell yes, I mind. But Cole wasn't about to say that. "Course not. I have to get to work soon, but you can come up for a bit since you're here." Again, Cole smiled, wondering if the forced expression looked anything like a chimp's face.

The elevator doors rolled open, and Tommy followed him inside, too close. Cole pressed the button for his floor, wondering if he was making a mistake.

TOMMY STAYED for the rest of the morning, right up until Cole had to leave to catch the "L" to Evanston for his shift at Pier One. Cole was surprised Tommy didn't get on the train with him.

Cole had to hand it to Tommy—the guy could talk. Endlessly. He'd said he was in law school at DePaul, and Cole thought his vocation choice was a good one for someone who so loved to blather on and on. And on.

Cole had barely said a word, but aside from his school, he'd also learned from Tommy that he was:

Third-generation Italian-American. "Sicilian, actually.
My people come from a little village called Cianciana. It's in the
Agrigento region. And before you ask, yes, there's mafia in the family
history, if the stories I've heard around various kitchen tables are to
be believed."

An avid runner. "I've done three marathons, six half marathons,
and more five Ks than I can remember. Running is my Zen. If a couple
days pass and I don't get at least five miles in, I go a little crazy."

A frustrated wannabe writer. "Yeah, I'm in law because of my
papa. He's a lawyer, and I think he dreamed of me being one since I
was in kindergarten. Someday I'm gonna have to break it to him that
things like torts, wobblers, prima facie, depositions, mens rea, and so
on are about as interesting to me as watching the hair on my legs grow.
Speaking of hair on legs, you're kind of like a little monkey, aren't you?
I actually wouldn't mind watching the hair on *your* legs grow! Anyway,
what I really want to do is write novels. Psychological suspense. Where
we get up close and personal with the victims of crime, their stories,
their terrors and dangers. See? Even the writer in me has no interest in
police procedure or courtroom melodrama. I definitely wasted a shitload
of my family's money, and that breaks my heart. It really does. But I
think if I have to settle for a life of reviewing contracts or even working
on criminal cases, I'll go fucking nuts. Eventually I'm going to have to
cut the cord, to mix metaphors, with my papa and tell him the truth. But
not today."

A voracious eater. "I get it from Mama. She loves to cook and
seldom leaves the kitchen. You want food that's better than sex? Come
to my house someday for Sunday supper. The best red gravy and braised
pork you ever had. And when she makes her own gnocchi! God, you'll
die, you'll just die. Little pillows that practically float out of the bowl.
But I'm an equal-opportunity eater too. Sushi, banh mi, pot stickers,
pancakes, BBQ, hell, just about anything you can think of—you put it in
front of me and I'll eat it up and ask for seconds."

Gay. "I know we already established it, but just wanted to be sure
you knew I am out and proud. Everyone in my family knows, everyone
at school knows, and I have no interest in hiding it or in being any other
way. To me, wishing you're straight is like wishing you were a different
height—it's unnatural!"

Single. "I know you don't care at this point. But if that ever changes...."

TOMMY HAD been yammering since he followed him in the front door. He continued throughout the shared cups of coffee Cole made, and even stood outside the bathroom door while Cole got ready for work, jabbering. It might have been funny if it weren't so damned annoying. Was Tommy always like this? Cole wondered. The conversation—or more accurately, the monologue—continued as Tommy walked beside him to the "L" station at Howard Street.

"Well," Cole said at the entrance to the station, "I need to be on my way. Thanks a lot for checking on me. People aren't usually so concerned, especially ones that I don't really know well."

At the mention of not really knowing him well, Cole saw a little light go out of Tommy's eyes. To make up for it, Cole gave Tommy's shoulder a brief squeeze. "You're a nice guy, Tommy. I'm glad we ran into each other, no pun intended." Cole chuckled. "Well, maybe a little." He turned. "But really, if I don't bolt up those stairs right now, I'm gonna be late. And what with Rory's disappearance and everything, I've missed a lot of work. I can't rely on their understanding forever. I need this job! I took my apartment thinking there were two people to pay the rent." Cole felt a lump rise up in his throat. *Damn it!*

"Okay. Get to work. Maybe I could see you later?" All that radiated from Tommy's face was hope.

Cole really wanted to tell the guy "That's not gonna happen. Look, we're two characters thrown together by some odd circumstances, but it's panned out as much as it's going to. Leave it alone, dude." But what he actually said, in deference to time and Tommy's feelings, was "We'll see."

"Really?" Tommy started with him into the station.

Cole sighed. He struggled to get his CTA pass out of his messenger bag. Tommy followed him right up to the turnstiles. "Yes, call me. Whatever." Cole could hear the rumble of a train pulling into the station overhead. It would be just his luck that it was an Evanston train. "Gotta go!" he cried and dashed through the turnstile and up the stairs.

He didn't look back at Tommy but could imagine him standing there, watching him. Yes, he had an admirer, a not-very-secret one.

What was he to do with *that*?

CHAPTER 9

"I WAS sure I'd put him off that first morning when I went over there and couldn't stop talking. I was *so* nervous! But I know I came off looking like an idiot to him." Tommy turned in front of Dora. "But enough about me. How do *you* think I look?"

Dora snorted. "You mean you ran off at the mouth for, like, ten minutes straight without coming up for air? Like you just did?" Dora laughed. "If he's going out on a third date with you, he must either be able to tolerate your diarrhea of the mouth or he likes you, he really likes you." Dora snickered.

"There you go again, boosting my confidence. What would I do without you?"

"Honey, if anyone doesn't need a cheerleader for his confidence, it's you."

Belying the statement Dora had just made, Tommy asked her again, "Do I look okay?"

Dora cocked her head in appraisal. "If you looked any better, I'd date you myself. Not. That would feel too much like incest." She winked. "You look irresistible, even to your honorary sister." She laughed, then added, "But just to be sure you understand, I don't think any man on the planet ever looked better."

"Really?" Tommy looked down at the black jeans paired with a soft emerald-green flannel shirt.

"Now you're just fishing. But yeah, that green really brings out the color of your eyes—picks up the gold flecks. I'm sure he'll be putty in your hands."

"I wish." Tommy went to the mirror on the wall by their front door, fussing with his hair, wishing he'd splurged for a cut that afternoon. The truth was this was *not* another date with Cole. It wasn't a date at all. Cole had simply agreed to see him, as a buddy. And if Tommy was being brutally honest, he'd have to admit that Cole agreeing to see him was somewhat begrudging. They saw a movie once at the Music Box. They went out to Sidetracks on another occasion, on comedy night, and stood elbow to elbow in the crowded video bar while laughing together at clips from *America's Funniest Home Videos*, *The Golden Girls*, and *Designing Women*. The third time they just met for coffee at a quirky little café on Lincoln Avenue called the Nervous Center. They'd ended up playing one of the board games the café had lying around—Yahtzee—and really not saying much to each other at all.

That night Cole was having him over for dinner. And Tommy supposed that was progress. Progress even though Tommy had suggested the get-together—as he had every other one—and offered to bring all the ingredients to make his mom's *pasta e fagioli* for him.

It was the perfect night for comfort food like the Italian stew of tomatoes, white beans, and ham. Early October, and any pretense of summer was in Mother Nature's rearview mirror now. Temperatures were predicted to dip down near freezing. There was a frost warning out. The mist hanging in the air had a nip to it, and it made everything feel a little damp. It was the kind of cold that chilled a person to his bones, regardless of how many layers of clothes he wore.

Tommy was beginning to think he was wasting his time. If he didn't want to be the poor sap mooning over some unrequited love, he knew he needed to consider his options going forward. *Yeah, I'll do that, just as soon as I make him dinner.* Tommy stepped out of the Jarvis "L" station and looked to his left before hurrying across the street. He made note, once again, of the little gay bar, Charmers, on the corner at Greenview. Maybe he could urge Cole out for an after-dinner drink later? Get him good and liquored up and bring him back home and take advantage of his fucked-up state?

Tommy shook his head as he started east on Jarvis. *You know that's not like you. You're too nice. And damn you to hell for that.* In spite of knowing he'd never get a guy drunk to seduce him, the prospect of it with Cole did cause a boner to rise uncomfortably in his jeans.

TOMMY RANG the buzzer three times, causing him to worry he'd been stood up, or that Cole was lying comatose in his apartment, before being buzzed in. As he headed up to Cole's, he reminded himself not to talk too much, to try for once in his life to listen. Let his Italian genes guide his hands in the kitchen and not his mouth.

Cole was waiting at his door for him, leaning against the frame with his arms crossed over his chest. He was grinning, and Tommy couldn't help his thoughts. *God, he's gorgeous! I just want to throw down this grocery bag and pounce on him.* It was his usual thought whenever he came within sight of Cole. One part frustration, one part romantic longing, and two parts simmering lust that Tommy, in his darkest moments, tried to accept would never be realized.

"Sorry if I didn't hear the buzzer right off. I just hopped out of the shower. And then I had to scramble like hell to get dressed." Cole stepped back a bit to admit Tommy.

You needn't have bothered. Naked would have been just fine. Again, that pesky boner raised its purple-helmeted head at the thought of Cole answering the door naked, muscles slick, as rivulets of water dripped down, puddling on the hardwood at his feet. As it stood, the only thing naked on Cole were his feet, and even that was pretty damn sexy. As were the old, faded jeans, very worn, almost white at the crotch, and the inside-out sweatshirt he was sure Cole had thrown on hastily. His mop of dark hair, still damp, was also a sight to behold. And that dark stubble? Tommy imagined the sandpaper delight against his skin if Cole would ever deign to kiss him.

If Cole realized half of what goes on in my head when I look at him, he'd send me packing.

"Ah, no worries. I only buzzed once," Tommy lied. "I'll just set this stuff down in the kitchen." And he made good on that promise. In the kitchen, he began unloading the ingredients for their meal—a nice loaf of crusty Italian bread from a bakery on Broadway, a couple of cans each of San Marzano plum tomatoes and cannellini beans, celery, onion, garlic, carrots, and some elbow macaroni. A ham steak. He looked forlornly into the empty bag and, almost under his breath, said, "Shit. I meant to bring wine. I really did. I had a bottle of chianti set out...."

"No worries," Cole said, coming up behind him. "I already started on this." Tommy turned to look and was surprised to see Cole holding up a bottle of cheap red wine—Riunite Lambrusco.

Inwardly he shuddered, but he made himself smile. "Ah, you think of everything. That looks great. Pour me a glass. And then just grab a seat at the table. You can keep me company while I cook."

"Yeah, I bought four bottles at the liquor store over on Sheridan. It was on sale—two for five—I couldn't resist."

Tommy was of the mind, perhaps the Sicilian mind, that no one should ever drink bad wine. But tonight he'd make an exception, especially since Cole looked so cute and pleased with himself, holding up the bottle. It wasn't just that he'd gone out and gotten wine that delighted Tommy, but the simple fact that he'd done something proactive for their getting together. It seemed like a small step, but it was one in the right direction. *Now just try not to read too much into it....*

His little head, toward the south, reminded him once more of what a bit of the grape could do for inhibitions. Tommy failed to keep the grin off his face. Right up until he tasted that sickening sweet wine....

"This is delicious," he managed to choke out, holding up his glass. "*Salute!*" He got busy doing his prep—chopping onions and garlic, slicing up celery, and dicing carrots. "You like to cook, Cole?" Tommy asked over his shoulder.

"I used to." He paused for a moment. "These days what I do best is call and order in pizza, Thai, and Chinese. I'm a wonder in the kitchen." Cole's eyebrows lifted.

Tommy chuckled as he threw the chopped vegetables in a pot he'd heated up with some olive oil. They began to sizzle. Tommy dumped some salt into his hand and sprinkled it over them.

"Make those onions sweat. Seriously, no cooking? How do you get by?"

Cole's silence, after a few seconds, told Tommy he'd said the wrong thing.

He turned away from the stove to look at Cole. "Ah shit, I'm sorry." *Why did I have to go and say something that would remind him of his old, and missing, boyfriend?* Tommy lowered the heat under the pot and then moved to Cole so he could stand behind him and massage his shoulders. To his surprise, Cole's head lolled back, his eyes closed.

He looked so sweet and vulnerable that Tommy couldn't help himself. He acted completely spontaneously, not listening to his head but only his heart. Without allowing himself to think or hesitate, he leaned down and kissed Cole. He expected, even as he was pressing his lips to Cole's, that Cole would reject him violently, pushing him away, acting indignant. The chair would fall over as Cole scrambled to get to his feet. Maybe he'd even tell Tommy to get the hell out.

But what he did instead was grab the back of Tommy's neck and mash his face even more into his own. He thrust his tongue into Cole's mouth. The kiss went on… and on. The kiss lingered so long and so passionately that Tommy was actually getting a little breathless. But he'd have rather died than come up for air. He didn't want to break the magic of this first kiss. He didn't know how delicate the spell might be. From all prior indications, he feared Cole might "come to his senses," push him away, and do exactly as Tommy had imagined earlier. Tommy found himself trembling slightly from the sheer force of the kiss. All sorts of thoughts were caroming through his head:

Is this really happening?

Where will we go next with this? Is it the beginning of something or a remorseful—on Cole's part—end?

Will my mirepoix *burn?*

At last, though, due to the need for oxygen and the strain on Tommy's spine from standing for so long and so awkwardly, Tommy forced himself to break away. He stood straight, relieving some of the pain in his back, and stared down into Cole's eyes. Cole peered back, and the visual connection was, surprisingly, just as passionate as the kiss. Tommy didn't think that would have even been possible until just that moment. But here was the proof, in the gorgeous, smoldering lust in Cole's eyes.

Cole suddenly stood and grabbed Tommy's hand. Wordlessly he led him into the bedroom. For about half a second, Tommy thought he should run back into the kitchen, turn off the heat under the vegetables, but once again his fear that an interruption might break this magic spell made him think *Let 'em burn.*

The bedroom was shrouded in shadows with only slivers of light, orange-yellow, sneaking in through the partially open blinds at the window. Tommy stood and watched as Cole undressed, savoring each bit of flesh as it was revealed. Cole's body practically shimmered, looking pale and ghostly in the dim light. Tommy had to remind himself to breathe, let alone getting his hands to move to undress himself. Besides, he couldn't recall when he'd been a witness to a more enthralling show.

At last Cole stood naked before him. His expression was serious, almost somber, belying the erection that pointed straight up at the ceiling, so hard Tommy wondered if it would simply explode.

Cole made no move toward him. He just stood there, breath a little heavier, watching and, Tommy supposed, waiting.

"Oh," Tommy said on a whispered outrush of air. Nudged into action by Cole's silence, he rapidly undressed, leaving his clothes in a heap all around him.

Cole moved to the bed and then lay down across it. He stared not at Tommy but up at the ceiling.

What do I do? Tommy wondered. He knew generally the answer to that question, but not specifically. *Let good old Mother Nature guide you....*

He moved to the bed and then waited a second beside it, as though asking for permission. When Cole said nothing, didn't even look at him, Tommy chose to interpret the signs as acquiescence. He moved on his knees on the bed and, making of himself a big furry blanket, spread himself out on top of Cole. The tingle and spark of their two naked bodies pressed nearly head to toe felt like fire to Tommy.

He had to kiss him. And he did. It was almost as though they'd never stopped kissing. This one was only a continuation of the one in the kitchen, the same fierce hunger. Their bodies moved to mesh even more, though that was impossible. Tommy reveled in the heat, the tensed muscles, the smooth skin and rough hair beneath him. Cole's lips were sweet, yielding, and his tongue and mouth tasted like wine, but also like something indescribable, an essence that was uniquely Cole.

Tommy was in love.

He moved down then, hungrily kissing Cole's chin, his neck, ears, lingering at his chest to tease the nipples up out of their mat of dark hair and to bite them so, so gently at first, and then hard enough to make Cole seize up a bit and gasp. He moved away slightly, but Cole grabbed the back of his head, forcing his mouth back down on his nipples. Tommy could feel Cole's erection throbbing against him. And that made him move south more rapidly, pausing only briefly to savor the taste of Cole's navel and then onward....

Until he came to his dick, which rose, almost quivering because it was so hard, out of a mass of dark brown, nearly black, curls. Tommy swallowed him to the root in one gulp, and he didn't gag because he wanted it so bad. He began swirling his tongue around the shaft, moving his head up and down in continual liquid motion. Cole began to thrust into him, matching Tommy's rhythm, and it wasn't long before he was groaning. Little shudders erupted from him every few seconds.

"God, I'm close," Cole said on an outrush of breath.

"Don't." Tommy moved his head away from Cole's jerking cock and gripped its base tightly. "I want something else first."

Tommy struggled with the temptation to simply move up, continuing to grasp Cole's cock tightly, and to let himself sink down on it… bareback.

But he pushed the temptation away, powerful and demanding as it was, and forced himself to ask, "You have protection? I hope! Lube?"

Cole nodded. "In the nightstand."

In record time Tommy managed to get Cole sheathed, lubed, and ready to lower himself down on. When he impaled himself—slowly, deliciously, impatiently—on Cole, Tommy let out a long, low moan. *This is heaven. This is what I live for.* He began to move, rocking slowly at first, then with an urgency born from need, faster and faster. He alternated the rocking motion with bouncing up and down, his heart pounding, breathing coming quicker, sighs and moans erupting out of him without thought, with only the fire of his passion.

He looked down at Cole, whose eyes were closed. Tommy wished he'd open them. Cole mumbled something, and Tommy leaned forward.

"What?" he gasped.

"I'm gonna come," Cole moaned, thrusting up hard inside Tommy. And Tommy could actually feel Cole's cock pulsing as he emptied inside the condom—and him. He clenched down tightly on the base of Cole's shaft as the pulses slowed and, at last, died.

Finally Tommy felt as though he came back to earth. His breathing and pulse returned gradually to relatively normal levels. He looked down and was stunned to see long arcs of come lying across Cole's belly and chest.

He hadn't touched himself and hadn't even realized he was coming. He was so caught up in Cole's pleasure.

And then it all went south. Cole bucked, and Tommy wasn't sure what was going on but was hoping for round two, even though he wasn't ready, but by God, he could get there. But Cole bucked again, and with shock and sadness, Tommy realized the truth—Cole was bucking him off.

Tommy reluctantly dismounted. He lay down beside Cole, who turned away from him.

They lay in silence for a while. At last Tommy put a hand on Cole's shoulder and asked, "You okay?"

Cole's response was to shrug Tommy's hand away. A sniffle caused Tommy to realize Cole was crying. Even in the darkness, Tommy could see the tremors coursing through Cole's body as he wept.

"Hey, hey. Don't cry," Tommy said softly and, he hoped, soothingly. He rose up, close to Cole, and laid a hand gently on his shoulder.

Again Cole shrugged the hand away. Almost violently, he moved away, sitting up suddenly on the bed, his head in his hands.

Tommy wasn't sure what to say or do. It was obvious the man didn't want to be touched. All he could think to do was ask what was in his head. "What can I do to make things better?"

Cole said nothing for a couple of minutes—minutes that stretched out so long they seemed more like hours.

Finally he said, more levelly and conversationally than Tommy would have thought possible given the circumstances, "You can get the hell out."

The imperative took Tommy's breath away. After he could breathe again, he got awkwardly up from the bed and, with trembling hands, dressed.

He paused at the doorway to the bedroom, praying Cole would bless him with only a look over his shoulder. But his head remained in his hands, his spine hunched and trembling.

Tommy hurried to leave. As he headed to the front door, he remembered the start of his dinner and rushed back into the kitchen. Smoke was coming out of the pot, and when he looked inside, the contents were nothing more than black things, unidentifiable, almost ash. He pulled the pot off the burner, scorching his fingers in the process, and then turned off the gas.

He headed once more to the front door, thinking he'd just done the best thing in his life—and the worst.

CHAPTER 10

COLE LAY on his bed for a long time, doing nothing more than staring at the ceiling. He felt deflated, lifeless, a something rather than a someone. Paralyzed.

He noticed a minute crack in the plaster, spreading out from the light fixture to a corner of the bedroom, sheathed in shadows. A spider or some kind of bug, it was too dark to be sure, scurried across the ceiling.

He turned on his side, marveling at the little bit of yellow-tinged light that emerged from the crack at the bottom of the window blind where it didn't quite meet the sill.

He remembered lying there with Rory. His lips turned down in a frown, and tears threatened once more. The last time they'd made love was almost a mirror image of the time he'd just had with Tommy.

How could he?

In his head he knew he'd done nothing wrong. But betrayal, shame, and guilt ate up his heart. Rory still had to be alive out there somewhere, and Cole had cheated. Unlike most of his gay friends, young, some even in relationships, Cole was monogamous to his core. Even Rory, a true one-man man, had thought Cole a little old-fashioned for his judgment of their friends and their open relationships or their "monogamy with adultery" lifestyles.

"I want to give everything to you, sweetheart," Cole had told Rory once, most likely in this very room. "And that includes my body." Cole remembered shrugging and going on, "Sure, I'd be lying if I said I only had eyes for you. A hunky guy can turn my head. But that's all—it's just a visual appraisal, an appreciation. You're the only man for me."

And now he'd had sex with someone else. It was a thing, once he was together with Rory, he'd truly believed would never happen again. It didn't matter that the entire time the sex with Tommy took place, starting with that first heated kiss in the kitchen, Cole imagined Rory in his place, which was why he rarely opened his eyes. He and Rory had made love so many times in their brief period together, it was easy to cast Tommy in Rory's role. It was easy to imagine Rory there, so close.

When he'd come, Cole had actually, for the briefest and sweetest of moments, imagined it really *was* Rory he was thrusting up and into. He was surprised he'd enough restraint not to call out his name. He almost, almost believed that, when he opened his eyes, he'd look up and see Rory staring lovingly down at him. Rory would say something like "You've been dreaming," and they'd cuddle, rest for a bit, and then he'd flip Rory over and they'd go for round two, Cole being the bottom this time.

But when he opened his eyes, the illusion shattered. Tommy. He was a nice enough guy, and Cole realized Tommy was falling for him. In other circumstances Cole might have fallen right back, but he didn't know if he was over Rory, didn't know if he ever would be. It still felt like too much of a betrayal.

He mustn't see Tommy again. He couldn't give him what he wanted, and that wasn't fair to a man who only wanted to love him, to bring him joy and pleasure, to explore where their hearts might take them….

He could smell the burnt makings of their dinner wafting in from the kitchen, and it was on that odor that he, amazingly, drifted off to sleep.

THERE'S A *knock at the door. Groggily, Cole opens his eyes, wondering if Tommy has come back to try to make things right or even just to pick up the groceries he'd bought, since dinner was now out of the question—perhaps for good.*

The knock comes again, a little more insistent. Cole feels as though he's been drugged as he forces himself to get up. As another volley of knocks sounds, Cole manages to get to his feet and hurry to the front door, shouting, "I'm coming! Hold your horses!"

Why can't Tommy just leave him be? How has he gotten back inside the building anyway without buzzing?

Irritated, Cole swings the door open and...

It's him! Rory! He's standing there, head cocked, a crooked grin on his face. "I thought you'd never answer."

And he's in Cole's arms—as though he'd never left them.

COLE WOKE to cruel, bright sunlight, the dream images scattering. Of course he was alone. Even knowing that fact, he got up from the bed and hurried to the door. He opened it, and a little groan escaped him as he took in the empty hallway.

He rushed barefoot downstairs, hoping against hope he'd see Rory in the courtyard. But all outside was still—mockingly. No one else, obviously, was even up yet, save for a gray squirrel scurrying up a maple tree.

Feeling weighted down with heavy sleep and a disappointing dream, he headed back upstairs. The door was partially open, and the phone was ringing. He ran inside, a certainty that Rory would be on the line seizing his mind, his heart, his soul.

But when he answered the phone, it was only his sister, Elaine.

"Hope I didn't wake you," she announced.

Cole plopped down on the couch, all the hope leaving him, despairing. "No," he said, casting his gaze around the empty apartment, wondering how he'd manage to pay this month's rent on his meager retail earnings.

"What do you want?"

"Well, good morning to you too!" his sister said with a laugh. "Don't you have work today?"

The reminder was a grim one. He glanced over at the clock on the VCR and saw that it was a little after seven. He was due at the store at ten. "Yeah, work. Good old work. Pays me just enough to choose between a roof over my head or eating." He leaned back into the couch, suddenly longing for the meal Tommy was going to prepare for him. His stomach growled.

"Well, I'm glad I called, little brother, because I can help out with the starving. I was on my way out the door, and thought I should give you a buzz to see if you'd like to come over for supper tonight. I just put the makings for my famous chili in the Crock-Pot."

Cole wanted to just say no. The appeal of holing up here was simply too great.

"Before you beg off, I need to tell you I won't take no for an answer." She chuckled.

Cole sighed. *Whatever.* "Sure. I get off at six."

"Good man. We'll see you at my place sometime before seven, then."

"Before seven," Cole responded. And before she could ask him how he was, he hurriedly said goodbye and hung up.

He didn't want to dwell on the truth—that how he was, was miserable.

DESPITE FEELING wrung out and depressed, Cole had to admit the steaming bowl of chili his sister had just placed before him smelled awesome, almost transformative. Wafting up in the steam, he detected notes of cumin, chili powder, and Elaine's secret weapons—coffee and cinnamon. Elaine was a good cook. And chili was one of her showpieces. She made it without beans. She'd told him chili with beans wasn't "real chili." Hers was rich with tomatoes, peppers (jalapenos and banana), mushrooms, black olives, and chunks of braised chuck.

She busied herself setting out the accompaniments, her dark hair swinging in her face as she laid out bowls of avocado, shredded sharp cheddar, oyster crackers, and sour cream. There was also a cast-iron skillet with corn bread in it, to which Elaine always added sun-dried tomatoes and chili powder.

WXRT played in the background. Suzanne Vega was singing about Tom's Diner.

"This looks amazing," Cole said, feeling both obliged to be grateful to his sister and for the tiniest frisson of happiness the prospect of the food brought to him. He couldn't recall the last time he'd felt even remotely happy. No, what he experienced most days of late was... *nothing*. It was like everything about him—brain, body, emotions—was simply numb. He moved through his days like a zombie as they fell, one upon the next, like dominoes.

"What do you want to drink?" Elaine asked as she headed back into the kitchen. Out of sight, she called, "I have a red—Syrah—or you can have beer, it's Stella. Or you can have Coke, but I only have diet."

"What do *you* think, sis?" It was all Cole could do to restrain himself from tucking into the meal before Elaine sat down. He clutched his spoon tightly in his right hand in anticipation.

Elaine returned with two glasses of foam-topped beer and joined him at the table. She raised her glass, clinked his, and said, "To new beginnings."

Cole let that pass, or at least he let it pass for now. He wasn't ready for the "line" Elaine had been feeding him for the last week—that it was time to move on with his life. That he couldn't remain in this *stasis*, as she called it. He was only hurting himself, she told him. There was nothing Cole could do to make Rory return or not return, and it wasn't right that he was sacrificing his own life right along with Rory. There didn't need to be the loss of two lives!

So Cole changed the subject, sort of. "Yeah, I need a new beginning. As in a new job."

Elaine cocked her head, staring him down with her dark brown eyes. They were only a few years apart, and people often asked them if they were twins because they were so similar in appearance, even though Cole always reminded himself that fraternal twins needn't look anything alike.

"Well, you *are* working below your potential. Way below. You know that. I know that. The wall behind me knows it." She snorted and took a bite of her chili. She moaned "Oh my God" and continued, "There's an opening at my firm for a clerk. It's entry level, but you could go to night school and one day be a paralegal like me, or even an attorney. God knows you're smart enough."

"I don't want to work in a law office," Cole said sullenly.

"Well, what do you want to do? I know you didn't dream of pushing throw pillows and place mats when you grew up."

Cole sighed and ate some more. "I don't know. Seems I never know. I just need to find something else so I can pay the rent."

Elaine looked concerned. She was a straight arrow when it came to finances. Only in her late twenties, she already had a mortgage on the Ravenswood condo they were sitting in, a paid-off used Mitsubishi Galant, and no credit card debt. Cole's Visa, on the other hand, was growing every month. He now owed somewhere around three thousand on it. But what else could he do? He'd made different plans not that long ago, plans where bills were to be divided in two.

"You're having trouble paying your rent?" She covered his hand with hers. "Why didn't you tell me?"

"I didn't want to worry you. I'm a big boy. I should be able to take care of myself."

"Don't be stupid. You've been through an awful time. And you didn't budget for one hundred percent of expenses when you took those expenses on. Can you get out of your lease?"

"That never occurred to me." The idea of moving seemed daunting. For one, the sheer effort it would take was akin to rolling a boulder up the side of a mountain. For another, and this was the big one, what if Rory came home and Cole wasn't there?

"Well, it should have!" Elaine sipped her beer. "You don't need that expense. And the landlord, I presume, knows your troubles. They might be willing to let you out of the lease, especially if you can't afford it anymore. Or at least maybe they'd allow you to sublet until the lease was up. People in Chicago do that all the time."

"Where would I go? Back to Mom and Dad?"

"You don't have to be that drastic." She took a sip of her beer, belched, and then wiped her mouth with the back of her hand. God, he loved his big sister. "You'll move in with me. I have a second bedroom sitting empty."

Cole stared down into his bowl. The food suddenly didn't look as appetizing. He grabbed his beer and stood. He wanted to say something to Elaine, to thank her for her generosity maybe, but there were no words willing to come out through his lips right now. It seemed, in one way or another, his big sister had always been there for him. She refereed fights when he was little, staving off the ire of neighborhood bullies. She was the first person he came out to, and she even went to bat for him in that area. She was the one who sat Mom and Dad down to tell them their only son was gay, while he waited nervously in the shadows outside their pine-paneled family room, eavesdropping. It was Elaine, not him, who reminded them that he was still their beloved son and nothing, really, had changed.

He turned and went into the living room, sat in one of the chairs at either end of the coffee table, and drained his beer. Immediately he wanted another one.

Elaine followed. "You okay? I was just trying to help."

"You can help by getting me another beer." He held up his empty glass. "Please?"

She didn't say anything. She simply turned and went to the kitchen to fetch another Stella. She didn't bother with a glass this time. She handed him the green bottle before taking a seat on the couch.

"If you don't, or can't, move in here until you get on your feet, at least let me give you some money."

Cole didn't want to tell her how much he'd need—and that was just to get out of debt before starting the cycle all over again.

Cole didn't say anything for the entire length of time it took him to down the new beer. And then he set the bottle on the coffee table and looked at his sister. "Okay."

Elaine put a coaster under the bottle. "Okay what? You want a loan, or you want to move in?"

"I'll move in." And just like that, it was done. Cole stared down at the ivory rug at his feet, thinking how he was betraying Rory yet again. An image arose in his mind, Rory coming to the front door, trying to get in, but his key no longer worked. For some reason he imagined an Indian woman opening their door, a quizzical, slightly frightened expression on her face as she looked out at him, wondering who this stranger was, trying to get into *her* apartment.

He needed to move. He knew that. And life with Elaine wouldn't be so bad. They'd always gotten along just fine, probably because she babied him. So he'd move and chance Rory finding him when he came back, because he *would* come back—one day. Living with his sister right now made sense for so many reasons. Really, what else could he do?

COLE WAS surprised, as the days turned to weeks and the weeks into months, how easily he slipped into being his sister's roommate. He couldn't pay her, so he was super careful about taking care of everything—he cleaned the whole place once a week, vacuumed daily, never left a dirty dish in the sink. He even washed, dried, and folded her laundry. He didn't iron it, though. That was too much. Cole didn't iron. If one of his garments got wrinkled, he never wore it again. Rory thought this quirk was amusing and would iron for him. Now Cole had a closet full of wrinkled clothes.

He didn't cook for Elaine, because she was even better at it. Plus, it seemed to relax her. When she came home from work at night and they were both home, she'd slip into some sweats and an oversized T-shirt, pad barefoot into the kitchen, and turn on a classical music station. She'd pour herself some wine and start cooking. She didn't even need to know what she was going to make when she walked into the kitchen. It was always delicious, even when it was something as simple as what she called clean-out-the-pantry-and-the-fridge soup.

Cole always insisted, though, on clearing and cleaning up after every meal.

His days and nights blended one into the other as they headed into Chicago's cold and unforgiving winter. Work, home, TV, bed—that was the sum of his life these days. Well, save for the little "entertainment" he'd found for himself when he was home during the day when Elaine was at work downtown. He also indulged in this entertainment—or was it an addiction?—when he knew Elaine would be gone for an extended period on a date, which she had more often than he'd realized. That fact shouldn't have been surprising. His sister was a catch, pretty, funny, and smart, and of course the men came buzzing around, courting her hand and other body parts, Cole was certain, farther south. He didn't like to think about the latter, but it was hard not to when she left her diaphragm case lying around, not only in logical places like her nightstand or the edge of the bathroom sink, but he'd once found it on the living room windowsill and even atop the refrigerator. He didn't want to know....

Elaine was entitled to her secrets.

And so was he. His entertainment was his only one. And he tried not to think too much about it, except when he was actively engaged in it. It brought him temporary pleasure, a release of sorts, but then after, the guilt and shame would rise up and he'd make the same promise once again. "That was the last time, honest. I'm better than this." He might as well have that saying tattooed somewhere on his body, since it had become his litany over the end of fall and into winter.

Things would get better, he told himself. And then he'd shake his head and allow himself to engage once again in the behavior he hated himself for.

He got fired from his job at Pier One at some point in November, even though the holiday rush was building. But he'd been late so many times after moving in with Elaine that his boss could no longer ignore his tardiness, even when Cole explained desperately how he was now taking three "L" train lines to get to work.

He'd gotten on as a stocker, nights, at Toys"R"Us in Skokie. The commute wasn't any easier—involving a train *and* a bus—but at least his new hours meant he didn't have to travel when public transportation was at its height of business.

He liked the solitude of working in the store when it was closed. And he thought he was doing a great job. It wasn't exactly rocket science, so it was easy to accomplish his tasks in way less than the time allotted. And he'd been punctual. And cheerful to his boss and the few other folks with whom he worked.

It didn't matter. After the holidays they laid him off, telling him he'd be first in line for a position once something opened up. Yay. Something to look forward to.

The layoff, at the beginning of 1998, was really the beginning of his true downfall. He was able to get unemployment, which meant he could indulge his misery and his addiction even more. He added another addiction to the first—weed, which he purchased weekly from a former Toys"R"Us coworker, even though he couldn't afford it.

But the drug made it easier to cocoon. So did the snow, heavy that winter. He'd lose whole days indulging himself, even though he knew he should have been looking for work. But the unemployment checks kept coming, and those enabled him to be a sloth, especially since he could throw in a bag of groceries now and then or pay the cable bill.

And then came that early Saturday morning in February when Elaine marched into the living room and plopped down across from him in a hard-backed chair. He was stretched out on the couch, watching a rerun of *The Golden Girls*. She was in a quilted teal bathrobe, like something his mother would wear.

Elaine sighed. She groped into the pocket of the robe and brought out his bag of weed and threw it on the coffee table. The bag contained mostly seeds and stems, but Cole figured he could get one more bowl out of it.

He switched off the TV and looked at his sister with what he hoped were contrite eyes. He managed to sit up.

"Really, Cole?" His contrite eyes obviously weren't contrite enough. "This is how you're spending your time when I'm not here? Time you should be looking for work?"

"I told you, sis, it's rough out there. I've been looking, but—"

She held up her hand to cut him off. "But 'nobody's hiring.' I know." She got up and disappeared into her bedroom for a minute. When she came back, she held a section of the *Chicago Tribune* in her hand. She put it down in front of him and opened it up to the retail section of the want ads, where she'd circled in red dozens of help-wanted ads. "I think you need to check again, little brother. Apparently *somebody's* hiring." She tapped the paper. "Quite a few somebodies, actually." She sat back and crossed her arms over her chest. "I hate to be a bitch, Cole. But I can't let you do this. I can't sit back and watch you let yourself go."

Cole wanted to shrink into the upholstery. He knew what was coming, and it made heat rise to his cheeks. The words Elaine started to speak had been simmering in the tension-filled air around them for weeks.

"I don't want to be what they call an enabler. But I look at you and think—when's he gonna get his hair cut? Shave? How much weight has he gained? I never thought I'd see you with a gut, but now you have one." She lifted the bag of pot and set it back down. "Munchies, much? You might not think I notice, but I do—the chips bags, the beer bottles in the trash—and this is late afternoon, when I come home from work."

She sighed. "What are you thinking, Cole?"

He stared down. "I don't know." His voice was barely above a whisper.

"Well, you need to figure it out. When I offered you a place to stay, I meant for it to be a temporary thing, until you could get on your feet again, until you could maybe find a job that would allow you to get your own place. Be it ever so humble. I thought you wanted the same. The Cole I know has never been a well of ambition, but he's always been hard-working, he's always taken care of himself." She looked hard at him, leaning forward. "He's never been a leech."

Cole wanted to, but he couldn't look away from her. He couldn't remember the last time he'd felt this embarrassed. And the thought that really kept digging at him began with… *if she only knew.* "I'm sorry. You want me to move out?"

"Where would you go?" she asked. "I know you don't want to go back home. I don't blame you. What I want is for you to take care of yourself." Her lips kept moving a bit, like she wanted to say something else but couldn't. Her eyes brightened with unshed tears. "I know. I know. Losing Rory was hard. I loved him too, Cole. But he's gone. And as much as I hate to say it, we both know he's not coming back. Not after all this time."

The statement hung heavy in the air, like a monstrous thing, dark and wispy. Neither of them spoke for several moments.

Cole barely got out, "I know." And he did. Right then, he did. The probability—the truth—expanded and contracted before his eyes. It was the blackest thing he'd ever seen, smudging his soul. He matured at least ten years in that moment.

Sure, it still felt like Rory was out there somewhere. He could tell himself that, maybe even feel it a little bit, but Cole knew he'd have to accept in his heart that such notions were only wishful thinking. More than likely, Rory was dead. He was rotting in a shallow grave, who knew where?

He hiccupped out a sob and wiped angrily at his eyes.

Elaine was next to him, on the edge of the couch, touching his face and staring down at him with her own pain, a hurt so intense and piercing it only made Cole want to cry all the harder. "I was gonna be all hardass this morning, but I can't."

"You can." Cole smiled through his tears. "I need it. I know it."

"I was going to tell you I'm going away this weekend, up to Door County with Rob." Rob was the latest beau, an attorney from the office where Elaine worked and a guy who looked like he might have the potential to stick around. "But maybe I should cancel. You and I can hole up here, rent some movies—"

Cole stopped her. "No. I won't let you do that. You go. Enjoy yourself."

Elaine moved back to her chair. "Are you sure?"

Cole nodded.

She smiled. "I was also going to tell you to use my computer while I'm gone. And I think I should stick with that."

Cole forced himself to sit up. He sniffled a bit, took a deep breath, tried to calm himself. "And you were going to tell me to use it to answer some of those ads."

She nodded. "You need to get on with your life, Cole."

"I know. And I will."

"There's more than retail too, Cole. There are inside sales, customer service, administrative stuff that you're more than qualified for. And they'll pay enough so you can get your own place, even if it's just a studio in Rogers Park. You want that, right?"

He surprised himself by laughing. "Yeah. I need to get out of your hair."

She touched his hand. "My home is always your home. You know that. It's been nice—mostly—having you here."

"And I need to get out of your hair."

She flung a pillow at him. "Yes! You cramp a girl's style." She stood. "Rob's gonna swing by to pick me up in an hour or so. I need to get a move on."

"I'll look, sis. And I'll send out resumes. I promise. I'll show you the proof when you get home on, what, Sunday night?"

"Monday, actually." She grinned, and he could see the anticipation in her eyes. "It's a holiday. Remember?"

Cole had forgotten all about President's Day. Why should he recall a holiday? Hell, he barely could tell weekdays from the weekends lately. Everything merged into one undistinguished and unremarkable day.

"You don't have to show me proof. I trust you."

"Oh, but I do. And you're right. I need to find something. And something better than retail."

Abruptly, she leaned down and kissed his forehead. "I love you," she said softly.

"Me too," he said back. He reached up to touch her hair.

He watched as she disappeared into the bathroom and closed the door behind her. Cole picked up the want ads and glanced at them for a moment. Then he threw the paper back on the coffee table, picked up the remote, and lay back, settling in for another episode of *Golden Girls*. He had all weekend to answer help-wanted ads, right?

He waited for an hour after Elaine left to load up the one-hitter and to pick up the telephone.

CHAPTER 11

IT WAS when Tommy called the phone sex line for the third time that he actually forced himself to go through with it. *Third time's the charm.* The previous times, in the yawning space of ten minutes, he'd hang up on the second ring, heart pounding, a little line of sweat at his hairline. *This is stupid. This isn't me. I'm better than this.* But all week long, that full-back-cover ad on the *Gay Chicago* he'd brought home from the bars the previous weekend taunted him. Not only was the shirtless, stubbled, brown-eyed hottie in the ad mouthwatering and hard-on inducing, the ad for the 976 number promised he'd have more hookups than he could handle. Guys just like the one the ad pictured were impatiently waiting for Tommy D'Amico to get over his nervousness and make that call.

He could smell a ripe aroma coming from his pits as he was connected at last. Somehow he'd managed to never have this phone sex experience before, never dared to. He met his hookups the old-fashioned way—after staring at them across a crowded bar for hours until they finally showed mercy and came over and said hello.

But damn it, he was horny. And it was snowing outside—hard. The flakes were fluffy and huge, enough to make blurs of the slow-moving traffic outside and the poor pedestrians who tried to hurry through the snow and wind, heads bent low. It was actually very pretty—if you were inside.

The weather forecasters were saying that tonight, with the windchill, all of Chicago might shiver through double digit subzero temperatures. Tommy likened getting on the phone sex line to ordering a pizza—which he'd already done, earlier, from Giordano's. With both, he'd get his pepperoni. He grinned.

Plus, he had the place all to himself for the weekend, with Dora at her parents' way out in Wheaton until Monday afternoon.

There was no reason *not* to give the phone sex line a try.

And now he gave out a little frightened yelp as a deep-voiced man answered, beginning his spiel. Of course it was only a recording, which relieved Tommy a bit. The butch voice told him that he'd reached the "manline," a place to "mainline" all his steamiest fantasies with the hottest guys around. Presumably, they were all just waiting behind the shield of this recording.

There were two options for connecting—one involved providing a credit card number and would get the user "unlimited cruising" for up to twenty-four hours for the bargain-basement price of $9.99. That was still too much for Tommy, who knew full well he might just hang up after a few seconds on the line, especially when the second option was a free sample line, which limited his connections and how easy it would be to get into the rotation of other guys. He shrugged and pressed two for the free option.

The signal was busy. *You get what you pay for.* He hung up, went through the process again; still busy. He repeated the process once more. Again. Finally, on his sixth attempt, when he was about to fork over the ten bucks, he was connected.

Immediately he was hooked up to a rotation of short recorded messages, made by guys who all had one thing in common—every one of them, it seemed, strained to deepen their voices and to use terms like *buddy* and *dude* to get across that they were macho men. Tommy would have thought it was funny, if he weren't so desperate himself.

He'd done the same thing when he recorded his own message. "Hey, buds, laid-back, good-lookin' Italian American here with a fat uncut seven and a half inches, five around, looking to get a little piggy tonight. Decent bod, five feet six inches, moderately hairy. Mostly bottom, but versatile. What are you up for?" He'd had to restrain himself from giggling the whole time he recorded the message, and in fact, it took him three tries before he could actually go through with it—you should pardon the expression—with a straight face.

It seemed like the line was an endless loop, though, of "hungry" "piggy" "nasty" and "insatiable" bottoms, like Tommy, which made him wonder if he'd ever find a match or if tops were a myth—like unicorns.

Hope forced him to stay on the line for a lot longer than he really should have. He listened to the same messages over and over. After a while he recognized the voices and could almost repeat their pitches word for word. Finally a new voice emerged, this one a little high and breathy, but at least he said he was a "total top," despite the effeminate cast of his voice. Tommy wondered, "Should I?" and then just couldn't bring himself to punch the pound key, which would allow for the option of talking live.

He was about to hang up when a strong possibility came on. "Hey there, just a regular guy in Ravenswood looking to cut through the bullshit and meet up for a solid connection. Good-looking, mostly top, dark hair and eyes, nice dick, height and weight proportionate. Not in this for conversation, just get it up, get it off, and get out. No strings. Can host or travel. Party friendly, weed only."

Tommy wasn't much for partying, but he liked the sound of the guy's voice, which seemed *naturally* deep and masculine. And in spite of his emphasis on a no-strings-attached encounter, he sounded like someone Tommy felt like he could have a beer with afterward. That is, if an afterward was even in the offing.

Before he could punch pound and request a live connection, though, the rotation moved on. Tommy had to wait a full ten minutes for the catalog of horny male voices to run through again before the man he hoped was his Mr. Right Now emerged again. Tommy was certain he'd lose him in that time span, especially with the ratio of bottoms to tops.

He punched the pound button as soon as he heard "Hey there" and recorded his message: "Hey, man, I like what I hear. Hot redhead bottom in Edgewater looking for just what you're offering tonight. You willing to travel? Hit me up, okay?"

The message sent. And then Tommy waited... and waited. He figured the guy didn't like the sound of his voice, didn't like redheads, didn't want a bottom—just like almost every other guy on this line tonight, it seemed. But after an interminable five minutes passed, a voice told him, "You have a connection."

Tommy got a short recording that made him smile. "Yeah, man, I like what I hear too. And I love a hot redhead. *And* I can travel. Let's make this happen." The facilitator told him to press one if he wanted to talk live. He did.

"Hey," Tommy said, kicking himself inside for not thinking of a more provocative opening.

"Hey," his new friend said back, relieving Tommy, at least from worrying about his lack of wit.

The guy went on, "So what are you up for?"

Tommy nearly burst into laughter, because the first thing that came to his mind was Parcheesi. And then a good old-fashioned quilting bee. Maybe a big bowl of chocolate ice cream. He had to pinch himself to undermine the giggles that bubbled up inside. "Just looking to hook up. Horny."

"Sounds good, man. You lookin' for company?"

"Yeah. You want to come over?" *What is wrong with me? This guy is a complete stranger. He could be a pervert. A serial killer. A Republican. You're not just gonna invite him into your house, are you? That's nuts!*

"Sure. Address?"

Oh Lord, what do I do now? The good boy in Tommy, the one who respected his mother, the one who was always punctual and gave regularly to charity, told him to hang up *right now*. If he wanted sex, he could brave the snowstorm and go out and get it. A short ride on the "L" would take him to the bathhouse on Halsted if he wanted a quick and easy connection—or many, many quick and easy connections, some of which would even respond later to penicillin, if he was lucky. Or he could go to Roscoe's and pick someone up or get picked up. In spite of his shyness, he seldom had any trouble procuring male companionship.

With his finger hovering over the button that would disconnect him from "regular guy," he stared out the window at the cone of snow coming down hard outside in the light from the streetlamp.

He gave the guy his address. The guy told him he'd be taking the train on account of the weather, but that he should be there inside an hour.

Tommy regretted his decision the whole time he showered, cleaned himself inside and out, and straightened up the apartment, including a quick change of sheets. He hoped against hope that maybe the guy wouldn't even show up. Then he could throw some porn in the VCR, jack himself off, and be done with this nonsense. Sleep.

But after about an hour had passed, the buzzer rang. It startled Tommy so much, he actually gave out a little scream.

When he opened the door, Tommy sucked in a breath. "Oh my God," he said without thinking. "It's you."

Cole blinked and then smiled at him with that sexy grin of his. He made no attempt to come in, just stood staring back at Tommy, hands at his sides. "I thought you sounded familiar."

Tommy said, "Me too," but he was lying. If he'd known it was Cole, he wasn't sure what he would have done. He'd spent the tail end of fall and all of this winter trying to get over the guy. He'd fallen hard for him—inexplicably, painfully, a real-thing kind of love. And ridding himself, or so he thought, of that encumbrance was the most painful and daunting work he'd ever done. He thought he'd wiped out the fierce feelings Cole had evoked in him, but there was seldom a night when Tommy had fallen asleep or a morning when he'd awaken without seeing that beautiful face in his mind's eye. He hated himself for it. *The guy isn't interested in you. He's got a cargo hold full of baggage* were just a couple of the common-sense reminders he gave himself on a regular basis.

But there was a reason Tommy had called the phone sex line tonight. There was a reason his bar hookups, one-night stands, even proper dates all died on the vine. And that reason was standing right in front of him, snow rapidly melting from the furry flap-eared hat he wore, the cheeks above his dark sandpaper stubble a bright red from the cold.

Tommy was amazed how much could go through his head in just a couple of moments. He honestly didn't know what to say, so he simply stood back, making clear by body language that Cole should come in.

There was an awkward pause as Cole stood there in front of him, dripping on the little Persian rug Dora had found at the Brown Elephant thrift store on Halsted. A clear, sensible voice inside of Tommy told him to let Cole warm up and then explain that this wasn't going to work. Maybe he could even offer the guy cab fare to get home since he'd gone to the trouble of coming across town.

But even as he had these sensible thoughts, he knew he wouldn't act on them. He couldn't. He was helpless in front of this man. "Let's get you out of those wet things."

"Thanks." Cole removed his shearling coat, his red wool muffler, his furry hat—handing each in turn to Tommy, who hung them up in the front closet. Tommy stood waiting while Cole hopped around, getting out of his black boots. Tommy procured a newspaper from the coffee table for Cole to put them on. Otherwise Dora would have a fit when she got home to see the salty snow stains on the hardwood.

Tommy shrugged when Cole stood before him in jeans, flannel shirt, and woolen-stockinged feet. This was obviously a situation neither of them had anticipated, even if Cole had really thought Tommy's voice sounded familiar. It was a nice thought, but he doubted it. Normally, if there was a normal for this situation, Tommy would have turned things immediately sexual. After all, fooling around was the aim for both of them. There were a thousand other things each of them could have been doing on a cold Saturday night aside from throwing caution—and dignity—to the wind on a phone sex line.

Tommy thought he needed to be more of a host and less of a horndog. After all, he wasn't really sure he wanted to get into bed with Cole. Oh sure, his libido would beg to differ, the half a hard-on he'd had since he opened the door to Cole would beg to differ, but the truth was Tommy had a self-protective streak when it came to his heart, and he knew, if only in his mind, that sleeping with Cole again would very much be like ripping a scar open. He'd made little progress in getting over the guy, but he'd made some. He wasn't sure he wanted to ruin that. So he said, "You want something to drink? A beer?" Without waiting for an answer, Tommy turned away and went into the living room.

Cole followed. "That sounds good."

"I have Bud Light. And there's a bottle of vodka in the freezer if you want some."

"Cool. How about a shot of vodka with a beer?"

"Party hearty," Tommy said, without much conviction. He told Cole to grab a seat on the couch and went into the kitchen to get the drinks. He was surprised his hands were shaking a little as he removed the beer and vodka from the fridge. Somehow he managed to crack open a couple of bottles of beer and to pour a juice glass half full (or was it half empty?) for Cole. No way was he doing anything stronger than beer. Tommy needed a clear head. He wanted to make a smart choice.

Would his heart allow him?

He returned to the living room to find Cole on the couch, rolling a joint. "Smoke?" He looked up at Tommy and grinned.

"Nah, man. I haven't done that stuff since college. All it does is make me hungry… and then fall asleep." Tommy set the beer and shot down before Cole. "But don't let me stop you."

Cole licked the joint shut but didn't light it. He set it aside on the coffee table. He took a sip of his beer, and Tommy noticed something that touched his heart and gave him a little comfort. Cole's hand was shaking too.

Tommy sat down next to Cole, took a big gulp of beer that he just barely managed not to choke on, and stared ahead for several moments before taking the plunge and asking, "What are we doing here? I mean, I thought we were done. Not that we ever really started…."

Cole didn't answer for a long time. Long enough for Tommy to wonder if he'd said the wrong thing. *Why can't I just be like other guys? I should be on my knees between his legs getting busy on his dick. I want that. I need that. But I want too much more.* "It's okay. Stupid question." Tommy drank some more beer. *Maybe I should just ask him to leave.*

Cole set down his beer and turned toward Tommy. "It's not a stupid question." He paused, looked away, then looked back, locking gazes. "You know what I thought when you opened the door?"

Tommy shook his head.

"I thought, 'thank God it's you.'" He sighed. "I've been messing around on this shitty phone sex line for the past few months, hooking up way too much with way too many people, a lot of them that I wouldn't even look at twice if I saw them on the street. Bad on me. And when they leave or I leave, I'm left feeling even more unsatisfied than I was before."

"Why?" Tommy asked. He hoped the reason was the same for Cole as it was for Tommy, because he just couldn't get over him. Because none of the guys—and Tommy felt a deep, cutting twinge of jealousy when he thought of these hordes of anonymous, unfulfilling lovers in Cole's life—were Tommy.

"I don't know. Maybe the sex just underscores how alone I really am." He paused, his eyebrows furrowed together in thought. "It sounds corny. But there's something weird at work here. I want love, but at the same time, I push it away. To love someone else makes me feel guilty, like I'm cheating, like I'm betraying Rory." He downed his shot, let out a breath. "I'm talking too much. You don't want to hear this."

"No. No, you're not. It's just enough."

They drank in silence for a few minutes. Tension, almost palpable, hung in the air.

Cole nodded toward the window. "It looks like there's no sign of that snow letting up."

"Forecasters say we could get as much as ten inches."

Cole grinned. "Well, even I can't promise that much."

The quip made them both laugh, probably much harder than the situation warranted. When the laughs slowed to a trickle, like the final pops of popcorn in the microwavable bag, Tommy looked seriously at Cole and said, "I'm glad you're here."

Cole opened his mouth to respond, but Tommy cut him off.

"I'm also *not* glad you're here. Does that make any sense?"

Cole eyed the joint on the table, and Tommy could see the want in his eyes, but he left it alone. "Yeah, I suppose it could—make sense. Why don't you explain a little more just to confirm that I have the right idea?" Cole settled back into the couch, arms spread across the back and his legs also spread wide. The image before him was enough to make Tommy just want to straddle him. Talk was overrated, anyway.

But Tommy thought for a moment and did what he guessed was the right thing. "Last fall? When we met? I really liked you, man. A lot. Couldn't get you out of my head. I'd wake up in the morning thinking about you. I talked endlessly to Dora about you, about the future I imagined and where things could go with us. So much so that she told me that if I took the word 'Cole' out of my vocabulary, I wouldn't have anything left to say." Tommy smiled, and his gaze darted down to the floor. Heat rose to his cheeks.

"I knew you weren't into me—" Cole leaned forward, ready to speak again, and Tommy raised his hand to stop him. "Don't deny it. You weren't. You couldn't be. You were grieving, and maybe you still are, but in a different way."

Cole sat back on the couch. Something went out of him. Tommy wasn't sure what to call that particular something. He knew only that Cole looked defeated. Where before there had been a little spark, even if was only lust, now there was a kind of slackness about Cole. *Boy*, Tommy thought, *I'm really well on my way to royally screwing things up. Why can't I just be like every other gay guy my age and concentrate on simply screwing? But I need to be honest with him. I need him to know how I feel. And I don't need to make a choice with my dick. I'll just be hurting myself.* So Tommy continued.

"I'm sorry. You came over here for some quick and easy sex, which is totally cool, and I'm going off on a tangent." Tommy turned to put a hand on Cole's knee. The touch immediately felt like an electric shock. It turned Tommy on. He took his hand away. "For my sake and yours, though, I need you to know how I feel, what I want." He shrugged. "Maybe after I *go off* on this tangent, we can *get off*… together." *Lame.* Tommy smiled anyway.

Tommy tried to compose himself by taking a few deep breaths. *Where was I? Oh yeah.* "I knew you weren't into me, but I thought if I just tried hard enough, my charm, my freckles, my irrepressible joie de vivre would wear you down." He laughed nervously.

"And then we did crawl into bed together. I thought it was amazing. Until after. Until I saw how hurt you were and how selfish I was.

"I was pretty sure I'd ruined everything. And even though the sex was mind-blowing for me, I regretted it, because I thought I'd ruined any chance I'd have with you.

"And then tonight, of all things, a phone sex line hands us a second chance." Tommy wriggled closer, until their shoulders touched. He leaned into Cole a bit, pressing. "I still don't know what I want. I still don't know what you want. I still—"

Cole cut him off. "Maybe if you'd shut up for a minute or two, I could tell you." Cole smiled at him. "Sorry. But you do have a tendency to go on."

"Guilty. Dora tells me the same thing. So does my mom. Even some of my professors say—"

"Dude. You're doing it again."

Tommy laughed. "I'll bite my tongue. The floor is yours, sir."

"Thanks. Look. I'm probably in a similar place as you, Tommy. In spite of what you thought, I was into you, *am* into you. Two things, though, bugged me about that. One is that you look like him, like my Rory, and that hurts. And that doesn't seem fair. I don't want you to be a fill-in. You deserve more than that.

"The other thing is that I felt guilty about being with you. Not the sex, but because I did feel something more than physical for you. Sex is easy. Caring for someone in a real way is hard. What I felt when I was with you seemed like a betrayal. Does that sound stupid?"

"No, no. I get it," Tommy said, his heart ripping a little because he felt like this conversation couldn't lead anywhere good, at least not for him.

Cole blew out a big sigh. "Yeah, yeah, I think it *is* stupid, especially now, since I've been using this dumb fuckin' line on an almost daily basis, hooking up with dozens of guys, being a real man whore." He chuckled, but Tommy couldn't detect much mirth in it. What he could detect was the nauseous stab of jealous pain in his gut. "Not that there's anything wrong with that—*if* your head's in the right place. And mine isn't. Wasn't. Whatever. I know now, right now, that I was just using all that spectacularly unsatisfying hooking up as a Band-Aid. And as a Band-Aid, it wasn't working worth shit. Isn't. Whatever.

"I didn't realize that, really, deep in my soul, until tonight, when you opened that door. And when I saw you standing there, I was so happy because I thought, 'here's a guy who's the real deal.'"

When Cole looked over at him, grinning, foot tapping hard on the floor, Tommy swore he felt his heart drop into his gut. He also felt a burst of sunshine deep within him that he could only describe as joy. Yet his head told him *tread carefully here*. Tommy wondered what he should say, could say. He was great at running off at the mouth, which was one of the reasons he'd agreed to a law career. But now it seemed like there were no words in his brain, leastways none that would spill down into his mouth. So he stared dumbly at Cole, wanting to kiss him but not daring to.

Cole reached out, touched Tommy's cheek gently. "You want to kiss me. I can see it in your eyes."

Tommy nodded.

"It's funny. I don't know if I'm ready. Not for the door that kiss might open. Because every kiss opens a door, and sometimes what we find behind that door can be wonderful, and sometimes it can be disappointing. If you kiss me and open that door... will I want to set foot in the room behind? Or will I want to run the other way?"

"It's always a risk, isn't it? Making a connection?"

Cole didn't answer. Not right away. Tommy thought he could see him tremble—just a tiny bit. He knew Cole was perched on the brink of a big decision. Tommy kept quiet as Cole finished his beer. He watched Cole as he stood, turning off the lights in the room.

He sat down again—close—and put his arm around Tommy in the darkness. The window in front of them was an illuminated rectangle, and the snow seemed to pour down more brightly in contrast to the deep shadows, making Tommy feel even closer to Cole, sheltered, comfortable. He let his head loll onto Cole's shoulder.

After a while Cole said, "Can we not do anything tonight? No kissing. No sucking. No fucking. Can we just hold each other and watch the snow? Can we just fall asleep together?"

Tommy felt like Cole had proposed the perfect date. "Those things aren't nothing, Cole."

"I know," Cole said.

"Okay. Let's just settle back together."

Cole placed his other arm across Tommy's front, making Tommy feel enfolded, safe. And then Cole said, "Right. And we'll see what the morning brings us."

PART TWO
PRESENT DAY

CHAPTER 12

"YOU KNOW, sweetheart, a day doesn't go by that I don't think of you, even though it's been twenty years now since you've been gone." Cole set down the bouquet in front of the headstone. Irises, yellow daisies, a couple lilies, baby's breath, all wrapped in green tissue paper. He did this every year on the anniversary of Rory's disappearance. He still wasn't able to reconcile himself to the fact that Rory was dead, even though a headstone was right in front of him. Black granite, solid, bearing the simple legend "Rory Schneidmiller, 1974—1997."

He hadn't died, Cole told himself. *I don't know what happened to Rory, but he didn't die.* His parents had only had him declared dead after waiting for seven years after he vanished. Seven years was the legal limit one had to wait in Illinois. They thought it would bring them all some peace of mind, but the only thing Cole thought that could possibly bring peace of mind were if Rory were to return.

Cole had never stopped *feeling* Rory through all the years. Oh yes, he'd accepted he was gone and wasn't coming back (most likely). But he knew, somewhere deep in his heart, that Rory still existed. Even if it was only his spirit, he was always nearby. Cole couldn't have managed to go on if he didn't believe that.

It was a hot and humid day, the moisture in the air making everything seem close, damp. Insects buzzed, delighting in the oppressive heat and wet. This was what August in Chicago was like, when it was saying "Here, take my worst. Live with it." The sky was a milky grayish-white. To the west, a bank of gray, almost black, clouds massed. Cole's face was slick with sweat, and droplets of the stuff leaked down from his armpits, tickling his sides.

Heat lightning flashed, and thunder, low, like grumbling, sounded behind it.

Now, on this day, Cole felt Rory's presence especially strongly. Through the years he'd wake with thoughts of that awful night playing like some bad Lifetime channel thriller movie. He'd drive by their old place off Sheridan Road, maybe walk the beach they'd been so excited to live so close to. There were even times when he'd go have dinner at Moody's Pub, which was, as far as Cole knew, where Rory had had his last supper. His waitress that night, Dora, left the job about a year after Rory went away, to have babies and live in the suburbs (Deerfield) with her attorney husband. She and Tommy had remained good friends throughout the years. She would often call or even drop by, but they never discussed Rory. At least, not as far as Cole knew.

And in spite of his tenuous yet solid connection to his first love, Cole had found another love. He was as comfortable as a pair of old slippers, reliable as the sun rising over the lake in the morning. He was oatmeal on a rainy, chilly morning. He was a flickering fireplace. He was the embrace of a hot bath. He was everything—but exciting. Yet, at age forty-six, what need did Cole have for excitement? He'd had his share, like everyone, in his twenties.

He stiffened a little as a car door clunked closed behind him, followed by whispering footfalls on the grass. His husband, as always, had been patient, indulgent of Cole's annual ritual here at Graceland Cemetery in the heart of Chicago. But even Cole knew, enough was enough. He'd been kneeling here in front of Rory's tombstone for almost an hour, just chatting. A quick glance at his iPhone confirmed the timing.

A shadow fell across him—and the grave. Cole turned to peer up at the man standing behind, only a silhouette, backlit by diffuse sun, the man he loved and with whom he shared a home, a condo in Evanston. Cole's eyes swam with tears, trapped here in a very literal way between the past and the future and the love of two very different men.

He smiled at Tommy. "Sorry. You're usually the one who tends to run off at the mouth. But I had so much to say to him."

He searched Tommy's green eyes for signs of hurt and found only understanding. *God, how did I get so lucky?* This was why Cole loved him—he understood. Tommy had made peace with the fact that there'd always be a third presence with them, no matter what. Tommy also knew, Cole made certain, that Cole loved *him*, maybe not with all his heart, because all his heart was never a commodity he had to give, but with a deep and unwavering devotion.

He allowed himself to size up his husband once more—remembering how what initially attracted him to the man was his resemblance to Rory. Now, at age fifty-three, Tommy bore little resemblance to the guy Cole had thought looked so much like his Rory. Tommy's flaming red hair had dulled over the two decades they'd been together, becoming dryer, a sallower color, streaked with gray, wispy on his crown. His trim body, although he still ran twenty to twenty-five miles a week, had become less taut. He had a little paunch, which Cole only said made him look "well-fed" and sexier. His eyes were hidden behind a pair of tortoiseshell horn-rims. The edges of his eyes and mouth were lined with deep-etched wrinkles, from all the smiling and laughing he did.

He was a good guy.

Cole got to his feet, which drew attention to reminders of his own aging—the pain in his knees and lower back. *Remember when standing up was an effortless thing?* Tommy was forever on him about exercising, that he could stave off some of the joint pain if he were only more active and thus, fit.

But Cole had always been a classic couch potato. At forty-six, he wasn't about to leap off that proverbial couch and become a fitness buff. Tommy claimed to hate him because, over the years, dedicated runner Tommy had gained more than twenty pounds while Cole, whose most grueling exercise was lifting the remote to change the channel, stayed the same weight he always was, his waist size an enviable thirty-two.

He smiled at Tommy.

Tommy said, "You want to go get lunch somewhere? Or you just want to go home?"

Cole knew what he really wanted was the latter—where he could hole up in the bedroom and pull out the few photos of Rory he had in a closet. Aside from visiting the gravesite, looking through the photos was another annual ritual Cole indulged in on this day. The photos, though, were something he kept secret from Tommy. Tommy would understand, but that didn't mean he wouldn't be hurt. So Cole said, "How 'bout a little lunch? I'm craving a burger."

Tommy pulled his keys from the pocket of his joggers and jingled them. "Yeah, sounds good. I'm craving a burger too." He turned and started back to their car, a black Lexus crossover. Over his shoulder he said, "But I'll get a salad."

"Lucky Platter?" Cole caught up with him, naming a restaurant that was right around the corner from their condo on Lee Street.

On the drive north up Lake Shore, Cole was quiet. This day always made him pensive. He'd thought that, over the years, the memories of Rory would rust and fade away to little more than dust. Gritty, but manageable. After all, he and Rory had only been together for less than a year.

But… Rory was his first love. His first real, head-over-heels limerant love, the kind they write songs and poetry about. And Cole realized, too, that if they'd stayed together, who knew how things might have gone? That spark they had might have flickered and died within a year. And these days Cole would hardly ever think of him. But the thing, the tragedy, the disappearance, made Rory, or at least his memory, firmly occupy a hallowed space in his mind. Forever, Rory would be young, charming, sexy, his man. His true love….

He looked over at Tommy, his eyes hidden by the shades he put over his glass lenses. The day was dull, yet washed-out sunny. Cole touched his shoulder, feeling strength beneath the worn gray sweatshirt he wore. "Thank you," he said softly.

"Ah, I don't mind running you down to Graceland. It gets me away from my desk, the characters that are driving me crazy. There's this one kid at the school I'm writing about. He's the quarterback, the big man on campus, but he's still in the closet. Even though—"

Cole interrupted. If he let Tommy go on, he would talk until he parked the car behind their building and turned the engine off. He'd go on and on about the characters he was writing about and project their entire story arcs. "I meant thank you for understanding. Not many guys would put up with me and these little annual rituals I have, especially around somebody else I once loved." *Still love*, his mind corrected.

Tommy took his eyes off the road for a second to glance over at Cole. "It's okay, honey. He's a piece of your history. I get that. I'm not threatened. Never have been." He looked back at the road. "Besides, without Rory, you and I might have never met. Not the first time, anyway."

Cole took a little comfort in what his husband said. He still couldn't help but feel guilty when he knew that, later today, he'd wait for Tommy to shut himself up in his office, where he cranked out a series of young adult novels revolving around a fictional inner-city Chicago high school, and pull out the box of photos and notes from Rory. He'd touch them with the tenderness of a lover, and for a moment, he'd be twenty-six again.

He looked out at the lake as they whizzed by. They were at Hollywood, where Lake Shore Drive morphed into Sheridan Road. The gay beach was in view to the right. It was sparsely populated on this drab weekday afternoon marching resolutely toward summer's end. Cole felt wistful, a sudden image of him and Rory at the beach on a windy summer day, trying to tame the old pinstriped sheet they'd brought long enough to get it down on the sand, where they could weigh it down with their boom box and flip-flops. They were laughing as the wind twisted and upended the sheet, threatening to snatch it away.

And then Cole's view of the lake was suddenly replaced by the canyon of high-rise apartment and condo buildings lining Sheridan. He reminded himself he was in the car with Tommy.

Cole circled back to lunch, hoping to get his—and Tommy's—mind off Rory, off the somber memorial today had become. "A salad isn't bad at the Platter," he told Tommy. "They have that tandoori salmon one that you like."

"Don't try to make me feel better," Tommy said. For a moment Cole thought he was chastising him over the day and the longing taking place in Cole's mind. But then Tommy added, "I'm going to be drooling the entire time you eat your cheeseburger. And your damn sweet potato fries!"

"I can't help it if I can't gain weight," Cole said, patting his still-flat stomach.

"Shut up," Tommy said, laughing as he switched lanes to avoid a CTA bus ahead.

WHEN THEY got home from lunch, Tommy stretched, refilled his Camelbak water bottle, and told Cole, with a wink and a smile, "I'm going to head off to work." *Heading off* meant going a couple of hundred feet to the third bedroom in their condo, where Tommy had his home office set up. It was where the magic happened—the Clinton High Books—the young adult bestsellers that had made Tommy rich and famous, relieving him of the burden of proving to his family that he was *not* cut out to be an attorney, as they'd originally wanted, but was to be a free spirit, an artist, a man who earned his bread and butter by his imagination.

Cole interrupted Tommy only when he had to. Tommy had told him that his work was like a kind of self-hypnosis, that he "went under," living his characters' lives and getting caught up in the trials and tribulations of adolescent life. Apparently, whatever he did worked. Tommy's books had been translated into more than a dozen languages, two had been made into feature films, one was in the works as a television miniseries for MTV, and whenever he deigned to do a book signing, overeager pubescent fans and their parents would line up for blocks for a glimpse of their hero and a chance to get his autograph. He wasn't J.K. Rowling, but he did all right for himself and for Cole.

Cole touched his shoulder. "You go to it, lover. Bring home that bacon. I'll fry it up in a pan." Over the years, Cole had become a virtuoso cook, good enough for Tommy to sometimes rumble that Cole should think about going to culinary school to become a chef. But they both knew that Cole was right where he belonged—at home. Over the years he'd tried on several different careers—retail, outside sales, and even dog walking/sitting—but nothing had ever stuck. He'd gone to school for a couple of stints—once to pursue a degree in marketing and the other time, six months at cosmetology school, believe it or not. Again, nothing stuck. He found no spark, no passion for the work. Sometimes Tommy would say Cole should get out of the house, even if it was just for volunteer work, but both of them knew he didn't really mean it. All his talk about too many recluses under one roof was just that, talk. They were both settled in their quiet home-centric life in their vintage condo there in near-to-the-city suburbia. What with Amazon, restaurant, and grocery delivery, they hardly ever needed to leave the house. And that suited them.

Cole listened to the close of Tommy's office door, the start of the new-age music he listened to as he wrote. Today it was Yiruma. Cole waited a moment, in case Tommy should open the door, and then headed down the hall to the master bedroom. He knew Tommy would not emerge until dinnertime, or even later, if he really got involved.

He sat down on the king-size bed, running his hand over the orange and gray quilt. Part of him simply wanted to collapse backward on it, close his eyes, and sleep for hours. The hum of the window air conditioner was soothing, and he knew he could be under within minutes if he allowed himself.

But no, it was the *anniversary*. He would do what he always did on this day. He pushed himself up and off the comfortable memory-foam mattress and walked to his closet. One of the advantages of the condo, which was built in the 1920s, was its massive size, a total of nearly 2500 square feet. Their bedroom was enormous and included two walk-in closets, one here and one they'd added off the en suite master bath.

Cole's was in the bedroom, and even though he knew Tommy wouldn't hear it, he opened his own closet double doors quietly, wincing at the familiar squeak of the hinges. Cole felt a rush of heat rise to his face, despite the frosty air-conditioned chill all around him. Guilt induced that heat, Cole knew. Like an addict, he'd told himself dozens of times he should put away his obsession with Rory. It wasn't healthy, not for him, and certainly not for his marriage. Secrets never were. Tommy was understanding, sure, but Cole knew he didn't realize the depth of Cole's feelings for Rory, not after all these years. Tommy didn't realize how much he still yearned for Rory, especially around this time of year.

Cole squatted down on the floor, pushing aside his rather sizable collection of running shoes, Cons, and sandals—no wingtips for this boy—and from the far back recesses of the closet, hidden by shadows and garment bags, pulled forth the old black Reebok shoebox. The box held his and Rory's entire history. Sad thing was, there wasn't even enough to fill it halfway.

As he opened the box, Cole wondered why he even bothered. In more logical moments, he told himself that the Rory he still loved didn't even exist anymore, no matter what had happened. If he was alive, he would have aged, just like Cole, by twenty years. So much could happen, physically, emotionally, spiritually, to a person in two decades. Most people weren't even close to the selves they were twenty years ago.

Still, he dug into the box. There were only a half dozen or so items inside, and Cole knew each and every one of them by heart. He could just as easily have sat in the kitchen and brought each item out in his mind, examined it, and put it back.

But there was something about touching the mementos. There was an electric connection to each item. He likened it to movies he'd seen about psychics—and how they could get a certain energy from a person off an object they'd touched.

First, there was his old ID for the Bally gym at Century City mall. Cole fingered it and laughed, remembering a time when he *did* have the energy for going to the gym on a regular basis. Thank God he did, because it was where he'd met Rory. At first sight, he knew that all he'd wanted to do was kiss the guy. He believed, and still did, in a way, that to kiss this kind of nerdy, uncoordinated, bespectacled young man would be a revelation and a kind of salvation for him. He'd be home. His wish had come true later that same day. And Cole had not been disappointed.

What they shared had been far too brief, but it had been real.

Next, there was a cereal box top Cole had hung on to through all these years, simply because it was Rory's favorite breakfast food. It was kind of endearing that Rory loved Froot Loops so much. Cole used to kid him about how childish it was, that he should eat something more grown-up, sensible, something with a little fiber, for Christ's sake. "Real men don't eat Froot Loops," he'd tease, playfully whacking the back of Rory's head as he sat on their thrift-store couch, hunched over a mixing bowl full of the stuff, just going to town. "You want me to put some cartoons on?" Cole remembered asking, and Rory had nodded, grinning through a mouthful of milk and unnaturally colored, fruit-flavored confetti.

As the weeks and then months passed with no sign of Rory, he'd hung on to the cereal in the pantry. It wasn't until he moved in with his sister, Elaine, and she was helping him pack up for his move, that he rescued the box of cereal from the trash, where she'd thrown it.

"Oh no, not this." He'd snatched it out of the wastebasket.

"You and your sweet tooth," she said, taking the box from him. She opened it and dug around inside, grinning at him. When she put some in her mouth, though, she spit it into the sink. "That stuff is stale, Cole. Tastes like sugary cardboard." She replaced the box in the trash.

He waited until she was in the bathroom to rip off the top of the box as a souvenir. Even then it was stupid. But somehow the cereal was a concrete reminder of Rory, who could sometimes be a little kid in a very smart man's body.

There was a poem Rory had written him, late one night after the third time they'd made love. It was scrawled on a yellow Post-it. Bad rhymes and nearly short enough to be a haiku, it was still the only poem a man had ever written to Cole, about Cole. Even Tommy hadn't, and he made his living as a writer. Cole got a lump in his throat as his fingertips danced over the six lines and the words "You're all my heart."

He missed his sister too, although not nearly as much as Rory. She'd passed away the year before, much too soon, a victim of breast cancer. He knew he should get out to Arlington Heights more often and see his nephew, Bobby, who was in high school now.

He returned his attention to the contents of the box. Here was the photo of Rory unpacking in their new apartment. He wasn't looking at the camera, his glasses had slipped down his nose, and his reddish-brown mop was a mess, sticking up in several different directions. Cole recalled Rory didn't even know when Cole snapped the picture. He was too absorbed in what he was unpacking—his computer game software, his most treasured possession. Back then Cole thought the photo would be funny, something to rib Rory about once he'd had it developed at Walgreens.

But now, with the sunlight hitting Rory's head just so, the youthful exuberance on his face, even the bend of that lithe young body, the photo had become sacred to Cole, a reminder of their beginning a new life together.

How short that life had been! If he had known it would all be snatched away just a few weeks later, would he have behaved any differently? That was the thing about life, though; we were never given the courtesy of a warning when something bad was about to strike. We could only mumble bitter what-ifs, which tasted like ash in our mouths.

Cole set the photo back in the box, eyes welling with tears. *Why do I do this to myself?* Once upon a time, it seemed there was a point to it, but no more. He was a middle-aged married man mourning a too-brief love from when he was in his prime. Pathetic.

He didn't look at the rest—a takeout menu, a note Rory had left on the nightstand shortly before he disappeared, letting Cole know he'd gone to the gym—he simply put the lid back on the shoebox and then sat for a moment, cross-legged on the floor, staring at it.

As he did every year, he thought *I really should get rid of that box. Burn it, maybe.* And just like every year, he shoved it to the back of the closet, hiding it behind and under shoes.

It was his history. No one could take that away.

"Hon?" Tommy called from the hallway. "What are you thinking for dinner?"

Cole got up, taking extra care to close the closet door quietly. He glanced at the clock on the nightstand and saw that it had magically become six thirty. Weird—it seemed like only minutes had passed. Feeling the shame of the infidel, he walked slowly to the bedroom door, composing his face, taking a deep breath. When he opened the door, he rubbed his eyes, then stretched and yawned. "Fell asleep."

"My little dormouse," Tommy said.

And Cole felt a rush of love for this man, promising himself that next time Tommy was out of the house, he'd take that shoebox and put it in the dumpster downstairs.

Tommy deserved more.

"I'm thawing some pork chops. How about that with some new potatoes and a red cabbage slaw?"

"Kind of German for this dago kid." Tommy grinned. "But I love it. Call me when you need me to set the table. We have that riesling in the fridge."

"Perfect," Cole said, watching as Tommy disappeared back into his office.

He lingered for a moment, half in and half out of the bedroom, then shrugged and headed toward the kitchen to begin making dinner.

CHAPTER 13

HOW HAD it become daylight? It was dark…. What? A minute or two ago? And when did that high-rise apartment building become an empty hole in the ground with a chain-link fence around it, with a lonely crane suspended over the hole?

Rory shook his head, trying to clear it of the cobwebs of just waking. Everything about him—limbs, mind, even his eyes—felt heavy, weighted down. He blinked a couple of times, rubbing at his burning eyes. When he opened them again, he thought he'd see something different, but no.

He leaned back against the brick wall of the building near him, back and hands supporting him so he didn't simply collapse.

It was morning. Traffic whizzed by somewhere close. The familiar rumble of the "L" sounded, a few blocks away.

He glanced down and looked at his clothes. At least they were still the same.

The last thing he remembered was leaning against a dumpster and taking a piss—and then bright lights. What was that about? The dumpster, he noted, was still there. But it was green now instead of blue. The top was black plastic instead of rusting metal. Last night there was a bunch of trash spilling out of it, but now, as he looked down, the bricks of the alley were clear, free of debris.

He shook his head again, as though doing so would free him of the headache he could feel beginning just in back of his eyes. "Okay, what happened?" he asked himself, his voice sounding too loud there in the alley. It must have been early morning, because there was a mist near the ground; everything was covered with a light sheen of dew. The brightness in the sky, to the east, was diffuse, eerily bright, though.

Had he passed out? *Sure. That's what must have happened.* He'd read somewhere about seeing bright lights just before having seizures or any sort of brain episode.

God. What if there's something wrong with me?

He groped through his pockets. Wallet and keys were still there. Inside his wallet, the same things—his Illinois driver's license, a library card, a picture of Cole on Fargo beach, and a lonely looking dollar bill. It was all the cash he remembered having last night.

Had he slept there, on those grimy bricks, all night? He surveyed himself and noticed a puzzle. If he had slept on the ground or passed out, he was surprisingly clean. No dirt. No debris. He ran a hand through his hair and it came back empty.

He felt a little nauseous. Bile splashed at the back of his throat. *Something* had happened, yet he had no idea what. He remembered the burger at Moody's the night before, a few beers... not enough that he'd pass out from them, even though Cole always taunted him about being a lightweight when it came to booze.

Cole. My God, Cole! It's morning!

Rory realized he must have been gone all night. What would Cole think? How worried must he be right at this very moment? Rory pictured him coming home from work late and finding the apartment empty. He imagined him on the couch with the TV on, waiting for the sound of Rory's key in the lock, unable to concentrate on what was on the screen. He would have paced. Called Rory's parents. Oh, and then they would have gotten in on the worrying too.

He felt even sicker as he thought of the sleepless night Cole and his mom and dad must have spent as the hours ticked by, as the darkness of the sky morphed into the milky gray it was right now.

He needed to get home, needed to get in touch with Cole and let him know he was okay.

And he was. Okay. He looked down at himself once more. Clean. No scratches, cuts, or bruises. He hadn't even had his pockets rifled through as he lay here—that was lucky. And other than the cloying queasiness in his gut, he felt no worse for the wear.

He took a few deep breaths and exited the alley.

It must have been early in the morning, because the traffic there on the side street was light. Where was he? Rory looked around for a street sign. He was on Albion, just north of the Loyola campus.

Cars were huddled on both sides of the residential street, and Rory stopped for a moment, mouth open. The cars. They looked familiar, but different somehow. More streamlined. He could barely recognize some of them. Ah, it must be an aftereffect of whatever had befallen him the night before. Why was he thinking about cars, anyway? He needed to get home to Cole, or at least find a pay phone and call him.

He headed out of Albion and found himself on Sheridan Road. He looked around for a pay phone and didn't see one anywhere. And the shops and restaurants around the Loyola "L" station? He could have sworn they were all different now, as though someone had come in during the night and changed all the signs.

No matter. Most of them were iron gated at this early hour. A city bus, also looking weird, swept by, heading south. He stood for a moment, frozen, as though the world had tilted on its axis and no one told him.

A young woman, probably a Loyola coed, hurried by. She'd almost run into him. Crazy bitch. She was talking to herself and staring down at some black rectangle in her hand. What was it? A little mirror? It was as if she hadn't seen him.

Was he invisible? He laughed out loud at the prospect and the possibilities that could come with it and then decided, no, he wasn't invisible, but he probably looked like a nutcase, standing in the middle of the sidewalk, laughing and talking to himself.

He eyed the train station across from him and a little to the south. There would be pay phones in there. But he didn't have change. And the walk to his apartment on Fargo was only a mile or so from here. A dollar wasn't enough for a ride on the "L."

He'd just hoof it. The morning air would clear his head. Hell, he could run most of the way. The effort would be worth it when what he knew had to be a very worried Cole opened the apartment door. He imagined his face morphing from surprise to relief, his smile broadening as he opened the door wider. "What the hell happened?" he'd ask. And Rory wouldn't answer because, well, he wished he knew.

Single-mindedly, Rory headed north. He barely noticed other people on the street, although he did take in that most of them were staring at the same little black rectangles the Loyola coed had held. What was that about?

It took too long, but eventually he got there—to their building on Fargo. Once again, someone had left the gate open. It was a common thing, and it always irked Rory because it compromised everyone's safety. *That's something to worry about later.* He closed the gate firmly behind him and walked to their entrance, on the left.

He pulled out his key and tried to insert it into the lock.
What now?

The key wouldn't fit. He turned it upside down, tried again, and got the same result.

He stepped back, away from the wood-and-plate-glass door, seeing his reflection in the glass. He laughed bitterly. *At least I'm not invisible. At least I still look like me. But what goes on here? Have they changed the locks overnight? Why would they do that?*

With a feeling of dread that caused a cold sweat to break out on his face, he wondered how long he'd been passed out. He couldn't have lain in that alley for days, could he? *That's just not possible! But what to do?*

Just then he saw a dark figure in their lobby coming toward him. He hoped it would be a neighbor he'd recognize, but it was just some middle-aged guy with a salt-and-pepper beard, in running shorts and a tank top.

As he exited, Rory grabbed the door before it closed. The guy looked back at him, eyebrows together as though to say "What the hell?" Rory just shrugged and gave him his best, most honest smile and said, "I forgot my keys."

"Whatever." The guy did a little skip and began his run from the courtyard.

Inside, the air in the tile lobby was noticeably cooler. Rory noted that the Persian rug, red and cream, that used to lie on the floor was gone. Maybe it was being cleaned?

He headed to the elevator. At least it looked the same. He got in and pressed the button for his floor.

As he headed down the corridor, sure that the carpeting used to be dark brown and not this light beige now before him, he began to experience a sick feeling of foreboding.

He didn't want to think about it.

When he got to their door, he again produced his keys from his pocket.

And again, they didn't work.

"What the fuck?" Rory cried out, unable to help himself. Frustrated, he hammered the door with a volley of knocks. "Cole!" he yelled.

After a moment or two, the door opened. The woman inside peered out at him quizzically, keeping the chain lock in place. She was middle-aged, with straight bleached-blonde hair and a spray of reddish-brown freckles across her nose. She had on a blue terry cloth bathrobe. Rory had never seen her before in his life. What was she doing in his apartment?

With some indignation, she asked, "Can I help you?"

"I'm looking for Cole."

"What?" She cocked her head, groped in the pocket of her bathrobe, and produced a pair of black horn-rims. She put them on, looked Rory up and down.

"Cole. Cole Weston. My boy—" Rory stopped and corrected himself, "My roommate."

"Are you high?"

"What? No, no of course not." Rory didn't think so, but maybe he had the wrong apartment. He stepped back a couple of paces and looked at the number on the door. No. This was the right place. Frustrated, he blurted, "Who are you?"

She gathered her robe tighter to her chest and said, "I could ask you the same. And I could also ask why the hell you're hammering on my apartment door before seven in the freakin' morning!"

"*Your* apartment? What are you talking about? I live here, with Cole." Suddenly Rory was having trouble getting his breath. His stomach was doing somersaults. He felt like he might burst into tears. Or throw up....

The woman cast a brown-eyed gaze to the left. "What's going on here? I am *not* letting you in, if that's what you think this whole ploy is about."

"It's not a ploy. This is my home."

"Buddy. You need help. I've lived here for the past five years. And before me, an old lady who ended up in the home over on Sheridan was here. Now, I don't know what your problem is, but I need to get ready for work." She closed the door in his face.

Rory immediately raised his hand and knocked on the door again.

She opened it, without the chain in place. He could see sympathy mixed with fear in her eyes. "What? I don't know what to say to you."

"You don't know me? You don't know Cole?"

"I have no idea what you're talking about." She reached out, like she was going to touch him, but then dropped her hand. "Really."

"This is the tenth floor, right?"

She nodded.

"I don't know what's happening," Rory confessed, his voice quivering just a little bit. "Honest to God, last night this was my apartment. We'd just moved in!"

"Honey, that's not possible. As I said, I've been here, like, five years. Are you sure you're in the right place?"

Rory recited the address, and she nodded. "I don't know what to tell you," she said. "You seem confused. Is there maybe somebody I could call for you?" She groped in her other robe pocket and brought out one of those rectangles everyone on the street seemed to have.

"What is that?" Cole pointed down at the rectangle.

"This?" She showed him the face of the thing—glass with little square pictures lined up in rows on the surface. "This? Are you serious?"

Rory nodded, staring down at the thing. It looked like a little TV to him.

"It's my phone."

Rory stepped back. Since when had phones become so small, so weird looking? He shook his head; add another mystery to a day that was shaping up to be an unending series of enigmas. Regardless, maybe she could use that thing to call Cole. Sure, if she could reach him, maybe they could get this whole thing straightened out.

"That's awfully nice. Could you maybe call my roommate, Cole?" Rory recited the number and watched as she tapped at the glass screen. Amazing….

She listened for a moment, pressed a button at the bottom of the phone, and then tapped the screen a couple of times. She tapped the button at the bottom again and frowned at him. "That number goes to a breakfast joint over on Morse."

"What?"

"Look, I need to get to work. I don't have time for this." She smiled sadly at him. "I wish I could help you. I really do, because…. Oh, I don't know why. I just get a read on you that you're not some scammer, but you're kind of lost." She cocked her head. "And I'm still not gonna let you come in. I'm sorry." She started to close the door.

"Wait. Maybe Cole's at work. Could you call the Pier One in Evanston? I forget the number, but it's in the book."

"Pier One? On Davis?"

Rory nodded.

The woman looked like she didn't know whether to laugh or cry.

"What?" Rory asked.

"Sweetie, that place closed *years ago*. Your friend couldn't work there, not unless he has a time machine."

Rory felt a little dizzy. The store closed years ago? How could that be when Cole just had to stay late last night, doing inventory? And…

they'd been in the store the weekend before because Cole wanted to get some place mats he liked. Orange ones.

He stood in front of the closed door for a minute or two, and then he turned and slid down the wall until he was seated on the floor, his legs spread out before him. He felt numb, like it was too much effort just to think. So for a while he simply sat and stared, thinking nothing. Or maybe, he realized, it was more that he was avoiding thinking. There was an answer to the riddle here, but that answer was so momentous as to be truly terrifying. So he just sat and listened. Noises from other apartments he hadn't noticed before rose up—toilets flushing, the rolling doors of the elevator opening and closing down the hall, the creak of floorboards, a couple arguing just below him.

He jumped as a door opened down the hall. A young African American guy, dressed in chinos, a white shirt, and running shoes emerged. He had a messenger bag of some sort, maybe canvas, slung over his shoulder. He bent a little to lock his door and then turned—and stopped at the sight of Rory.

"Who the fuck are you?" he asked, nearing Rory. "You need something?"

Rory said the first thing that came to mind. "I'm locked out."

The guy narrowed his eyes, making it obvious he didn't believe Rory. "Right. You need to get your ass out of here."

Rory was afraid he'd do something more forceful, but he simply hurried away.

After a while the woman opened the door and gave out a little cry when she spied Rory sitting there. She put a hand to her chest. "What are you doing?" She was dressed for work, Rory guessed, in a pair of jeans, a loose blouse, and a bright blue blazer. She had a cream-and-blue scarf around her neck, a yellow leather bag over one arm that Rory thought she clutched just a little too protectively.

"I'm sorry," he said. "I don't know where to go."

"Well, you can't stay here. Do you need some money for the train? A bus?" She opened her purse, groped around it, and came out with a ten-dollar bill. "Here. Take this."

He was going to refuse, but then he reminded himself he only had a dollar to his name and now, apparently, no home. He took the money from her hand. "Thanks," he mumbled.

She held out her hand. "You can walk out with me."

"Oh, okay." He didn't touch her, simply stood. He could only begin to imagine what she must think of him—some lunatic. He realized he was beginning to think the same thing about himself.

They started down the hall together, and Rory finally allowed a realization to burrow into his psyche—he'd blacked out and lost some serious time. He wanted to ask the woman what day it was but thought that would make him seem even more crazy.

As they rode down in the elevator, though, he did summon the nerve to ask her one more thing. "Um, I don't suppose we could run back upstairs for a minute?"

"What for? I'm late for work."

"I'm sorry to cause you all this trouble. But I just thought, if you'd just indulge me with one more huge favor, we could call my mom and dad. They're in Wilmette."

The elevator landed in the lobby, and she stepped out. Rory thought she was refusing him, so he stepped out behind her.

"I have my phone right here." She dug it out of her purse. She held it out to him.

"It works down here?"

"Yes, what century are you from?" She laughed, but he could see she was uneasy.

He pushed it back toward her. "Would you mind dialing? I don't know how to use that, uh, telephone." He recited his parents' number.

She tapped it in, listened for a second, and then held it out to him. He hesitated, and she said, "Just talk normally. It's voicemail."

He held the phone to his ear. His mother's voice, sounding different somehow—a little hoarse, weaker—was speaking. "I'm not home right now. Please leave me a message, and I'll get back to you just as soon as I can." Rory didn't have time to think about why she was saying "I" instead of "we," but the beep had sounded and he needed to leave a message.

"Mom? It's me, Rory." *Like she doesn't know! What else do I say?* "I'm gonna come see you today. Hope you and Dad are home!" The beep sounded again. He handed the phone back. "Thanks."

"Sure. I'm glad you got hold of her. Is she close to the "L" station?"

Rory nodded.

"Then you should go see her. Just take the Purple line at Howard. Just follow Fargo up to Paulina and make a right and you'll see the "L" station. You can get a train for Wilmette there. Okay?"

Rory knew how to get to the "L," for fuck's sake. She was talking to him like he was mentally challenged or something. "Okay."

She smiled. "I'd take you myself, but I called an Uber."

Rory didn't want to ask what an Uber was, so he simply thanked her again for her patience, her understanding, *and* her ten dollars, and tried to appear normal as he began walking west on Fargo.

Maybe Mom will have some answers.

CHAPTER 14

GRETA SCHNEIDMILLER had the same routine Monday mornings—she'd get up, take Minnie, the rat terrier mix she'd rescued from the Humane Society, out for a short walk, feed her, and then sit down to a breakfast of one poached egg on toast and a cup of Earl Gray tea. While she ate, she'd read that day's *Chicago Tribune*.

After breakfast she'd go upstairs, change into a tracksuit—she had one in about every color imaginable—slip into her Nike cross-trainers, dab some lipstick on, and head out for her walk. She always headed east, ending up at Lake Michigan, where she'd sit for a while, if it was nice out, on a bench overlooking the water. Some days she'd bring her Kindle and read a few pages of whatever romantic suspense novel she was engrossed in at the moment. Other days she'd simply stare off into the distance, noting the color of the water, how it changed from the shore to out in the far distance. She'd sometimes imagine what the clouds looked like.

It was an easy yet humdrum existence.

Then she'd return home. To an empty house. It had been an empty house now for more than a decade, since Homer had passed away shortly after retiring from his stressful job as a floor trader at the Mercantile Exchange. Oh, how Homer had looked forward to retirement—puttering around in the garden, growing tomatoes and peppers, maybe taking a cooking class, finally beginning some sort of exercise. He was eyeing mountain bikes at the Target on Howard when he'd dropped over from a heart attack. Dead almost immediately, right there in the store. And he'd only been retired for two weeks.

And then, what with Rory, their only son, being gone, well, Greta wondered if she'd ever look at the Dutch colonial residence as anything more than an empty house. The women in her book club told her she should sell it. She could make a hefty profit, they said, and then she could buy a nice new condo near downtown Evanston. No fuss, no muss.

But even though the pain of its emptiness haunted most of her days, she couldn't bear to leave. It was where Rory had grown up. It was the place she and Homer bought when she found out she was pregnant—after trying for years and finally giving up, after living in an apartment in Chicago, in Edgewater. There were so many birthdays celebrated there, so many Christmases, Thanksgivings, and Easters around the big walnut dining room table.

The empty house certainly wasn't empty of one thing—memories. And Greta simply coveted those too much to let go.

She liked her routine, monotonous as it was. It gave structure to her days, made her feel less lonely, made her feel like her life had a purpose.

As she returned to her house that August morning when everything would change, she'd recall that she felt nothing different when she unlocked the door. It seemed a day just like any other—like all the days and the way they ran into each other with sameness, making them indistinguishable except for how the seasons watermarked them.

She went inside, put down her Kindle on the coffee table, intending to come back with a second cup of tea and immerse herself in the latest Nora Roberts. Minnie danced around her heels, and she let her out into the fenced backyard, where she could count on finding her later sunbathing, or roasting in the sun was more like it, tongue lolling out and panting. The poor thing wasn't smart enough to find herself some shade!

When she came back in, after she set the kettle on the stove to boil, she noticed the message light on the cordless phone blinking. She paused to throw a tea bag in the cup she'd used earlier and crossed to the wall-mounted telephone. She lifted it and pressed the button to access voicemail. Tomorrow night was her book club, and she wouldn't be surprised at all if it wasn't the always-harried Monica Habuda calling to ask her to bring hors d'oeuvres.

But it wasn't Monica. The familiar voice made her gasp and then reach out blindly for one of the stools at the kitchen island so she could plop down on it before she fainted.

"Mom? It's me, Rory. I'm gonna come see you today. Hope you and Dad are home!"

Mouth suddenly dry, Greta pressed the button that would replay the message. She had to have had some sort of aural hallucination. The new message would be a roofing contractor offering a free inspection, or from the Democratic party wanting a donation, or even Father Frank at St. Ann's, wondering if she was coming to bingo next week at the parish hall.

But it wasn't.

"Mom? It's me, Rory. I'm gonna come see you today. Hope you and Dad are home!"

No. The voice was so familiar, but it *couldn't* be Rory. She threw the phone across the room, where it shattered on the tile floor. Even though she was breathing hard, it felt as though she couldn't get enough air into her lungs. She stared, openmouthed, nearly groaning, at the charcoal gray phone on the floor, broken, as though it were a monster that had somehow managed to get inside her house.

It was on the tip of her tongue to cry out for Homer. But no, he was gone. And so was Rory!

But the voice had sounded so like her son's! A mother knows the voice of her only child There were few things certain in this life, but parents knowing their children, their voices, their smells, the color of their eyes and hair, was one of them.

But it couldn't be. Her Rory was dead. Someone was having a sick joke at her expense after all these years. Who would do such a thing? Why would they want to?

The simple message replayed again and again in her head, taunting her, making her cover her gasping mouth with her shaking hand, causing her eyes to well up with tears.

What was the greater horror? That it really was him?

Or that it wasn't?

Somehow Greta managed to get to her feet. She crossed the kitchen and stumbled through the french doors out onto the deck. The day was already heating up. The weather folks on Channel Two said it was going to be a scorcher. "Minnie!" Greta called. The dog came running, tail wagging, tongue out, mouth opened in what looked like a huge smile. "Get inside!" she snapped at the dog, shooing her in through the open french door into the air-conditioning. "Drink some water, for God's sake."

She watched the dog scamper for its stainless-steel bowl on the terrazzo tile floor and then shut the door. She sat down hard on one of the deck lounges, still gasping for air.

In time, she thought, she could go back inside, listen to the message again from the extension in the den, and see for herself that it wasn't Rory. It couldn't be Rory.

He'd been gone for twenty years.

He was never coming back.

She'd accepted that a long time ago. They'd had him declared dead so they could move on.

But they couldn't—couldn't ever move on. The loss was a hole in the fabric of her and Homer's world. Sometimes she envied him for dying.

She had just lowered her head to her hands so she could sob when the doorbell sounded.

CHAPTER 15

RORY SHIFTED his weight from one foot to the other as he waited for someone to answer. Of course, this was his own house, the one he'd grown up in, and he could simply walk right in. And he'd tried, but the door had been locked. And, just like the key to his apartment, the key for this front door no longer worked.

Out of the corner of his eye, he thought he saw the lace curtain at the front picture window shift just a little bit. He drew in some breath, waiting, trying not to get too impatient.

What if someone new lived here too? What if they were just as confused as the woman now inhabiting his and Cole's apartment on Fargo? What if he or she or they called the police on him, thinking he was a nutcase or a scammer? Where would he go then?

A dog barked inside, and he thought for sure that his parents no longer lived here. Growing up, it seemed like the one thing he'd always wanted and yet could never have was a dog. Too messy, his mom, Greta had said. Too much work and responsibility, his dad had always patiently explained. "What would we do with it when we want to go on vacation?"

After a couple of minutes passed, he rang the doorbell again, listening to those familiar chimes. Then he knocked on the door, not hard, but loud enough to be heard.

He was just about to check the mailbox to the left of the door, just to see if there was any mail there and to whom it might be addressed, when the door opened.

His mother looked out at him, a hand to her chest, her mouth open in a little O of surprise. Surprise? More like shock.

"Mom—" Rory started.

"No!" she cried. "It's not you! It's not you!"

Rory's hand was half upraised, to do what he wasn't sure, when she slammed the door in his face.

Rory stood staring at the door for a long time. She'd slammed it so hard it seemed to be vibrating in its frame. After a moment he heard the turn of the dead bolt.

His mother looked so different—she'd aged. Her hair, for one. It was once the same reddish-brown as his own, and she kept the roots and stray hairs touched up, but now it was white, like an old lady's. Her face was careworn, the creases in her forehead, around her eyes and her mouth, were deep. She'd gained weight—and she never would have worn that gray-and-pink tracksuit she had on.

He knocked again. And again.

Finally, in despair, he simply turned and plopped down on the front steps, head in his hands. He had nowhere else to go. Nowhere to find answers that might begin to solve the mystery that seemed to have turned his life upside down.

After a while the door creaked open. He turned slowly, peering at his mom over his shoulder. She stood, arms limp at her sides, staring, jaw slack. Her eyes, even from where he sat and even behind her glasses, were rimmed in red, as if she'd been crying.

"Mom?"

"It's not you," she repeated, her voice dull, that of a zombie. "It can't be. You're, you're—gone."

Rory stood, making his movements slow, as he would to ensure he wouldn't frighten a wild animal.

A little dog, lemon and white, panting, danced around her feet, whining and trying to get out the door.

"You got a dog?" Rory asked.

She shook her head. "I needed the company," she said simply. "I was so alone." He could see her throat work as she tried to swallow.

He took a step toward her. "Mom? I don't know what's going on. But it *is* me. It's your boy, Rory." A lump formed in his throat. She cowered as he neared her, and that stopped him in his tracks. He noticed her hands shaking.

"Get back in, Minnie!" she shouted harshly at the dog. And the dog vanished into the shadows behind her, although Rory could still hear her whining. Greta looked him up and down, as though looking for a clue. "Who are you?" she asked, but Rory could detect the defeat in her voice.

"You know who I am, Mom."

She slumped to one side, letting the doorframe support her. "You certainly look like my son."

"I *am* your son." He raised an arm to tap the port-wine birthmark on the inside of his forearm. "Surely you remember this? And the time, when I was six, I tried to wash it off with Lava soap."

She shook her head—hard. "You can't be my son, young man! And *that's* why—you're young! My son, *my son*, if he were still alive, would be forty-three years old."

Rory stepped back and almost fell off the edge of the porch. "What?"

Her cry, an accusation really, came out garbled, desperate. "My son would have some gray in his hair! A few lines on his face. Maybe a little paunch on him. My son might need bifocals. My son, my son! Can't be *you*. You just can't be him." She reached out her hand and then let it fall. In a whispered rush of breath, "It's not possible."

"It's me, Mom. It's me. I think you know that."

What was going on? Rory didn't dare even wonder, although the pieces, impossible though they were, were beginning to slide into place, even though Rory couldn't accept them.

After a bit she simply closed her eyes and stepped back. "Come in," she said, voice barely above a whisper.

He followed her into the house. It looked familiar, yet not. The only piece of furniture he recognized was the leather recliner in the corner his dad loved. Its buttery surface was worn, darkened by body oils. There was a large black screen over the fireplace. What had happened to the seascape his father so loved?

The dog rushed up to him, anxiously sniffing his ankles.

"Minnie!" Mom cried. "Get away."

Rory squatted down to make friends with the little dog. "It's okay." He reached out his hand to let her sniff. She did—and then she licked it. He scratched her behind the ears and while doing so, looked up at his mom and smiled. "It's okay. It's okay, Mom," he said, even though he knew it wasn't. "I don't understand what's going on either. No more than you do. But I do know you don't need to be afraid."

She didn't say anything. She turned and disappeared into the kitchen. There was the sound of the pilot light on the stove clicking on, a faint whoosh. She came back. "I'm making tea. Come in the kitchen and we'll talk."

Rory followed her into the kitchen. The room was unrecognizable. Where once had been a white stove, refrigerator, and dishwasher, there were now ultramodern-looking models crafted from stainless steel.

Where there had once been a large picture window looking out on the backyard, there were now french doors. The cabinets he remembered had been maple—now everything was white, and the upper cabinets had glass windowpane fronting. Even the old maple table was gone, replaced by a center island with barstools.

Rory felt something clench inside. Where was he? He looked down at the floor. The linoleum, a pebbled beige surface, had been replaced by terrazzo tile.

He turned around, in an almost complete circle. "It's so different. When did you do all this?"

Mom, near the stove, lowered her head a bit to peer at him over the tops of her glasses. "We remodeled a few years ago, just before your father—" She stopped herself in midsentence.

"What?" Rory took a step toward his mother. The house, he noticed, was so quiet. He looked out through the french doors and saw Minnie chasing a squirrel, barking at it as it scrambled up a tree.

"Nothing." Greta turned and began pouring water into mugs. "Come. Sit down." She placed a tea bag in each mug and brought them both to the table.

Like normal people, when the situation was so far from normal that Rory didn't know of a word that could describe it. He sat down with his mother at the kitchen's center island. For a long time, neither spoke, nor did either touch the tea in front of them. Along with Mom, Rory simply stared down into his tea, watching as it slowly deepened in color and the steam rose from its surface.

At last Rory spoke. "I don't know what's happened. I woke up this morning in an alley in the city. It seemed like only a night had passed, but, but—" Rory couldn't go on, couldn't make himself say the incredible, unimaginable words, although they were there, poised at the tip of his tongue. *But it looks like, somehow, and I have no idea how, twenty years passed in what seems to be a single night.*

Greta, he could tell, was unable to say any more herself. After several awkward silent moments passed, she got up from the table, the legs of the stool scraping against the tile floor. She hurriedly left the room.

Rory watched her go. Listened to her footfalls as she made her way up the stairs off the entryway at the house's front.

He knew enough not to follow her. He was left with the anguish imprinted on her features for company. He waited for the longest time, thinking she would return. When she didn't, he got up from the table and let the dog in. She scampered through the kitchen, and then he heard her running up the stairs, following her mistress.

He looked out into the yard. It seemed like a typical August day in Chicago. He had no thoughts. What could he possibly think, anyway? He'd woken and stepped into an episode of that old TV series he sometimes caught on TV late at night, *The Twilight Zone*. There were simply no words to explain the chaos in his heart and mind.

After what seemed like an hour or more, his mother, sniffling, came back down the stairs. She entered the kitchen, Minnie trailing behind. Rory looked up. His mother's eyes were fiery red. She clutched a Kleenex in her right hand.

He started to speak, but she held up a hand. "No. Don't say anything. Not now. I've been upstairs, thinking. And the only thing I can imagine is that this, *you*, are a miracle. A true miracle. The Good Lord has seen fit to return you to me. Now, I don't know how. And I sure as hell don't know why." She started to cry again as she spoke. "But Rory, sweetheart, I'm so glad you're here." She stood before him, hanging her head, sobbing.

Rory took her in his arms, and she clutched him, weeping into his chest.

After a bit of sniffling, she pulled away, stared into his eyes. "It's really you, isn't it?"

Rory, emotions threatening to overtake him as well, simply nodded.

"We can't tell *anyone*. No one would understand. But we have to accept this miracle somehow. This gift…." She looked away, staring outside. "I never thought I'd see you again."

"It sounds all right, Mom." Rory didn't know what else to say. The truth hit him hard—twenty years *had* somehow passed. He had all the proof he needed. And in that time, he had not aged, and the world had gone on around him. For right now, her plan, a pathetic one at best—keeping him a secret—seemed like the best option, or maybe their only one.

There would be time enough to figure things out later on. If indeed anything *could* be figured out. Right now he was overcome with exhaustion and emotion. The fatigue came on suddenly, like a lead weight over his entire body. His eyes burned. "I'm so tired," he said. "Is my old room still set up?"

She smiled through her tears, nodding. "Of course it is." She shrugged and smiled shyly. "I think there was always a part of me that kept it the way it was just in case…."

"Can I just go sleep?"

She pointed to the ceiling.

He started from the room.

"Don't go away, son."

He paused at the doorway. "I'm not going anywhere. Not if I can help it."

And he headed for the stairs. Maybe, when he woke, he'd discover this had all been nothing more than a bad dream.

CHAPTER 16

"I DON'T know if he'll ever get over it, or him, rather," Tommy said to his best friend, Dora. The two were having lunch outside, on her flagstone patio in the northern suburb of Deerfield. Tommy had picked up a big salad from Whole Foods in downtown Evanston before heading north on the Edens Expressway. Dora was on yet another diet, and he knew she'd appreciate the effort, if not the greens.

Dora took a bite of her salad, looking thoughtful as she chewed. Tommy thought she didn't need to diet. Sure, what with having children and the relentless passing of the years, she'd put on a fair amount of weight. But the extra pounds looked good on her. She carried them well and knew how to dress for a lady of a certain age and carriage. Her face was still unlined, and she kept her blond hair, though now short, colored and highlighted so it, at least, still looked as though it was in its twenties. She asked, "And that doesn't bother you?"

They had this same conversation, it seemed to Tommy, every year around the anniversary of Rory's disappearance, when Cole would make his annual pilgrimage to Graceland. Tommy didn't really get why it bothered him so much, because after a few days, Cole—and their non-Rory lives—would return to normal. During the remaining 360 or so days of the year, Cole never mentioned Rory and, as far as Tommy knew, never gave an indication of thinking about his first love. "Well, you know it does. A little." He took a sip of iced tea. "I mean, I should be tolerant, right?"

Dora moved some of her veggies around on her plate, peering down at them as though they were maggots or cockroaches. "What I'd really love is a big juicy burger with bleu cheese and crispy bacon, with a huge heap of fries alongside. A beer. And after, a cigarette."

She laughed, but Tommy witnessed a kind of longing in her features. Mention of the burger made him think, once again, of Rory. A Moody's burger had been his last meal, served up by none other than the woman sitting across from him. Tommy wondered if she was aware of the connection and then immediately doubted it. Most people didn't put such things together, especially after twenty years had passed. But he wasn't married to most people....

Dora choked down some more of her salad. "No. You shouldn't be tolerant."

"What?"

"I said it. I've been holding it in for years. I'm not going to listen anymore. And neither should you.

"You don't need to be tolerant. Not for another year, not for another day. Tommy, it's been *twenty years*! That's a nice round number and way beyond what anyone would have a right to expect from you, anyway. Twenty years. You're done. He needs to get over that boy, especially when he has a gorgeous, smart man who loves him with all of his heart right in front of his nose. You just need to tell him to get over it. You've been patient, kind, and understanding more than long enough."

"You're heartless."

"And you have *too much* heart, Tommy. You always have. We all know that boy was most likely dead within hours of my waiting on him. That's very sad—tragic—but it's true. And to my mind, it's a little sick the way Cole pines after him. I think anyone with a reasonable mind would agree with me that you've gone above and beyond the call of duty in the understanding department. For your sake and for his, Cole needs to let this go."

Tommy knew she was right. They'd had a similar conversation every year around this time for the past ten years—yet this was the first time she'd told him he was being too tolerant, too kind, too understanding. And every year, he came away from seeing Dora with the same resolve— that he would speak with Cole, tell him how much it hurt him that he still had these feelings for Rory. Tommy knew that if Cole and Rory had simply run their course, they might not even be together today—young, hot love often had a way of burning out as quickly as it flared up into lusty flame. But then, if Rory hadn't disappeared, Tommy might have never met Cole. And Tommy couldn't imagine a life without Cole. He was his husband, his family, his best friend.

His everything.

Which was why it was hard to have a talk with him about this annual "thing." How could Tommy take it away? And he knew that's exactly what he'd be doing. Cole was a nice man, a pushover, really. He'd give in. He'd promise to let things go, to not commemorate the anniversary.

But would he keep the promise?

"Yeah, you're right," Tommy said. "I should have a talk with him."

"And you know you won't." She laughed. "Every year, you tell me you feel bad and every year, I bite my tongue, letting go of my own good judgment and not telling you to have it out with him—that his memorializing this guy goes above and beyond. This year, I made myself speak up. And it doesn't seem to have had much effect." Dora shrugged. Tell you what, next year let's just skip talking about it."

Tommy grabbed her hand. "Oh, can we? Pretty please! I'll treat you to that burger and fries. And we'll get a pitcher of Leinenkugels!"

"It's a plan," Dora said. "We'll get drunk off our asses and raise a glass to when we were roomies and our place needed a revolving door for all the men we had stoppin' by."

Tommy joined her in laughter. "Oh, those were the days."

"You were quite the slut." Dora nudged him.

"Oh my! Talk about the pot calling the kettle black!"

"But it all came crashing to an end when you met Cole. At least for you. My wild oats days continued for a couple more years, especially after my moved out. Gave me even more freedom to get my freak on." She snorted. "But after Cole? You were a different man. I didn't think there *was* any such bird as a one-man man, or even a one-woman man. I believed men were helpless little babies when it came to their libidos. No control." She leaned in close to Tommy. "You ever get a little on the side? You can tell me."

Tommy reared back in his chair, a hand to his chest. "Me? Never!" He burst into more laughter, and Dora eyed him, the surprise on her face plain.

"That's sarcasm, right?"

He shook his head. "It's sad. I haven't touched another man's cock in two decades. I've eyed a few, of course, at the gym and when I bring up some porn on the computer, but I can't imagine myself with someone else. There've been a couple close calls here and there over the years, but I always think, why should I go for hamburger when I have steak at home."

Dora reached over the table to tweak his nose. "You're adorable. Why is it that it always seems to be the gay guys who are the sweetest?"

"Oh, I've met some pretty vinegary gay guys, believe me. Gay men have not cornered the market on sweetness, take it from one who knows." Tommy laughed and then leaned in and asked, "What about you? Any dalliances?"

Dora gave him the side-eye. "Honey, don't nobody need to see these droopy tits, stretch marks, and flabby thighs." She shook her head. "Besides, I can barely find the energy to make love to David a couple times a month! I can't add anyone else into the equation."

"You're a beautiful woman."

"Oh, go on!" She looked away for a moment. "And you're a beautiful man. And I love you."

They finished their lunch in comfortable silence as the warm breeze, with just a hint of the coming autumn, washed over them.

Tommy thought, really, he had so much to be grateful for. And all in all, there was much that was right with his world.

WHEN HE got home from Dora's, Tommy found Cole asleep in their bedroom. Naps were a pretty regular occurrence around their household, since neither of them worked outside the house and they had the luxury of enough time to indulge the habit.

The TV was on, the volume low. Cole had put in one of their *Golden Girls* DVDs. They had all seven seasons, and Cole referred to them as his form of Ambien. Televised comfort food. Cole once confessed that he rarely saw the end of an episode anymore because the show put him to sleep, usually within five minutes. It wasn't that it was boring—quite the contrary—but that it just felt so warm, familiar, and comforting that he could relax and let go, the wisecracks and laugh track lulling him off to dreamland.

Tommy moved quietly into the room. It was peaceful. The sun's dying light filtered in through their honeycomb blinds, and he could see tinges of lavender and tangerine through them in the dusky sky. The trees were sharpening in definition, becoming black silhouettes as the sun set.

He sat down on the bed, still trying not to make any noise, and bent to remove his running shoes. He was glad Cole was a deep sleeper. He liked having this time—stalkerish though some might consider it—to simply drink in the beauty of his man.

Cole was on his side, on top of the quilt, wearing only a pair of gray plaid boxers. His body didn't look much different from when they'd first met. A little hairier, perhaps, a little saggier in places for sure, but whose wasn't? Tommy looked down at his own paunch, thinking once more he needed to start logging more running miles.

Five miles every other day no longer kept the weight away. Maybe he'd think about doing that next week....

But Cole, for the most part, still had the body of a much younger man. Lithe, lean, fit, almost boyish. Tommy was lucky.

His gaze moved up to Cole's face, and in repose Cole looked very young, his brow not creased by worry, his lips gently parted as he inhaled and exhaled. Even the little line of drool on his cheek was adorable. Tommy thought you really had to love somebody to find their spittle cute. Here, though, Cole's forties showed up a bit more readily. His hair, once so thick and dark, was now thinning, especially on his crown. He wore it in a buzz cut for exactly that reason. And the buzz cut also helped hide the gray at his temples. Tommy could see more and more of it every time Cole let a haircut go too long.

Tommy didn't mind. The gray was silvery, distinguished. Tommy thought growing old with his man wasn't something to be cursed, but a gift to be grateful for. He remembered how, when he'd first met Cole, marrying him wasn't even something he allowed himself to dream of. It simply wasn't in the cards for gay men back in the 1990s. It didn't even seem unfair because it was so far out of reach as to be invisible.

But when the same-sex marriage movement began gathering momentum in the twenty-first century, he and Cole had both fought hard for their right to wed. No longer did something like a "domestic partner" have any appeal. They refused to be second-class citizens. And they'd won. Tommy would never forget the day the Supreme Court ruled in their favor.

They'd had a small wedding, right here in this very condo, in front of the fireplace, the Christmas tree, and a handful of friends. They'd read poetry to each other and said their vows with tears in their eyes.

It had been the happiest day of Tommy's life.

He hoped the same was true for Cole.

Quietly, Tommy took off his shorts and T-shirt and then lay down beside Cole. Why did it always seem there was this third presence hovering around their relationship? Would Tommy always doubt that Cole loved him best? Could he compete with a memory, a memory Tommy was sure had had its rough edges eroded over the years into a kind of magical perfection?

He snuggled close to Cole's warm body. He was like a little furnace. Did any of this matter? Once upon a time, a teacher in college, a wise and white-haired old man named Milton White who taught creative writing, had told him there were always two parties in any relationship—the lover and the loved.

If Tommy was the lover, that was okay by him, as long as Cole was around to be loved. There was such joy in the *giving* of his love.

He flung his arms around Cole, spooning, and Cole stirred, mumbling and smacking his lips. "You home?"

"No, it's Ryan Gosling. I couldn't keep away," Tommy whispered in Cole's ear. He bit the lobe, and Cole squirmed, laughing.

He flipped over so they were facing each other and peered into Tommy's eyes. "What do I need him for when I have you?" He bumped against him, letting Tommy feel he was erect. "Gosling's got nothing on you."

Tommy reached down and squeezed the head of Cole's cock through the fabric of his shorts. The simple action produced a similar effect in his own boxer briefs. "My, my," Tommy said, his voice gone a little hoarse. "Sweet dreams?"

"Not as sweet as what's about to happen." Cole growled and forced Tommy onto his back.

Above, Cole smiled down at him. There was such warmth—and fire—in those eyes, that gaze. Tommy felt like he could see Cole's soul.

"And what's about to happen?" Tommy asked.

"Close your eyes and find out."

And Tommy did. The first thing he felt was Cole's mouth on his own, his tongue prying his lips apart. How could it be that, after twenty years together, this moment was still so filled with excitement and promise?

Tommy knew better than to question it.

As he lost himself in the feel of Cole's hot embrace, his tongue, his lips, his limbs entwining themselves around Tommy's body, he could hear Blanche, the slutty Golden Girl, saying something about how she loved a tight man.

Tommy thought he couldn't agree more.

CHAPTER 17

IT WAS the end of October, and Cole peered out at the day from the floor-to-ceiling windows in their condo's living room. He could almost feel the warmth of the sunshine and the crispness of the breeze through the glass. Only autumn, Cole thought, had such blue skies, such brilliant sun. The breezes rustling the trees seemed alive with morning promise. The scene, one for a postcard, filled him with a kind of peaceful bliss.

He barely heard Tommy come in behind him. But then, all of a sudden, he was there behind him, a hand on his shoulder, squeezing. "Ah, I wish I didn't have those edits due back this afternoon. I'd love to get outside today, but unfortunately all I'm going to be seeing is my computer screen. I'm way late on the deadline for this one."

Cole said over his shoulder, "Ah, poor you. I wish I could help. But you're so secretive with those books!"

Tommy chuckled; they'd had this conversation dozens of times over the years. Besides his trusted editor in New York, Tommy couldn't let anyone see his work until it was in print. Not even Cole, who, bless his heart, bought e-book and paperback copies the moment a new book came out, just to show his support. "Oh, you know, the mystery of the creative process." He let his hand slide down Cole's back before he took it away. "But you don't have to be stuck in here today. Weather app says it's gonna hit the upper sixties with clear sunshine all day. It's almost Halloween, and we both know what that means in Chicago."

"It could be snowing next week," Cole said.

"Right. So you should get out there and enjoy it. Take a walk along the beach. A bike ride? You haven't gotten the old Cannondale out in ages."

"Its tires are probably flat, and it's covered with cobwebs."

"And you can fix those things in a matter of minutes." Tommy sighed. "Do what you want—but enjoy yourself and know that I'm just a tiny bit jealous of your freedom." He turned toward the hallway leading to his office. "I got to get to work. That book's not gonna edit itself." And just as quickly as he'd come into the room, Tommy left it. Cole listened for the sound of his office door closing.

It did look nice out there, inviting. The fall colors were in their full glory, and Tommy was right—the onset of winter could be capricious, and late October or early November were not unknown for demonstrating that. Even as early as tomorrow, the skies could turn dark, temperatures could plummet, and what felt like end-of-summer bliss could morph into early winter misery.

Cole had seen it happen more times than he could count.

Tommy was also right about the Cannondale commuter bike mounted on the wall by their car in the garage downstairs. With a couple of cloths, a can of WD-40, and his handy-dandy bicycle pump, he could have that thing roadworthy in twenty minutes or less, barring any serious setbacks like a punctured tire.

And really, what else did he have to do today? He thought he might go to Whole Foods. Maybe clear out his closet, looking for stuff to donate to Goodwill. Look for part-time work on Craigslist—that *never* worked out. Binge-watch the latest hot series on Netflix?

In the end he listened to his heart and knew what he wanted most was to be outside. Tommy wouldn't emerge from his office fully until dinnertime anyway. He'd sneak out to grab something easy from the fridge around lunchtime—a sandwich or the leftover shells with pesto and ham from last night—and then duck back into his office with it. Cole shook his head as he went back to the bedroom to change. Tommy, who'd once been an earnest yet miserable and uninspired law student, could have never been an attorney. Cole had yet to meet even one person more suited for a career that included so much solitude than Tommy. In spite of his friendliness, he was a true, 100 percent introvert, so holing up in an office by himself and creating people, places, and situations out of his imagination was perfectly suited to his temperament. If he didn't get his alone time, through work or some other means, he was wrung out and definitely not a pleasure to live with.

Unbidden, a thought popped into Cole's head—*Just like Rory used to be.*

In the bedroom Cole tried to drown out the thought quickly by putting his Bluetooth earbuds in and bringing up his "Move" playlist on his phone. It included songs by Lady Gaga, Britney Spears, Janet Jackson, Madonna, and even oldies like Tone-Loc, Donna Summer, the Average White Band, and Anita Bell.

Cole danced around the bedroom as he donned a pair of jogging pants, a Cubs long-sleeved T-shirt, a pair of black Cons, and a black baseball cap. He appraised himself in the full-length mirror. With the cap hiding his balding head, he thought he could even pass for his early thirties, hell, maybe even his late twenties.

What did that matter, anyway?

He grabbed his phone off the dresser and texted Tommy that he was going to take advantage and use his idea about the bike ride, indicating he'd head north on the Green Bay Trail to better see the color changes of the trees. He texted because he'd learned, long ago, one did not interrupt Tommy when his office door was closed, at least if you wanted to keep your head.

Tommy texted back a hands-clapping emoji and a kiss-blowing one.

Cole set off.

COLE WAS so glad Tommy had urged him to get out and ride his bike. He couldn't remember the last time he'd had the thing out, and it felt good—the pull of his leg muscles working, the steady in and out of air. Cole could imagine his lungs as bellows. The breeze against his skin felt warm when he was in the sun and almost cold in the shade.

It felt good.

The air was crisp and clean and, before noon, was only in the low sixties. As he coursed through Northwestern University's campus and its lakefront setting, he savored the teal blue waters of the lake against the sky's brilliant backdrop to the east. To the west the gray buildings on campus looked stalwart, imposing, and a little Gothic. Students hurried between them, to and from classes.

Before long he was off the campus and on the Green Bay Trail, pedaling alongside the railroad tracks on a paved path, beneath a canopy of trees sporting red, orange, and yellow leaves. Sunlight dappled the asphalt before him, and he felt the heat of it on his shoulders.

He figured on the way back, he'd stop at one of his favorite North Shore restaurants, the Pantry in downtown Wilmette. It was a little place, not far from the train tracks, that had been there for years. Three older women, sisters, Cole had heard, ran the place. And for years, their simple formula had worked well—you walked in, ordered a sandwich—always the same three choices: chicken salad, rare roast beef, or turkey breast,

Havarti cheese optional on the latter two—ordered soup if you wanted it—usually homemade chicken noodle and something more exotic, like borscht—and a drink, and paid one of the sisters sitting at a folding table with a cashbox. You picked out a table, sat down, and one of the other sisters—who all looked like the Polish grandmas you wished you had—would bring out your sandwich on homemade sourdough bread, and you'd be in hog heaven.

Cole was getting close to Ravinia Park and had it in his head to go farther when the pull of the Pantry—and the growls in his stomach—became too strong. He turned around and began heading south again.

He was nearing the Pantry when he saw him, on a side residential street near downtown Wilmette.

Cole slowed his bike so he didn't crash, blinking and peering at the young man walking down the street, a couple of books under his right arm. He allowed the bike to coast to a stop and then put his feet on the ground so the bike didn't tip over—or maybe so *he* didn't tip over.

Cole's heart, ahead of his head by a minute or two, pounded in his chest so hard he thought that, if he looked down, he'd see it cartoonishly pressing the red cotton of his T-shirt up and down as it contracted and released. A line of sweat beads popped up on his forehead, and another group of them formed rapidly in his underarms, to crawl in a tickling way down his side. His mouth was dry. He blinked several times to assure himself his eyes weren't deceiving him.

He laid the bike down on the grass at the edge of the sidewalk and turned to peer again at the young man, who was now farther away as he headed east and toward the lakefront. He didn't want to think about it, but the recognition was unavoidable.

He looks just like Rory. Not just similar—exactly.

Cole squeezed his eyes shut tight, trying to clear his head of insane, hopeful, and irrational thoughts, and looked again.

It can't be Rory. He's too young. And besides, if Rory came back, don't you think he'd at least get in touch? Where would he have been all these years?

No. That can't be him. That guy's just a kid.

Still, Cole couldn't help himself. His appetite had vanished. He became consumed with a singular purpose. Quickly he found a street sign to lock his bike to. It wasn't the most secure way to prevent having his bike stolen, but it was quick, and it would have to do—for now. Besides, this fool's errand he had in mind shouldn't take long.

When he turned back around, the young man was gone. At first he thought the passing of a black pickup truck simply blocked his view, but when the vehicle roared away, Rory was nowhere to be seen.

But he had to find out where he'd gone! Everything about the guy, even from the short glance Cole had, was just like his Rory, right down to the slight pigeon-toed way he walked. Cole broke into a trot, heading east on the street, looking down side streets on which he might have turned, heading north or south.

As he got to within a couple of blocks of the lake, he spotted him to the north, a good block ahead. Was this the right one? Cole questioned himself. But the camo cargo shorts he wore and the red in his hair, glinting in the sunlight, helped Cole know for sure he was looking at the same guy.

Wait a minute. Another coincidence. Isn't this the street where Rory grew up? Where his parents lived?

Cole paused briefly at the corner to look up at the street sign. Fourth Street. Yup, even through the passage of all those years, Cole still remembered that the Schneidmillers lived on Fourth Street. He remembered coming over with Rory for family dinners and backyard barbeques. His mother made the best German potato salad Cole had ever tasted. He remembered walking from the house over to nearby Gilson Park with Rory.

Their house, a large brick bungalow, was just a few blocks up from where he was standing, if Cole remembered right. He stopped for a moment, watching the figure in the shorts and the faded, dirty-white T-shirt head away.

Stop it. Go back. Pick up your bike and get yourself some lunch. You're just hungry, and it's bringing on hallucinations. Cole took a few more steps toward the retreating figure on the sidewalk ahead. *Yeah, right. Hunger never caused me to have hallucinations before! Just let me catch up and have a quick glance at the kid. I'm sure once I see his face, all doubt will be erased. I'll know, unequivocally, that it's not him. Of course it's not him. It can't be.*

Even as his logical mind was feeding him these very credible and reasonable thoughts, his intuition was telling him no one had a walk like that. It was unique. No one had hair like that, with the cowlick that stuck up out of the crown on his head.

Cole stepped up his pace. As he got closer and closer, his mind sort of went numb, because each step revealed to him that this guy *was a carbon copy of Rory*. He could tell himself, over and over again, that it couldn't possibly *be* Rory, but the resemblance was simply too astonishing. And too on target.

Cole broke into a run, hoping the *slap, slap, slap* of his Cons didn't alert the guy that someone was pursuing him. Cole imagined him turning around, looking perhaps a little annoyed, with a face that was nothing like Rory's.

He slowed as he got really close. He had to stop himself from crying out "Hey, Rory!" just to test and see if he'd look.

Cole almost stopped or he'd run right by the guy. He slowed not because he didn't want to catch a glimpse of the young man, but because they were now on the block on which Rory had grown up and on which his parents lived, just at the corner of Washington Avenue.

He spied the house. It was essentially the same. The trim had been painted a dark red instead of the cream color Cole recalled. The grass needed cutting. The front blinds were drawn.

Could Rory's parents still live there? Were they even still alive?

And then the young man did something that sucked all the air out of Cole. He turned at the house and made his way up the front walk. Now Cole's heart was beating so hard and fast he feared an attack was imminent. He watched breathlessly as the young man mounted the steps and then groped in his pocket, presumably for his keys.

Distantly, he heard the jingle of a set of keys as he brought them out.

And then he turned and looked. Perhaps he felt Cole's gaze on him.

Oh, my God. That face. It's him. It's really him. Their gazes connected for what seemed like a long time but had to have been only a couple of seconds. Cole knew he was the only one on the street.

Cole didn't see recognition in Rory's face—only a mild curiosity. He cocked his head, as though to ask "What are you staring at?" And then he turned, unlocked the front door, and went inside.

Cole stared at the closed door for a long time. He wondered where his ability to speak had gone. In his head he'd wanted to call out to him, saying something stupid, like "Rory? Is it really you?" But the ability to combine voice box, tongue, and mouth together to form words seemed a skill Cole no longer had.

Should he go up and knock? He shook his head. Something kept his feet rooted to the sidewalk below, as though an invisible force pressed him into place. He waited and waited for the door to open again—to see, maybe, Rory standing in the open door, smiling and beckoning as if all those years hadn't passed.

The door didn't open, and at last Cole's common sense, his logical brain, took over. Despite the coincidence of the house and the young man who looked *exactly* like Rory, he told himself the man couldn't be Rory. It wasn't possible because he was far too young.

He wanted, wished so hard, that it were true. But it couldn't be. It just couldn't be.

After much deliberation, he found the will to move his feet again and head back west, toward the little downtown.

He was no longer hungry. He would mount his bike and ride home, hoping that, by the time he got there, things would fall into place. That his memory of the young man would supersede the reality of him and Cole would realize that he looked nothing like Rory.

That, Cole thought, would be a blessing.

CHAPTER 18

RORY SLAMMED the door behind him, locked it, and then leaned against it as though he were holding back a horde of zombies. He was trembling, gasping for air. Stars danced in his vision. His scalp prickled.

He'd dreamed of the moment almost from the time he'd returned— once he'd sorted out that two decades and not two days had passed. He'd imagined their reunion over and over. On good days, it would be a happy one where Cole had waited for him. On the worst days, Cole would see him and barely recall their association.

It was this latter part that scared Rory so much, scared him enough to let days pass without looking, for fear he'd find Cole was with someone else or he was far away or even that he'd died. Any of those things was possible.

But he was here. Close by! The shock of it made Rory go cold.

Greta glanced up from the couch, where she was perched with her legs folded beneath her, Kindle clutched in her hand. Her pince-nez glasses, for a moment, flashed when she looked up, from the sunlight pouring in through the picture window. "What's wrong with *you*? You look like you've seen a ghost."

Rory couldn't answer. He wasn't ready.

Just so she wouldn't carp too much, he held up a placating finger, indicating she should wait for a second. He went into the kitchen and filled a glass with water. He drank it down in one long swallow. Filled it again, did the same. It felt like his whole body was vibrating. In spite of the water, his mouth was dry. For a moment he stared out the window over the kitchen sink, as though he expected to see Cole lurking among the pots of asters.

But there was nothing going on back there save for Minnie stretched out on her side, asleep in a shaft of sunlight on the flagstone patio.

He set the glass down and hurried back to the living room. He crept to the front door again and peered out through the trio of windows at the top. The sidewalk in front of the house was now empty. A couple of leaves, brown and gold, pirouetted gracefully down to the sidewalk. A black Volvo sped by.

Maybe he was never there. Maybe I just imagined it.

"Are you going to tell me what's going on?" Greta had risen and walked over to him. She stood on tiptoes to look over Rory's shoulder out those same windows. "What? I don't see anything. Was someone following you?"

"No. I mean, yes." Rory put a hand to his forehead. Nausea welled up in his gut. He looked at his mother, her concerned features. "Can we sit down?"

Greta nodded and resumed her place on the couch. Rory took a chair kitty-corner to her at the end of the coffee table. He tried to slow his racing pulse with a few deep breaths with dubious success. Finally, when he thought the suspense was just about to kill his mom, he said, "I saw him."

"Who?"

"Cole." As though she might not remember, he supplied Cole's last name. "Weston. Cole Weston." He licked his lips nervously. "Swear to God, he was just outside. He followed me home."

"Really? Are you sure it was him?"

Rory nodded. "He's older—of course. But I'd know those eyes anywhere."

"Did you talk to him?" Her voice had a slight tremor, and Rory knew it was because she was afraid he had.

"Talk to him? No! No, I was too shocked. I think he was too."

Greta let out a little sigh that sounded like relief. "That's probably for the best." She toyed with the shut-down Kindle on the coffee table, as though she wanted to pick up her reading where she'd left off.

"What? Why do you say that? I loved him once, Mom." Rory looked down at the Persian rug, cream and blue, at his feet. "I still do." He moved the Kindle away from her so she'd be forced to peer into his eyes. "I thought we were a forever thing, you know, like you and Dad. I really believed we'd grow old together, maybe end up in rocking chairs facing the mountains in Palm Springs, tan and shriveled but still holding hands."

Greta gave him a smile he knew was intended to be kind. "That's sweet."

"I need to talk to him, Mom. I need to see him."

"It's not a good idea. He wouldn't understand. How could he? *I* don't even understand." She pulled her Kindle away from him and held it in her lap. Rory knew the book she was reading, *The Grays* by Whitley Strieber. He didn't want to ask her about why she chose that particular book.

Rory stared at her. She looked so worried, so concerned. He'd been living here, a secret, practically a prisoner with a very benign jailer, for two months now. Greta told him that, until they could figure out how to explain him, they should simply avoid contact with anyone who'd known Rory before his disappearance. Her reasoning was shaky, Rory thought, but he abided by it—to a point—because he felt a deep-seated guilt for shaking her up as he'd done, even if he was in no way responsible, even if he was as stymied about things as she. But still, his return was akin to someone coming back from the dead. And Rory couldn't imagine how that must feel. Nor could he imagine how others might deal with it.

And the truth was, he'd tried to look for Cole—in secret, when he could get out from under his mother's watchful eye. Many days, he'd simply hop on the "L" and wander around their old neighborhood in Rogers Park, hoping against hope he'd run into him in one of their old haunts. But the bar they favored, Charmers, was now gone—and so, apparently was Cole. The café on Sheridan Road they liked was filled now with Loyola students, not one of them nearly the age Cole would now be. None of the directories in the Wilmette library listed him. And the few feeble searches he'd done furtively online had also yielded nothing.

But until they could figure out an explanation for his presence? He didn't believe that day would ever come. He wondered daily about what that explanation would look like. In his mind there was only an empty gray mist where nothing moved. Sometimes, at night, he dreamed of weird stuff, stars, great moving clouds that looked alive, and most curiously, a sparse white-tiled room with stainless-steel fixtures. He didn't recall much about the room upon waking but felt an ineffable peace, a kind of embracing warmth.

So he felt he had no choice but to go along with her notion of keeping things quiet. To not let relatives and neighbors know. When, after a couple of weeks of feeling claustrophobic in the house, he demanded that he at least be allowed outside for walks, for fresh air, and to see human faces other than his mother's, grudgingly, she relented.

"And if you run into any of the neighbors," she told him, "who knew you from before, you just tell them you're my nephew, visiting me from Seattle while you check out colleges. You're thinking of Northwestern."

"You're crazy, Mom. We don't need that much of a backstory. Besides, haven't most of them moved, anyway?"

"I suppose you're right. But just be careful. Things are different now in the world. It's not as friendly, with everyone plugged into their phones or iPads or whatever. It's more dangerous. And I just don't know how people would react to seeing you, if they knew. They'd think it was some kind of resurrection. And I don't have a clue how on earth we'd spin that!"

Rory cut her some slack because, even though she'd never admit it, he suspected he knew the real reason for her wanting to keep him close, keep him all to herself—she was terrified of losing him again. It made sense. He had disappeared without warning, without a trace before. Who was to say it couldn't or wouldn't happen again, just like that?

He knew there was nothing to counter her fear. It wasn't irrational. And sometimes, late at night, as he gazed out the windows at the stars, the same fear crept up on him, as if an invisible presence had tiptoed behind him and placed an ice-cold hand on the base of his spine.

So he couldn't fault her for being afraid, for worrying that she'd lose him once more. He knew how much she loved him and how lonely she'd been, losing first him and then her husband, the only man she'd ever loved.

And his dad? What a shock to learn of his death. Rory was still trying to believe it was true. Coping with that reality was another whole issue—dealing with his grief and shock over the loss. His death was as fresh to Rory as if it had happened yesterday. Rory still expected to see him eating bacon and eggs when he came downstairs in the morning, that day's *Tribune* folded neatly into a quarter before him. Every time he saw his mother alone, fussing over Minnie, his heart clenched with longing for his dad.

Not that he didn't grieve for the loss of Cole. His dad was different, though. Dad was truly gone—Rory had visited his grave. Cole was out there somewhere. Rory could feel it in his bones—Cole was alive. He might have moved on, might have even forgotten Rory, but he knew he was still among the living. Rory wasn't ready to let go of that hope yet. And so he had yet to feel grief at Cole's loss. Where there was hope, Rory thought, there was less room for grieving.

He'd gotten used to his hidden-away existence. Sometimes, with the blackest of humor, he'd refer to himself as a latter-day Anne Frank.

The other issues Greta raised—how he would explain his appearance should he ever want to do anything practical like get a job, open a bank account, drive a car—made some degree of sense, but Rory knew this limbo would have to end at some point.

Maybe he'd shave his head and grow a beard to try to look older—though passing for fortysomething was a stretch. Could plastic surgeons *add* crow's feet and laugh lines, maybe a bit of a jowl? Would a hairdresser be willing to add a touch of gray to his thick auburn hair?

Maybe folks would come to accept him as the world's youngest-looking forty-three-year-old?

And these thoughts of aging brought him back to the present. Because Cole, the Cole whom he'd just seen, was now in his forties. Though still very attractive, he looked his age. Rory couldn't really be certain it was him. But that was only for a second. *We know people when we see them. It's almost instinctive. It's certainly intuitive. And it's always right.*

He looked levelly at his mom and repeated what he'd said before, knowing his wish had the potential to instill terror in her, to motivate impassioned protest. But she needed to hear it, and more, she needed to understand.

"I have to see him. I have to talk to him."

"Oh, why?" She couldn't keep the annoyance and frustration out of the short query. Her eyebrows came together in concern. She sat up straighter, placing both feet on the floor. "It's been such a long time, Rory. Even if that *was* Cole, which I doubt, he's moved on, sweetheart. Don't you think he has someone else by now? Don't you think he's made a life for himself without you? He could be married. Maybe he even has children. What good would it do to upset that particular applecart? You'll just open yourself up to heartache. And God knows what it would do to *his* life!"

The thought of Cole with someone else made Rory feel sick. It caused tears to spring to his eyes. Twenty years might have somehow mysteriously passed, but it didn't feel like it. He felt like he and Cole were still a couple, like the last time they'd laughed together, made love, shared a pizza on the couch, was days ago instead of years. "That's mean, Mom. Don't you know I really love him?"

Her features softened. "Which is exactly why you should leave him alone, son." She leaned forward so she could reach out and grasp his knee for a moment, squeeze it. "Twenty years, sweetie. Two decades. So much has had to have happened for him. No one—" And she cut herself off to let out a sharp bark of bitter laughter. "No one, save for you, stays the same for that long. Everyone changes. Physically. Emotionally. Spiritually. However you want to look at it, people *change*. Even their chemical composition is completely different. We slough off those old cells and replace them with new ones until we're someone else entirely."

"Yeah, yeah, I learned that in biology freshman year at New Trier."

"My point is—no good can come of you getting in touch with Cole, even if that *was* him you saw. What? You think you'll just pick up where you left off?" She shrugged, and her lips came together to make a little trembling frown. The expression telegraphed how much she ached for Rory. She leaned back into the couch cushions, her gaze down. After a moment she said, "I should let Minnie in. I've never seen a dog that loves the sun so much. She'd roast herself if I'd allow it."

"Quit changing the subject. I need to talk to him. I need to let him know that I'm not still missing, or dead, or whatever he thinks happened to me. I owe him that. As much as I loved, *love* him, I know he felt the same for me. He must have been out of his mind with worry when I went away."

His mother looked pensive. "He was. We searched for you together. I remember talking, comforting each other in the weeks and months after…." Her voice trailed off. "He was devastated." She gnawed at her lower lip. "We stayed in touch for a while, but gradually that petered out. Christmas cards. And then nothing." She let out a small shuddering sigh. "I don't know where he is anymore." She looked at Rory with hope. "Maybe he moved away?"

"I told you, Mom, I just saw him. I don't doubt it. I'm going to find him." Of course this wasn't the first time the idea of finding Cole had occurred to Rory. He'd pored through lots of resources online to locate Cole Weston, but he didn't show up, not anywhere, which made Rory worry that he was not simply off the grid, but dead.

But he couldn't be. He'd been outside. And Rory could just kick himself for not speaking to him when he'd had the chance. But if that was Cole, and Rory knew in his heart of hearts that it was, he could be found. Even if Rory had to hire a private investigator, he could find him.

"I don't know what will come of my finding him," Rory told Greta. "You're right—I'm sure he has his own life and we *won't* 'pick up where we left off.' But don't you think he deserves to know I'm alive? That I'm okay?"

Greta nodded. "I suppose so. In spite of all the mystery around you, I'm so glad you came home to me." She blurted the last of the words out in a little burst of a sob. She gathered herself up pretty quickly, reaching beneath the lenses of her glasses to dab the tears away. "But how will you explain you haven't aged?"

Rory felt compelled to joke, "You think he'll mind? Most fortysomething guys fantasize about attracting twentysomethings, right?"

"Oh, Rory." His mother shook her head. "That's not funny."

"No. I suppose it isn't. I guess we'll deal with that issue when we come to it. How did you and I know how to deal with it? How do we deal with it every day? Say it, Mom."

And she smiled a little, taking her cue. "It's a mystery."

Rory nodded. "And a miracle. Don't forget a miracle." And if he was a miracle, maybe Cole would be too. Maybe the real miracle would be that Cole was still alone and pining for him. Maybe Cole, in the absence of verification with something like a body, had hung on, waiting for him. And maybe, just maybe, they *could* pick up where they left off. And wouldn't that be a wonderful miracle?

Stranger things had certainly happened.

"Will you help me, Mother? Will you help me find him?"

She nodded, and in her exhalation, Rory heard defeat. "I don't think I have any choice. You're going to go down this road no matter what I think or say anyway. And besides, I spent most of my life as a librarian. Finding information comes second nature to me."

Rory stood. "Can we start right now?"

CHAPTER 19

COLE PEERED out the window at the courtyard. The first flakes of winter were falling, gentle, fluffy things, melting as soon as they hit the ground. The sky was an expanse of drama, bright blue here, dark gray and ominous there. Even though it was only November, it looked cold out there, and the fluffy snow could morph into a storm. Anyone who'd lived in Chicago for any length of time knew that.

It was eleven o'clock on a Thursday morning, and the condo was curiously silent. No TV on. No music playing. Tommy had left via Uber that morning for O'Hare to catch an 8:00 a.m. flight to Los Angeles, where he was the keynote speaker at a popular fan convention, built around new adult and young adult fiction. He'd be gone until Monday.

Cole, once such an extrovert, had, over the years, narrowed his world down almost exclusively to this one person, his husband. Sure, they had friends, mostly made by Tommy through his connection with Dora—straight suburban couples they'd have dinner with once a month or so. Otherwise their life together was pretty insulated. Tommy sometimes joked that, if one looked up the term "homebodies," there would be a picture of him and Cole. Cole would laugh and describe the scene—Tommy in the leather recliner, his iPad open on his lap, and Cole on the couch, remote in hand, scrolling through the latest offerings on Netflix. Once he found something suitable on which to binge, he'd pick up his phone and tap the UberEats app and order dinner. What with restaurant and food deliveries, the latest movies on Amazon Prime and Netflix, downloadable music and books, what reason, other than a medical emergency, did they have to leave the house?

Cole liked it that way, and each excursion out lately found them getting home earlier and earlier, pining for the simple comforts of their well-appointed but never lavish home.

So this morning, once he'd seen Tommy off outside, he came back and felt a little lost, as though a part of him were missing. Maybe it was, he thought, time for them to go down to the animal shelter in Chicago and give some lucky dog or cat a new and reliable home. They were both certainly around enough to dote on a little critter and to ensure its proper training!

He'd rattled around in the oversized condo for hours, drinking coffee, nibbling on some bacon he'd fried up earlier, scanning through hundreds of offerings on their big-screen TV and finding nothing he'd want to watch. Sometimes it seemed like the more there was on offer, the less appealing it became.

Cole knew he was just lonely, already missing Tommy. It was crazy, he told himself; he shouldn't be so dependent on another person. It was sad.

But it was the truth. Their life was, in a word, dull. But it was theirs. And it was enough. And though it lacked thrills and chills, it was all Cole wanted.

As he was making his way into the kitchen, hoping there was still some of that pastrami left in the fridge, he happened to look outside. It had stopped snowing, and the sky had brightened. Some of the clouds had been swept away by the wind. He also saw the mailman rolling his trolley through the courtyard.

Cole smiled and remembered the anticipation seeing the mailman used to bring. These days, though, there was rarely anything in the mailbox other than junk. Even bills didn't come in the mail anymore.

He'd forgotten the mailman sighting until much later, when he was stuffed full of a pastrami and Swiss on rye with spicy brown mustard and a bag of cheddar and sour cream chips that was definitely *not* meant for one person. The movie he'd finally landed on, an old Lana Turner weeper called *Imitation of Life*, had left his nose running and his cheeks wet. He was glad, in a way, Tommy wasn't here to witness the pathetic spectacle he was at the moment. Cole chuckled at himself.

He'd gone into the bathroom and was just beginning to fill the claw-foot tub with water when he remembered seeing the postman. He squirted a healthy amount of an herbal soak liquid Tommy had bought over at Lincoln Square into the water and headed off to run downstairs to check the mail.

In the marble-and-tile foyer, with its mica fixtures, Cole expected nothing less than a handful of fliers, envelopes gussied up to look official and/or important to trick you into opening them, and maybe a free offer from Jewel.

But there was only one envelope in the box, and wonder of wonders, it was something Cole hadn't seen in years—a hand-addressed letter. He turned it over curiously in his hands, considering sniffing it. It seemed like something that had time traveled, like a rotary phone or a black-and-white TV.

His name and address were half written/half printed on the front in black ink. The letters were blocky, a bit architectural—and vaguely familiar. Cole didn't know quite why, but the familiarity was there in his head, like a clue just out of reach. *This is from someone I know.*

There was no return address.

Cole simply stood there in the lobby for the longest time, staring down at the envelope. It incited both a giddy feeling of anticipation and also what he thought of as an inexplicable harbinger of dread. Warring within him was a desire to rip the envelope open right there in the lobby or to shred it up as much as he could in his hands without ever looking at it and deposit it in the blue recycle receptacle in the lobby's corner.

It wasn't until old Mrs. Borque came in, shaking the snow from her gray hair, that Cole was reminded he'd left the bath water running upstairs.

"Think we'll get more than eight inches?" she asked, her bright blue eyes regarding him, standing there in sweat shorts, a black T-shirt, and barefoot.

Cole panicked and answered in a way that could be taken the wrong way, but he didn't really think so. Mrs. Borque was over eighty.

"One can dream!" Cole called over his shoulder as he scampered up the stairs, hoping against hope he'd not find a flooded bathroom or—worse—his downstairs neighbor pounding on his door because her bathroom ceiling was bulging with water.

There was no one outside his unit, which was the first good news. The second good news was that, when he rushed to the bathroom, he got there in the very nick of time. The greenish water was just at the very top of the tub, a little of it trickling down the side. None of it had reached the floor yet. Cole grabbed the two porcelain handles and twisted them forcefully and suddenly. They both squeaked. Then he plunged his hand into the water and pulled out the rubber plug in the drain.

Just to be sure the tub didn't magically fill up again when he wasn't looking, Cole watched as the water drained down to about three-quarters full, arms folded across his chest.

And then he left the bathroom and went to sit on the bed with his letter. He didn't know why he had this eerie, prescient feeling about it. Maybe it was just because it seemed like an artifact from a bygone time.

Who got letters in the mail anymore? Why wouldn't someone just email, or text, or Facebook message—that's how people got in touch in the twenty-first century, for cryin' out loud!

The lettering also bothered him—he could have sworn he'd seen it before.

"Oh, for the love of Christ!" Cole shouted to the walls. "Would you just open the damn thing already?"

And he did. His gaze went immediately to the signature. And his mouth dropped open.

This has to be a hoax. A sick joke.

He started reading.

And stopped breathing. After, he'd guess he'd managed to hold his breath for the entire length of time it took to read the one-page letter. It started off with a shock and then simply continued on and on with a domino effect of shocks.

> *Dear Cole,*
>
> *Yeah, it's me, Rory. I know you'll be surprised to be hearing from me after all of these years. And I know the first thing that may (or may not) come to mind is this letter can't be real. That I'm dead. Or at least gone for good.*
>
> *I'm neither, and you know this letter isn't a prank or a hoax because we both know the one true thing: we saw each other a couple of weeks ago.*
>
> *Yeah, you followed me through Wilmette for a bit and watched as I went in my mom's door. She's still kickin', but my dad, sadly, passed away while I was gone.*
>
> *I'm writing now because I didn't want to just show up at your doorstep unannounced. Didn't want to send you into cardiac arrest!*
>
> *And you might wonder why I took two weeks to write to you. For one, it took Mom and me a little while to find a private investigator to locate you, and then we had to wait for his results. He was thorough! And fast! He got everything we needed overnight.*
>
> *But I needed a few days to process what he told me. I suppose I shouldn't have been surprised that you'd*

found someone else. And, wonder of wonders, what with the impossible happening while I was gone, you'd married him. I never thought I'd see such a thing for our people in my lifetime!

Anyway, I want to assure you I'm not out to interfere with your current life at all. I'm getting in touch to let you know that I'm okay and alive and well (at least physically). I know you must have lots of questions, where did you disappear to for twenty years being principle among them.

I wish I could tell you I have lots of answers. The truth of the matter is my story is too mysterious and confounding to be believed—at least in a letter. Sadly, that also holds true for real life. I'm sorry to be so enigmatic. But I still think we need to talk—face-to-face.

Which is why I'm writing. I hope we can meet. One confusing tidbit I will tell you is that, although twenty years has passed in your time, it seems more like a few days or a couple of weeks to me. Don't try to get your head around that. You won't. I can't. My mother can't.

But I need to see you, to talk to you, and to at least make you understand some things.

I know this letter is shocking and maybe even frightening. I wrote it out rather than using the computer in the hopes you'd recognize my handwriting. I also wrote, instead of calling or some other means of communication, because I wanted to give you your space.

Because, even though it breaks my heart to say this, I want you to have the ability to opt out. To say that you can't, or won't, see me. You don't have to explain.

You can, of course, relegate this letter to the trash (or the recycling bin, I guess, would be more correct these days). You can convince yourself it's a prank from some twisted sicko.

Whatever your thoughts are, I beg that you do one thing—let me know. Even if it's a one-word answer—no— at least I won't be left hanging, worrying and wondering if you'll get back to me. My address (although you know

*that—I live with Mom) and my phone number are below.
There's also an email address for my mom, which you can
reply to. I haven't set one up for myself yet.*

*But I hope you'll want to see me. I want to see you.
And I repeat—I'm not interested in interfering with your
life. I just think we need to talk and connect at least one
more time.*

Are you willing?
Please, please let me know, either way.

All my love,
Rory

Cole sat, dumbstruck, on the bed for a long time, just clutching
the letter tightly in his hand. Several thoughts went through his mind,
ranging from *This can't be real* to *Oh God, it's really him, a miracle has
happened.*

One line from it made him laugh, although it was a bitter snort. It
was when Rory said he didn't want to interfere with his life. That was
rich. Whatever Cole did with the letter, however he acted on the request,
his life had definitely been interfered with. In spades!

He got up after a while and opened his closet. He got down on his
knees and moved some stuff out from the closet floor, at last pulling out
the old shoebox in which he'd kept mementos from Rory.

He had to be sure. The handwriting in the letter did look familiar,
right off the bat, but it had been so long since he'd seen Rory's penmanship,
there was no way he could know for sure. Well, there was one way....

With a trembling hand, he opened the box and groped around in it
until his fingers landed on that yellow Post-it where, years ago, Rory had
poetically professed his love for him.

He looked from the Post-it to the letter several times.

The penmanship was exactly the same, right down to the way his
*A*s looked like triangles with a line slanting upward through them.

The only thing that seemed a little hinky to Cole was that people's
handwriting tended to change a bit over the years. His certainly had. And
maybe this pair of documents, written two decades apart, were a little *too*
alike to be believed.

Cole's rational mind wanted to absorb the notion that this was a hoax. It had to be.

But his heart had told him it wasn't. And he trusted his heart. The voice he heard as he read the letter, he thought, was Rory's. He hadn't even realized it at the time.

He also trusted his eyes, harkening back to the day when he'd seen Rory.

Of course he'd see him. He had to. If only to get his questions answered.

And the universe had even cleared the weekend for it.

Cole got up off his knees and went to get his phone.

He pondered calling for the longest time. But once he had his iPhone in hand and was seated in the leather recliner in the living room, he just couldn't bring himself to call.

In the end, he wrote Rory an email.

CHAPTER 20

GRETA ALMOST deleted the email. She didn't recognize the sender name, "West1971," and the subject line, "Getting back to you," had the ring of someone phishing. Why would someone she'd never heard of be "getting back" to her? She sighed. Email these days was lining right up with what used to be junk snail mail. Marketers ruined everything!

Yet... if it weren't for the first few words of the email, which she *could* read, thanks to Gmail revealing the opening of every email, she would have thrown the message into the trash or marked it as spam. Those initial words were, to put it mildly, intriguing, because they mentioned Rory:

Dear Rory, I don't know what to think.

When she saw her son's name, she had no choice but to open the email. Clearly it was intended for him, because it began, "Dear Rory," just like an old-fashioned letter. Greta had been on Rory to set up his own Gmail, but he didn't seem inclined—she wasn't sure why. Maybe the fact that he knew no one anymore who'd get in touch with him? The thought broke her heart. She needed to help him find a way to reintegrate himself back into life. Somehow. Yet it always seemed that goal could be put aside for another day.

But right now she was faced with a bit of a moral dilemma. Did she read on beyond the salutation? Or did she let her son have his privacy and call him to the computer, leaving the room so he could read in private? Of course she'd mark it as unread before calling him into the little den off the kitchen.

Since he'd returned, she knew she'd been overprotective. But it was with good reason. And that's the excuse she gave herself to read the email. She was being protective. And even after reading the message, she could still mark it as unread. Rory would be none the wiser.

Still, she felt guilty as she started reading. This wasn't like her, she told herself as she scanned line after line of the email. But when she finished, she found herself glad she'd pried for her son's sake, and again, on the horns of a moral dilemma.

She had a choice—she could delete the email or share it. And then a third possibility arose in her head: she could answer for Rory and say what she determined was best for the situation.

Oh God, sometimes it's too hard to be a mother.

She'd actually started writing a reply, a very deceitful one, casting herself in the role of her son and saying, in effect, that he needed to move on, when she stopped herself, covering her face with her hands. *You are not this person. You love your boy. He's a grown-up, and this is his decision to make.*

She deleted her response, throwing it in the little garbage can and, yes, marking the original message as unread.

She got up from the old porcelain-topped table she used as a desk and went into the family room, where she found Rory eating a bowl of cereal and watching a DVR'd segment of *The People's Court.*

She had to chuckle at his viewing choice, and then she went serious as other thoughts intruded. *You're making him a shut-in. And the worst possible thing might be happening—he might be starting to feel comfortable in this reclusiveness you insisted on. A good mother, like the one you hope you are, or at least aspire to be, helps her child find his wings so he can fly. Even if that means flying out of this nest....*

"What on earth? You like this show?"

Rory turned to her, a little dab of milk still on his chin, and it made Greta's heart clench—only a mother could see such an image and visualize a little boy with freckles and a cowlick. It almost made her regret her decision to come into the family room, to tell him what she was about to.

"It's okay. I like it when that judge gets herself wound up. She's more emotional than Judge Judy, and I guess that's what I like about her."

"You need to get out more! I hate to say it, but—"

Rory turned the TV off. "*You're* telling *me* to get out more? Mother, it's all I've wanted since I came back."

"And I'm starting to see the wisdom and necessity of that, God help me." She stared at the blank TV screen for a couple of moments, then said, "I'm sorry, Rory. I've been being too overprotective. But like any mother, I just don't want to see my son hurt."

Rory's eyebrows furrowed together in concern. "Has something happened?"

"What do you mean?"

"You're sounding like you've had a change of heart. What about your wanting to keep me under wraps because of the weird amnesia and not-aging thing? That we can't easily explain? Your words, not mine."

"Sometimes life gives us the impossible to deal with, mysteries we can't hope to fathom, but we go on, don't we? We don't hide away from the world." She sighed and then blurted out, "You have an email from Cole."

Rory said nothing for a long time. She identified certain emotions passing over his features like sun and shadow. *There's relief; there's shock; there's happiness; there's hope.* "And what? You read it?"

Greta had to resist the urge to lie, even though the falsehood was at the ready on the tip of her tongue. But she couldn't allow herself any more deceit. "Yes. I read it. I'm sorry. I'd like to say I opened it by mistake, but I didn't."

"It's okay." Rory stood. "I'd probably do the same thing."

"Really?"

"Yes, you're not perfect. I'm not perfect. Nobody's perfect. You yielded to a little temptation, but in the end, did the right thing." He began to move toward the den. Over his shoulder, he asked, "What did it say?"

Greta was still a little dumbfounded at her son's reaction, like their roles had suddenly reversed. "Why, he said he got your letter, and of course, he wants to see you." She went over to the french doors and let in Minnie, who scampered around both of their feet, sniffing and licking, before hopping up on the couch. "But you should read for yourself."

"I will." Again, Greta could feel the hope emanating off her son. It was almost an aroma. Just before he disappeared into the den, she offered, "I can take you to him if you want. I can drive you down to Evanston."

Their gazes met, and something passed between them—acceptance, maybe, understanding, for sure. Rory said, voice barely above a whisper, "Thanks, Mom. I might take you up on that."

She nodded. "And I won't stick around. You know how to use the Purple line to get back home."

"I do." He vanished into the office, and she imagined his joy at the very positive words from Cole—how he was at first skeptical, then shocked, and finally excited. There was no big reveal about Cole's life now. If there was someone else in the picture, Cole didn't mention it. So Greta hoped and prayed that somehow, through the passage of all these years, Cole had never forgotten her son and was still, in his own way, available to him.

Wouldn't that be sweet?

CHAPTER 21

COLE SAW him on the path below, and it took his breath away.

It was obvious Rory was totally unaware he was being watched, which gave Cole the opportunity to stare, to let his gaze linger on the sight of his old boyfriend, just a couple of stories below. The feeling that rose up in Cole was one of unreality, as though he were watching a movie instead of looking out his window. There was also a sense of love, of hope, flickering like a candle flame Cole thought had been extinguished long ago.

"How does he manage to still look exactly the same?" Cole wondered aloud.

Wherever Rory had gone, whatever he'd done, he had to have had plastic surgery. There was simply no other explanation. No one, no matter how well they took care of themselves, no matter their diet, exercise regime, or moisturizing routine, was able to hang on to their youth as Rory had.

It wasn't just his appearance either, though that was the main thing. There was this kidlike exuberance in his step. There was also a charming curiosity as Rory looked around the courtyard, at the stately maple tree at its center, at the cement planters filled with greenery and orange, yellow, and red asters.

Cole could also see he was searching for the door that would bring Rory to him. When he found the right one and stood before it, he withdrew a piece of folded-up paper from his pocket, presumably to check the address he had written down against the one right in front of him.

And then Rory just stilled, shifting his weight from one foot to the other, hands hanging at his sides. He looked up, and for a moment Cole thought he'd been caught spying. But then Rory's gaze moved on.

Cole sucked in a breath as Rory did something unexpected—he turned and began to walk rapidly from the courtyard.

What's he doing? Cole's excitement, fear, dread, anxiety—all those emotions took a sudden plummet as he watched Rory take them with him as he headed toward the gate.

Oh shit! He's changed his mind. Maybe he thought no good could come from this meeting? And maybe he'd be right....

Seeing him headed for the courtyard's exit made Cole realize how much he'd wanted to see Rory, to come face-to-face with him once more, to hear him speak, to maybe even touch him. And that desire, burning bright, also made Cole feel a stab of guilt deep within his gut, as though he were betraying Tommy. *And aren't you? What would he think if he knew you were entertaining a young man alone while he was away?* Cole snorted at the thought. Tommy wouldn't care. He trusted him implicitly. And that last thought ratcheted up the guilt even more.

He let out a sigh of relief as he saw Rory reenter the courtyard, saw the purpose in his stride as he headed for Cole's front door. He moved away from the window to grab his phone up off the coffee table, and almost simultaneous with that action, the screen lit up with the word Intercom and the buttons to accept or decline the call.

Because he had no idea what to say, he hit Speakerphone, pressed the right button that would unlatch the lock downstairs, and then listened as the door opened and slammed, as it always did, too hard.

Cole hung up and went to wait by the front door. After a moment footfalls sounded on the staircase, then on level ground as they approached his door.

Again, there was a long pause before Rory knocked. Cole could hear him outside, moving around, maybe pacing. He took a glance through the peephole and saw him standing there in a denim jacket, chinos, and a plain black T-shirt. He looked like a kid, someone young enough, Cole thought with heat rising to his cheeks, to be his son.

This is too weird.

Without waiting for him to knock, Cole at last and impatiently flung the door open wide.

They stood there for the longest time, a distance of only a few feet separating them, but years and years of time apart an immeasurable void. Cole couldn't believe this was happening, and his mind did a quick catalog of all the things that had happened around Rory's disappearance so long ago—the searches, the sleepless nights, the dashed hope, the media stories, the tip lines, the offered rewards, the crashing sorrow when a body was found in a forest preserve or dragged from the frigid waters of Lake Michigan. *Could this be him? Will there at last be some answers, some closure?* But there never was, because, well, Rory was alive.

And standing right in front of him.

Cole felt dizzy. For the first time in his life, he thought he might faint. He saw stars. And the air around Rory seemed to shimmer. Maybe this *was* a dream, after all. This wasn't possible, was it?

Cole had no words. He simply stood there, clutching the doorknob with a hand he knew had gone bloodless.

It was Rory who spoke first. "Well? Aren't you gonna ask me to come in?"

What should I do? Should we hug? Tripping over his own feet, Cole stumbled a little backward while at the same time opening the door wider. He took a big gulp of air, air he felt was suddenly in short supply.

"Sure," he said, voice only a whisper. He cleared his throat and said with a little more volume and force, "Come on in."

Rory edged by him, and Cole knew this was no imposter. He immediately recognized his scent, something clean, something identifiable only as Rory-smell. Maybe there was a hint of mint in the smell, a bit of body odor, even. Rory had never believed in deodorant.

But the scent was uniquely him.

Cole closed the door, and the two of them once again stood, at a loss for words, in the entryway. Rory smiled. *Oh my God. It's you. Just as I remember. This isn't the work of a brilliant plastic surgeon. This is a fuckin' miracle.* Cole gestured toward the living room, sweeping his hand wide. "Come on in and sit down."

Rory took a seat on the couch, back rigid, not touching the cushions. *Why, he's just as nervous as I am!* Cole could think of nothing to do but revert to banal social pleasantries. Otherwise, what would he say? Part of him wanted to scream.

"You want anything? I could make coffee or tea. Or if you want, uh, I think there's some Diet Coke in the fridge. Maybe a couple bottles of Tommy's kombucha."

Rory looked up from the glass surface of the coffee table at which he'd been staring. "It's really you," he said softly.

Cole sighed and plopped down on the couch next to Rory. "I should be saying that to you."

Silence, like a cloak, hung over them for the longest time. Forget soft drinks and everyday hospitality. This encounter was anything *but* everyday. It was surreal. A page out of a book of fantasy or science fiction stories.

Sleet tapped on the windows.

Rory nodded toward the glass. "It's raining."

Cole glanced dumbly at the smeared windowpanes. "How is this possible?" at last tumbled from his lips.

Rory said nothing for a while, staring off into space. Finally, he said, "We can't ask that."

"Why?" Cole wondered.

"Because there's no answer."

"There must be. There has to be some explanation."

"If there is, I can't tell you what it might be. I went out one night to grab a burger while you worked late—inventory, you said."

"Moody's?"

"Yup." Rory cocked his head. "How did you know?"

"Your waitress came forward after you'd gone missing. She was the last person to see you—" Cole caught himself. He was about to say "alive" because he'd said it so many times before. "Her name's Dora. She's our friend now."

Rory leaned forward a little. "Our?" The hurt on Rory's face was apparent.

"Let's not worry about that now. How did you get here?" Cole needed to know, in spite of Rory warning him not to ask. There had to be an explanation. There had to be. Otherwise Cole thought he'd lose his mind.

"The Purple line."

"C'mon. You know that's not what I mean. Where have you been all these years? How did you finally come back? Why were you never in touch with me?" Cole suddenly felt at the brink of tears.

Rory licked his lips and gazed around the room for a moment. "Could I maybe have that Diet Coke you mentioned? Or at least a glass of water?"

Cole hurried to comply. He simply grabbed a can from the fridge, popped it open, and brought it back to Rory.

Rory took the can and downed a long swallow. He belched. "I'm surprised you have this stuff. You never used to like it."

"How do you remember something like that? How do you remember what I was doing at work the night you disappeared? I barely remember that job myself."

"It was at Pier One in Evanston."

"Oh yeah." Cole laughed. "I hated that gig. But then I've hated almost every bit of gainful employment I've ever had. Pier One, wow, they went out of business years ago."

"I know. I tried to find you there," Rory said.

"You did?" Cole scratched his head. "I quit that job shortly after you were gone. I was lost without you, Rory. Couldn't sleep. Couldn't eat. Where were you?" Cole repeated, even though it was beginning to sink in that asking that question was useless.

Rory put a hand on Cole's hand. The touch was electric, and for a moment Cole wanted to snatch his hand away, but he didn't. After a while he relaxed into the touch. It felt good. Cole let his head loll back on the couch. Closed his eyes.

Rory said, "I remember, because for me, it wasn't that long ago. Like yesterday, or maybe just a few weeks ago. Certainly nothing like years or decades." He shrugged. "It all seems so recent."

Cole kept his eyes closed, partially because he hoped it would encourage Rory to keep talking and partly because it somehow felt more real without the visual. He could imagine himself young again—or that Rory had aged. Whatever—he saw them as more equal.

"Okay. Let me try and make these muddy waters clear. And don't expect much. But I'll try. The plain and bald truth is I remember pissing in an alley." And Rory continued to tell the tale of the night of his disappearance. Cole assumed his memory was so clear because it really wasn't that long ago—for Rory. How that was possible made Cole's head hurt.

Rory finished up, "I remember a bright light above me. I remember feeling like my feet were leaving the ground."

"Weird," Cole said. He snickered. "Maybe you were abducted by aliens." He laughed some more, his voice going a little high, edging hysteria.

Rory fell silent for a very long time. When he spoke, his voice was deliberate yet very soft. "Yeah. That's what I think. Seriously."

Cole opened his eyes and sat up, peering over at Rory. "You're fucking with me."

Rory squeezed Cole's hand. "You ever heard of time dilation, as it pertains to space travel?"

Cole just shook his head. He felt an odd lightness and again feared he might faint. This conversation could not be happening.

"It's physics. Einstein talks about it in some of his stuff. It basically involves his theory of relativity. If you google it, you might come up with a story about a couple of twins. In Einstein's theory, there's no such thing as 'time.' Time passes differently for different observers, depending on the observers' motion. So you take these twins—one stays home, on Earth. The other goes into space in a superfast vessel, almost as fast as the speed of light, before coming back. When the one twin does return, the traveling twin is markedly younger compared to the one who stayed home. The exact age difference depends on the details. For example, it could be that, aboard the spaceship, two years of flight time passed, but on Earth, a whopping thirty years had passed between the spaceship's departure and its return." Rory let go of Cole's hand and stood up to cross the room. He stared out the window.

"Cole. This is the only thing I can find that makes any sense. That might explain why I'm still in my twenties and you're—" Rory turned to look at Cole. "And you're in your forties."

Cole could think of nothing to say. This was just too odd. Too, pardon the pun, out of this world, too incredible. But yet, what Rory said made sense. He could think of no other way to explain things. At least ways that weren't as far out there as this one. Finally he asked, "And what do you remember? I mean, like, after that feeling of being lifted up?"

Rory returned to the couch, sat close to Cole. "Nothing. The whole time—which I guess now was twenty years—is a blank. The next thing I remember is being in the alley again. But it was morning, and everything looked different." He smiled. "Because it *was* different. I just didn't know it. I thought a few hours had gone by, when it was apparently a couple of decades." He talked on—about how he found his way to his mother, her wanting to keep him a secret, how he'd frantically searched for a way to explain what had happened to him, especially when he knew he'd be coming to see Cole. "I needed to have something to tell you. I didn't want you to think I'd just run off."

"That's what I would have thought. No doubt. But then there was the pesky piece of the puzzle that didn't fit—"

"My age. I know."

"Yes." Cole felt as though his head might explode from the fantastic—literally—ideas he was trying to process. "And you remember nothing else?"

"Well, I do remember the night we moved into our apartment." And Rory tried to make sense of what he'd seen in the sky, the fog bank, the membrane, whatever it was, and the figures that seemed to be dropping from its churning, ethereal body.

"Wow. Why didn't you tell me?"

"You would have said I was dreaming."

"I think I'm dreaming right now," Cole said. And suddenly intellect shut down and emotions took over. He couldn't process logical thought anymore, but he could feel. And what he felt was that Rory was here now. Rory was home.

He was alive! His love! He was right next to him. And Cole had believed he'd never have that again. He hiccupped out a short sob and then blurted, "Will you hold me?"

Rory took him in his arms and held him close. And it was suddenly as though no time had passed—not twenty minutes and certainly not twenty years. They were the boys, the young men they'd been, in the giddy throes of first love. Cole kept his eyes shut tight as he clung to Rory, their bodies meshing and merging on the couch. He didn't want to think, didn't want to process this moment.

Something like joy tingled through his system. This was a moment he'd waited for most of his adult life.

Cole's lips found Rory's. His mouth was real, and he parted his lips eagerly to admit Cole's tongue. This kiss, this connection, was suddenly so big it filled Cole's world. He forgot where he was, who he was, what mattered—there was only the pure unadulterated bliss of finding what he'd thought was forever lost.

This was right. This was elemental, what he'd been longing for, an antidote to years of boredom with Tommy.

And the name Tommy, at last, stopped Cole short. He broke away from Rory, pushing against his chest with the palm of his hand, a little breathless.

Rory's face was flushed, full of wonder. "What's wrong?"

Cole groped for the right words. He felt sick. "I can't do this. Not yet. Not until I make things right." *Am I really contemplating breaking Tommy's heart?* "I, uh, I have a husband now. Tommy. We've been together—" Cole's voice trailed off, and he closed his eyes. Now he was feeling he'd betrayed not Tommy, but Rory. But he had to admit the truth. "We've been together almost as long as you've been gone. He helped me, at first, to look for you. He was there when I needed someone, when my world seemed to be crashing down around me." Cole eyed Rory. The hurt on his face was apparent.

"I shouldn't have come here," Rory said, his voice barely above a whisper. "Mom told me not to, for this very reason." He laid a gentle hand on Cole's cheek, then took it away, as if he hadn't the right. Tears welled in his eyes but didn't fall. "I should have known, I *did* know, that someone like you wouldn't wait, holding a vigil for someone who might never come back. I knew you were married—it was in the private investigator's report." Rory looked away and drew in a deep, shuddering breath. "I'm sorry. I didn't come here to upset your life, to shake its foundations."

He stood. "I guess my main reason for coming was to let you know I was all right. I am all right. That I'm... alive." He smiled, and Cole thought he'd never witnessed such sadness in an expression he'd always thought was reserved exclusively for happiness.

"Oh, Rory. I do appreciate that. You don't know how your death— and I'm sorry to use that word, but there's a marker at Graceland for you—has clung to me through all these years. I think always, in the back of my mind, there was this hope that you'd come back. I knew it wasn't rational. But you're standing here, right in front of me, a miracle, a mystery, showing me that my hope wasn't without meaning, wasn't in vain—not really."

Rory took a few steps away from the couch. "But what do we do with it?"

The question hung in the air for a long time, like a cloud of smoke. Cole knew what the answer should be—"I do have a life now. You need to go and find your own. I want only the best for you. And maybe one day, somehow, we can be friends." But something in him resisted saying the words, resisted mightily. At last he said all he could say, all he was able to. "Can you give me some time? I need to think about where I am now." He looked into Rory's eyes and saw his own despair and sadness mirrored there. "I still do love you, Rory. But I also love Tommy. And I'll be damned if I know what I should do right at this very moment."

Rory nodded. "Okay. When you find out, you know where to reach me."

Cole closed his eyes and put his hands over his face. "I don't know what to think," he said through his hands, voice muffled. "But I do know this isn't done yet." He removed his hands to find an empty room, the front door still open.

It was as though Rory had never been there. And maybe he hadn't. Maybe it was all a dream. Even though Cole knew that wasn't true, he wished it were so. It would make life easier.

COLE THOUGHT going to bed was futile. He'd never sleep, not tonight. Especially after the phone call he'd just gotten from Tommy, where he told Cole how much he missed him and how he couldn't wait to be home with him again, in their own little bubble, in just a couple of days' time. Cole mouthed all the right reciprocal words and hung up with an "I love you," feeling numb and dazed.

Around 1:00 a.m., though, he thought he should at least try to get some sleep. Even if he only rested, it might alleviate some of the nausea and fatigue he'd felt since Rory departed. *What if he'd stayed?* Cole wondered as he threw back the quilt and the top sheet and crawled into bed in his boxers. He settled himself and mused that they might be lying together in this very bed, warm body pressed to warm body, as though no time had passed, as though the two of them were young men again—randy and in love.

He shook his head, turned out the light.

Contrary to his expectations, he was asleep within minutes.

HE WAKES to the sound of voices in the other room. He stirs sleepily, wondering if Tommy has come home, brought a friend with him. He turns to glance at the pale blue illuminated display of the combination charger/alarm clock they have on the nightstand. It's a little after two in the morning.

He rubs his eyes and sits up in bed.

He hears laughter floating in from the other room, just a normal and happy sound. But it's not. He doesn't hear Tommy's voice. The voices he hears both confuse, delight, and scare the hell out of him. They make no sense.

He puts his feet to the chilly hardwood floor. He creeps to the bedroom door and opens it.

Down the hallway, he can see there are lights on in the dining room. He knows he shut off the lights before going to bed.

Trying and failing to avoid creaking floorboards, he makes his way down the long, narrow hallway that leads to the "proper" part of the house, living room, huge dining room. As he comes into the living room, he stops, stunned by what he sees at the dining room table.

It's a common scene, and in that commonality there's a bizarre sense of unreality, one that almost makes him scream. He's sitting there—

with Rory. The two of them stare into one another's eyes, and they're laughing. Before them sit plates of food, spaghetti and meatballs in wide bowls, glasses half-full of red wine.

The weird thing, besides the obvious, the thing that paralyzes his limbs and closes his throat, is the fact that they're both the same age. Both in their twenties. Cole's hair is once more dark, thick, and lustrous. His face is unlined. All this matches Rory's appearance.

"Did you get enough to eat?" Cole asks.

And Rory replies, "Yeah, but I think I'll switch to beer now. For dessert."

They both chuckle again, and it's as though no time has passed between them.

He closes and opens his eyes, and the food and drink on the table are different now. There's a box from Giordano's Pizza, its lid stained with grease. There are cans of Old Style beer.

Cole looks to the sideboard, where he knows there's a little gallery of photos of him and Tommy. But they're all gone. Now they are pictures of Cole and Rory—on Fargo Beach, at the Lincoln Park Lagoon, Halsted Market Days, the two of them shirtless, arms flung around each other.

The books of Tommy's, once stacked at the edge of the sideboard, have vanished. In their place is a row of boxed computer games.

Rory's.

He sinks down to the floor in shock and simply watches as the young men's laughter turns to soulful gazes. As Rory rises to come to Cole, to kiss him, straddling his lap. He stares, biting his lips, as the kisses grow more passionate, as clothes are shed and dropped carelessly to the floor.

They're naked now. Cole is fucking Rory, who lies on his back on the table. Cole's slamming causes one of the beer cans to tumble to the floor. An explosion of foam spurts from the can, staining the ancient Persian rug beneath it dark.

And as he sits there, in the half-dark, the room itself changes, by dissolving degrees, into their old apartment on Fargo.

Maybe, Cole thinks, the past twenty years never happened.

Maybe they were only a dream.

WITH THAT thought Cole was jolted into the present, into harsh, cold reality. He lay in bed for a moment, gasping, erect, and disoriented.

A bright light from the window illuminated the room. Silvery, a glow as though someone were flashing a spotlight.

A weird thought came to him in this strange pocket between dream and wakefulness. *Are there aliens outside? Looking for me?*

He got up and hurried to the window, heart racing. In his mind he had only one thought. *This can work. We can be together again.* He didn't question it. He leaned his head against the window's glass, expecting to see a spacecraft, something like, maybe, the one in *Close Encounters of the Third Kind.*

But all that was out there was a full moon, shining bright.

CHAPTER 22

WHEN RORY opened the door, Greta looked up from the couch. She set down her Kindle. "So you went through with it?"

Rory plopped down, a little breathless, on the opposite end of the couch. "I went through with it. We met up. We talked." He almost added "It was magic." Like no time had passed… and for him that was kind of true.

He wasn't going to tell his mom about the passionate kisses and caresses, the indecision and confusion. He didn't know what to make of them himself. It felt like there was a weight on his brain. He needed to think. For a long time, he simply stared straight ahead, feeling sort of numb and lost.

"Son? Are you going to tell me what happened?"

Rory debated. Maybe he should just make an apology, say he was really tired and needed time alone. He'd head up to bed now if she didn't mind. They could talk in the morning. All that was true—and certainly understandable, given the circumstances.

Instead, not quite understanding why, he told her, "You were right."

She nodded; her face looked expectant and fearful. She gently laid a hand on his arm.

"He's married now. Happy. I was a shock, but more, I was an intrusion."

But was I? Or was I a relief? Was I the key to rescuing some lost joy from his past? Was I the key to making everything in both of our lives good and real again?

Greta moved toward him. Ever since Rory was little, Greta had cornered the market on comforting hugs. She knew just how to envelop a person in her arms and with her warmth, her presence, and her touch. There was something all-encompassing about it. And Rory imagined letting himself surrender to the magic of a mother's arms.

But he couldn't.

He leaned away. "No. Thanks, Mom, but I can't take your comfort right now. I'm too torn up. You still don't get how little time has passed for me. This is breaking my heart." He knew if he didn't get away soon, he'd begin to sob, and he didn't want her to witness that.

He stood. "I, uh, need to get to bed. Do you mind?"

"Of course not." She looked up at him, and he could see the sorrow in her eyes. "You *should* rest," she said softly. Instinctively, he knew his pain was her own. She wished she could take it away from him, would even gladly absorb it herself, no matter how bad it hurt. That's what good mothers wished for, even if was never possible.

He started up the stairs, and Greta called after him, "I'm so sorry, Rory. Try to sleep."

He couldn't help it. He said the words as much as a reminder to himself as corrective news for Greta. "He needs time to think about things. He doesn't know what he wants to do. Nothing's really decided."

He was certain his mom would protest, so he hurried up the stairs before she had a chance to say anything. In his room, behind the closed door, he fully expected her to come knocking. He actually waited for a long time. But his room remained silent, the dark a comforting presence.

Rory stripped down slowly, remembering, savoring the feel of Cole's body against his own. He luxuriated for a while in the questions of regret—*Why did this have to happen to me? Why did fate intervene with a perfectly happy life? Why can't I simply get back to what once was? Why does there have to be someone else?*

Those questions offered no succor, nor answers. Even regular life, in the absence of strange and mysterious circumstances, was full of such wondering.

Rory lay on his back, staring up. His eyes had adjusted enough to see the ceiling, and he smiled. There were stars up there—stickers he'd put up as a boy that once had some kind of light-absorbing property so that when he turned off the lights, they would dully glow. He'd always been delighted by them. They made him feel weightless before he drifted off to sleep, as though he were floating in space. He'd tell himself stories about rising up into the night sky, the stars warm and welcoming. He'd imagine reaching out and touching them and discovering they were not fiery and hot, as one would suppose, but infused with a golden warmth. Those were the kind of thoughts that lulled the boyhood Rory to sleep on many nights.

In the morning he'd wake to the sun's bright light and forget about the stars.

Now the stars didn't glow, but Rory imagined rising up to meet them, actually feeling that old sensation of weightlessness, of floating.

He drifted off, feeling a golden warmth not outside himself, but within.

CLOUDS SHIFT, revealing blue, green, brown.

There it is, just below. He doesn't know how he's seeing it, but he is—the blue orb of the earth, mottled with clouds, the shapes of the continents beneath the wisps and clusters of white clear, defined. It's breathtaking in the most literal sense of the word.

He's lying on something, something soft yet firm, holding him. He's strapped down but doesn't feel confined. There's a kind of peace running through him—a faithful certainty that no harm will come to him.

He turns his head to look into the large eyes of a strange face leaning over him. The emotion in those large, nearly bulging, and pupilless eyes doesn't frighten. Somehow it tells him this: Everything is happening exactly as it's supposed to be. That Rory is chosen. Rory is special. There's no need for anxiety because harm and danger are simply out of the question.

Rory knows all this. He "hears" all this without the creature opening its tiny slit of a mouth at all.

In his ears—the sound of his own heart, beating steadily and surely. He feels half-asleep, and the lights behind the creature, pulsing in illuminant gold, red, silver, and deep blue, are some of the most beautiful things he's ever seen.

But this vision, whatever it is, isn't so much about what Rory's seeing but what he's feeling. His eyelids flutter as he wonders how to describe it. Words like serenity, joy, *and* peace *filter in, like soft neon light or the twinkling of stars. God qualities, Rory thinks, although the thought comes to him unbidden.*

Simply, he wants nothing.

When he closes his eyes, it's with a smile on his face.

RORY WOKE to dim light in the bedroom, grayish, revealing his maple desk, the recliner in the corner, and the maple footboard of his bed all as dark shapes. His imagination, at this low level of dawn light, could make the inanimate objects in the room into other things, morphing them, bringing them to fanciful life.

But no. He turned one way and then the other, the fragments of his dream coming to him like a montage from a movie.

There was a bright glow at his window, forcing its way through the slats of the plantation shutters, landing on the carpet in stripes. Rory sat up, feeling a pulse, a kind of hum, coursing through him. Mesmerized, he threw off the covers and wandered over to the window, although he didn't really feel his feet making contact with the floor. It was as though he floated over to the window.

He opened the blind, and it was out there. So familiar. So strange. Fearsome and comforting all at once. The membrane, the craft, Rory was never sure what to call it. To him it was simply an amorphous gray cloud with dark edges that formed it into a kind of oval. It spun in the dusky blue-gray sky, and Rory swore he could feel it calling him, not in words or signs but within a place deep inside him. Dare he describe it as his heart?

He felt only love as he stared out. Safety. Security. A place of belonging.

He pressed his hand against the glass, and the cold pain was a shock.

The cloud vanished at the moment Rory felt the cold, shooting upward into the still-dark night sky.

CHAPTER 23

COLE FIDGETED on the couch in the living room, a bundle of nerves. Outside, the sun shone brightly, streaming in their floor-to-ceiling windows with glorious and buttery light.

The illumination somehow seemed wrong and out of place. It didn't match the somber and fearful emotions coursing through him. To Cole, the appropriate look for the day would be gray, dark clouds massing on the horizon. A threat of a deluge. Thunder rumbling.

He'd come to a decision.

Today, he knew, would be a sad day, even if he hadn't come to the conclusion that this day would be a bridge to a happier and more fulfilled future.

But not for everyone....

Last night, he'd hardly slept. He'd tossed and turned for hours until finally, around 2:00 a.m., he rose and went into the living room, dragging a blanket from the bed behind him, with his pillow tucked under one arm. He'd made a bed on the couch, and then, after he'd lain down, he aimed the remote at the TV, determined to watch whatever came up on its screen.

It was an old episode of *Green Acres* on TV Land.

No. He switched off the TV, despite his determination, and lay in the dark, thinking until the room lightened, filling with grayish shadows, reminding him that this was home.

Yet at one point he must have dozed, because he startled awake, thinking Rory was sitting on the big leather chair and ottoman at the foot of the couch. His hand reached out for Cole.

Many things coursed through his head—memories of him and Tommy mostly from the start, right up to the other day, when he headed out for LA. There were many, many happy memories! Good times shared with others, better times with just the two of them. They were a couple in every sense of the word. They did the old cliché of finishing each other's sentences.

But in the end, his mind kept coming back to Rory and the powerful heat of first love he shared with him. At last he shook his head, feeling as though God, fate, whatever you wanted to call the universal force, was giving them a second chance. He could think of no other reason that— let's call him God for lack of a better word—God would put Rory back in his life again, after all these years of mourning and longing had passed.

It was like a resurrection.

Yes. Rory was a gift.

A second chance.

And it wasn't saying too much to say Rory was a miracle.

How could Cole just let that pass by? Continue with the status quo? He needed to be with Rory again, to see where things would go.

And once his mind was made up, he sat up, and the sun, like an omen, burst into the room.

He felt horrible for knowing how much he was about to upset Tommy's world, but he had to do this, had to follow things to their logical—no, *miraculous*—conclusion.

Maybe Tommy would understand. Maybe not. And despite how Cole's heart ached for Tommy, that same organ was also buoyant with joy at being reunited with Rory.

He'd already showered and dressed. Eating anything was out of the question. Now he was simply sitting on the couch, hands folded in his lap, waiting for the sound of Tommy's key in the lock. He thought he should be buzzing with nerves but instead felt an eerie calm, as if all of this was preordained.

Tommy had texted about forty minutes ago that he'd just landed at O'Hare and would cab it home, what with it still being rush hour and all.

Cole figured he'd be home in the next ten or fifteen minutes, maybe a little longer, depending on how bad the traffic was on Oakton.

He simply sat there waiting, not allowing himself to think. He knew if he permitted himself to wonder, to ponder, he might feel regret, and with regret, he might change his mind. There was a certain inertia that kept long-term couples together, Cole knew, and he didn't want to succumb to it.

He needed to be strong. For Rory. For himself....

At last the jingle of Tommy's key chain, the smooth sound of the door key inserted into the lock....

Despite the numbness he felt, Cole tensed at the sound.

Now there was no time for regrets, because Tommy opened the door much too quickly. Cole felt a rush of cool air on his neck from the hallway and smelled the aroma of Tommy's Old Spice deodorant.

He turned, and he sucked in a breath, shocked at what he saw.

Tommy stood in the doorway, his suitcase behind him, his keys still in his right hand.

His left arm was in a sling.

His face, the left side of it anyway, was a mass of ugly yellow-purple bruises and near-black cuts. A big goose egg rose out of his forehead, looking painful. His left eye was nearly swollen shut. Cole watched him swallow and then witnessed Tommy's good eye swell up with a tear that ran down his face.

Cole was on his feet in a split second, rushing toward Tommy. All the thoughts of the night before and the morning vanished, along with Cole's resolve. "My God, what happened?"

"I got hit by a car."

Cole gathered Tommy up in his arms, pulling him into the living room and hugging him at the same time. The heat and solidity of his battered husband's body against Cole's own changed everything. In that one instant, before they even sat down, Cole knew with a certainty beyond any doubt that his place was with Tommy. It always had been. Their years and years together—of good times and bad, of being rich and poor, of nursing one another through sicknesses and celebrating vitality, of dark nights and sunny mornings, of eggs Benedict and bowls of Frosted Flakes, of concerts, plays, nights out dancing and evenings sprawled in front of the tube with a bowl of shared ice cream between them, of all the elements of a life together—they were a couple, welded as one by history, by friendship, by caring, and by love.

Seeing Tommy hurt as he was put Cole's head on straight, so to speak, set his mind clear. There was no choice. In the end he knew he'd devoted his life to this man, and he couldn't turn away. Not today. Not tomorrow. Not ever.

"Come in, sit down." Tommy followed him into the living room and plopped down on the couch, wincing when his injured arm hit the back of it. He splayed his legs out in front of him. He glanced at Cole, who hovered above him, not sitting, and burst out laughing.

"What?" A frightened grin flickered across his features.

"You should see yourself. You look like you're the one who got hit by a car. You're as white as a ghost!"

Cole sat next to Tommy and put an arm around him. "You got hit by a car! In LA! You're lucky to be alive." Cole knew that was the truth—what if he had died? This was what clarified *everything* for Cole. He didn't know how he could stand a world without Tommy in it. He was obviously sorry Tommy was hurt, but glad in a way that his injuries made things crystal clear about what was important.

"I know, I know." He touched Cole's face with his good hand. "I hate to say it, but it makes me feel better just to see you so concerned. I didn't tell you when it happened because I knew how much it would worry you." Tommy shifted uncomfortably on the couch. "It's nice to know someone cares about me so much."

Tears welled up and spilled out of Cole's eyes. Guilt rose too, but Cole decided he wouldn't mention that. "Of course I care, honey. I don't know what I would do if I lost you." And he set free a single choked sob.

"Now, now. You didn't lose me. Yeah, it looks bad. I won't be winning any beauty contests anytime soon! But luckily, this is all stuff that'll heal." He lifted the sling. "My arm isn't even broken, just badly sprained. And the bumps and bruises? They'll fade." He paused, and Cole knew he was staring at him.

But Cole couldn't help it—he sat, head in hands, and sobbed. Sobbed with relief that he hadn't done something stupid, sobbed with empathetic pain, sobbed with the joy and sorrow of narrowly averting a course he now knew was wrong.

"Sweetheart." Tommy leaned forward. "I'm touched that you're so choked up, but really, this is superficial stuff. I'll be okay."

"Oh, I know. I know." Cole choked out the words. He grabbed Tommy and held him close.

And Tommy, God bless him, allowed the bear hug, fierce and frightened, for what must have been a couple of very painful minutes. Then he pushed Cole away, hard. "You're hurting me, buddy."

"Sorry," Cole said, moving back a little, sniffling and dabbing at his eyes, trying to rein in his tears.

"Hate to break the spell, but I'd love to get into some sweats and have my crybaby man here fix me something to eat." Tommy cocked his head, smiling. "Would you mind? The food on the plane was crap, and I'm starving."

Cole swallowed hard and nodded. "Grilled cheese? Tomato soup?"

"That sounds wonderful. Five stars! Yes, please."

Awkwardly Tommy tried to rise up, and Cole scrambled to help. Once he got Tommy on his feet, he shuffled toward the bedroom. "I'll slip into something more comfortable while listening to you rattle pots and pans in the kitchen." He took a few more steps toward the hallway. Without turning around, he shouted back, "Bliss! Domestic bliss. I love it. And I love you."

Cole, halfway to the kitchen, called, "I'm so glad you're home." *Maybe more than you'll ever know.*

Cole headed into the kitchen, glad they had the makings for the comfort food lunch always on hand. Glad Tommy was home, right there, with him.

CHAPTER 24

THREE DAYS passed that set Rory's anxiety level ratcheting higher and higher. Three days when he heard nothing at all from Cole. He really didn't know that he had a right to expect anything, but still, that indomitable force known as hope made his heart swell and his scalp tingle every time there was a footfall on the front porch or the phone rang.

Could it be so blasé as this? he wondered, sitting at the bar in the kitchen, eating a bowl of Froot Loops. Would Cole be just like some of the men back in Rory's limited dating days who made their lack of interest clear simply by disappearing? Would Cole never see him again? Never show up? Was a nonanswer the truest answer of all?

He had to allow for the possibility, painful as it was. Cole had a life now, a real history. Rory couldn't hate him for that, couldn't really, save in the privacy of his most selfish thoughts, even wish things were otherwise.

Perhaps Cole was scared, and the best way to deal with what Rory knew was a supernatural situation, in the most literal sense of the word, was simply to ignore it.

And then there was a knock at the door, and Rory dropped his spoon to the floor. No one knocked. Not even the mailman.

Before he could rise from the stool, he heard Greta rushing down the stairs, heard the door swing open and her querulous, "Well, hello."

The blood rushed so hard in Rory's ears he couldn't make out what was said next. He simply sat, numb, until Greta appeared in the kitchen with Cole trailing behind her.

Rory found himself unable to align thought, tongue, and lips enough to form speech. Seconds ticked by as he simply stared at his mom and Cole, the two people he loved most in this world, this confusing world that had been snatched away and was now returned in completely different form.

Greta looked from Rory to Cole and then back again. She appeared to be afflicted with the same loss of speech as her son. Finally she found a way to say, "I'll leave you two alone." And with those words she hurried from the kitchen, trailed by Minnie. Rory heard her going up the front stairs, the soft closure of her bedroom door.

After a moment Rory held up his bowl. "Can I fix you some Froot Loops? They're delicious."

Cole smiled—but Rory couldn't help but detect the sadness around the edges of that smile—and shook his head. Cole looked good. He wore a baseball cap, a worn gray T-shirt, and a pair of black jeans. Combat boots. Rory could imagine him as twentysomething again, and a warmth like love and a heat like lust welled up, along with his heartbeat.

What has he come to tell me?

Why did he wait?

What will happen now?

Why do we have to bother with talking?

Cole looked down at the floor for a moment, then up at Rory. There was that sad smile again. Rory hated it in that moment, even though his love for Cole burned fiercely. He also knew, somehow, neither of them needed to say a word. With a seeming sixth sense, Rory was sure he knew the outcome of this visit. It was, to use the old maxim, written all over Cole's face.

"So you've thought about things, and you've come here to say—"

Cole cut him off with a raised hand. "Can we go for a walk? Maybe down to the lakefront?"

"Like we used to?" Rory asked. He had a sudden flash of blowing Cole on the boulders bordering the lake one night, a dark sky with a harvest moon glowing behind them. He pushed the memory away.

"Yeah," Cole said and smiled. "You want to?"

Rory said okay and got up. He rinsed out his bowl in the sink. He went into the living room, where he'd left his sneakers by the couch. He sat down to put them on, saying nothing. "Just let me go the bathroom before we go."

"No problem."

Rory went into the little powder room just off the front door. He sat down on the toilet without lowering his pants and covered his face with his hands. *This is what it's like—a lamb led to slaughter, walking up the steps to the gallows.* He thought briefly he should just stay in there until Cole gave up and went away. At least that way he wouldn't have to hear the words he knew would cleave his heart in two.

No. You owe him. Go.

Rory stood, flushed, and made some perfunctory splashes under the faucet. He opened the door. Cole hovered outside. "Okay, I'm ready," he said, even though it was a lie.

ONCE THEY got to Lake Michigan and were seated on a bluff overlooking the water—pewter gray and choppy today, with a single brave sailboat far out on its surface—they at last spoke. All during their walk through the residential streets and to this lookout point, they'd been silent.

Rory stared out at the lake, so much like the sea. He drew in a deep breath and at last blurted the words out. He couldn't stand the suspense any more. "You're staying with him." He shrugged, knowing from a place deep within he was right.

He didn't look at Cole but could almost feel him nodding. "Yes. I have to, Rory." Then, after drawing in a deep breath and then letting it out with a sigh, he said, "I want to."

Rory glanced over at him, and his heart ached. He could see that he wasn't the only one hurting from this encounter. Just to alleviate Cole's obvious pain, Rory forced himself to speak, to say the words he was certain Cole would, if given the time. "You've been together too long." He couldn't look at Cole, so he stared out at the water and continued, "You're like a family. You've shared too much. Lived too much—together. Ups and downs." Rory stopped suddenly. The lump in his throat prevented him from saying anything more than "Right?"

Cole didn't answer for a while, and it gave Rory the chance to look at him—for what he knew would be the last time. He was still Cole, of course, but he was *not* the man/boy he'd fallen in love with. A middle-aged man sat beside him now, still handsome, still sexy, but not the same person he'd once loved. That middle-aged man had a whole lifetime Rory knew nothing about—happiness, sadness, joy, despair, highs and lows. He drank in the lines on Cole's face, especially around his eyes. And then he noticed a pale white line cutting through one of his eyebrows—a scar. Rory caught his breath. The scar hadn't been there when they were together, all those years ago. How had Cole gotten it? Rory shrugged. The reason for the injury was only one of thousands of stories Rory would never know.

Cole startled Rory by taking Rory's hand in his own, intertwining their fingers, just as he used to do back when they were young lovers.

The touch was sweet and, at the same time, distressing. Rory wanted to both lean in to the feel of Cole's warmth and yank his hand away.

After a bit Cole said, "Right." And then he stopped again. A breeze lifted Rory's hair off his forehead. The wind picked up, and Rory could attribute the moisture in his eyes to it. "I'll always love you, Rory. I did back then, and I still do now." Cole cleared his throat, and Rory wanted to scream *So why are you saying goodbye?* But he didn't.

Cole went on, each word like a knife, cutting deeper, deeper. "You're still young. I don't know how, but you are. You don't know about spending a whole life with someone, making that person not just a spouse, but a part of you. I can't leave Tommy. If I did, it would hurt just as much as ripping my own arm off. I know, because I went through that pain when I lost you."

Rory allowed himself a quick glance at Cole, saw for a moment the young Cole sitting there before he morphed back into the strange middle-aged man who was really with him, clinging too tightly to his hand. He thought about protesting and telling Cole he'd *never* lost him, not really, and then let the thought drift away. "It must have been hard," Rory finally said, referring to his own disappearance.

"Brutal," Cole responded. "I can't go through it again. Rory, I'm not the same man I was when you left, when you were taken, whatever. We change, constantly, even you, despite your being so the same as you were. You have in you the seeds of some experience I know nothing about and that I suspect I could never understand."

Rory's mind flashed on a clean white-tiled room, on large eyes, on a kind oval face, gray. Then he forced his view back to the familiar—the sandy brush of the bluff below him. He knew it was his turn to not only speak, but also to absolve, to set this man free.

It was what love dictated.

So he said, "You're doing the right thing, Cole. You love your husband. Go back to him, with my blessing. Treasure our time together in the way back"—he grinned—"and continue to make good memories with Tommy. Let go of me. I'm a kid. I have a different life ahead of me. We're no longer a couple. We're no longer even compatible." Oh, how it hurt to say the words, but Rory felt he had to speak them. "I was going to call you today and tell you—we can never be, not again. But that doesn't mean what we once had wasn't beautiful. You still have it. Just not with me."

Rory pulled his hand out of Cole's and let it lay in his own lap. "Go."

"What?" Cole leaned toward him. "We still have so much more to talk about."

Rory gathered up the courage, the will, the love to turn and look Cole right in the eye. "No. We don't. Not really."

After a while Cole stood and took a couple of steps away from the bench. He looked back. "Aren't you coming?"

"You go on. I want to sit here for a while. Okay?"

Cole started away. And then he returned. Quickly, he squatted in front of Rory and planted a kiss, brief, sweet, on his lips. And then, without any more words, he walked away.

Rory couldn't bear to watch.

He sat, unmoving, for a long time. The day grew warmer. People walked by on the trail behind him, laughing and talking. The lake, somehow, magically changed color as the sky cleared, becoming bluer, almost aquamarine in the distance. A bicyclist, in his best spandex, sat down beside him at the opposite end of the bench. They nodded, but said nothing to each other.

When the sun got too hot on his neck and he feared getting burned, Rory at last made himself get up. He realized he'd thought almost nothing for the hour or two he'd sat there, a feat he would have thought impossible. But he also knew why. He craved numbness; he was blocking out the pain, the feeling of exclusion.

He began trudging home, if he could call it that, no longer feeling that he was part of this world.

THAT NIGHT, Rory awakened from a restless sleep with a bright light shining in his bedroom window. He smiled. Even before he got up and walked to the window to peer out at the night sky, he knew what was out there. It wasn't the moon or the stars.

It was the ship, the thing Rory referred to as the cloud, the membrane, but it was a ship, a device for hurtling through time and space, its appearance and workings far beyond his simple human comprehension. His fingers splayed on the window's glass, as if he wanted to touch the thing hanging in the clear night sky, surrounded by constellations of stars.

He forced himself to turn away. He dressed quickly in the dark—jeans, a hooded sweatshirt, boat shoes. In the kitchen, he found a scrap of paper and a pen. He quickly jotted:

Mom. I no longer belong here. I'm going back. It's the right thing. Know this isn't your fault. I'll always love you. See you in the stars…

Outside, his once-upon-a-time suburb was still. Rory hadn't thought to check the time, but from the silence, with not even the sound of traffic on Green Bay Road a few blocks over, he could assume it was in the wee hours of the morning.

Time doesn't really matter anymore, does it? What is time, anyway? A hypothesis. A man-made measurement to try to capture something elusive and unreal. It's making demarcations with chalk—in the air.

With feet that were sure of purpose and a mind filled with determination and wanting, Rory walked toward the beach east of his mother's house.

I don't fit anymore was a bit of a mantra in his head as he continued on to the sand. The waves of Lake Michigan crashed against the shore. The membrane hung above him like contained smoke after a fireworks display on a humid night.

He thought of Cole, of his mother, his late father. There was really no one else. To each of them, he said goodbye. "I love you," he said, his voice barely audible above the roar of the surf.

He kicked off his shoes and simply stood, raising his palms upward. He closed his eyes.

After a moment there was heat above him, the distant sound of machinery working. First his hair rose, like static electricity had gotten hold of it. Then warmth—an enveloping heat—and he realized his feet were no longer touching the sand.

Eyes shut, he rose into the night sky, and he smiled, tears streaming down his face.

The warmth was like strong arms around him, all-encompassing.

He was going home.

Real Men. True Love.

RICK R. REED draws inspiration from the lives of gay men to craft stories that quicken the heartbeat, engage emotions, and keep the pages turning. Although he dabbles in horror, dark suspense, and comedy, his attention always returns to the power of love. He's the award-winning and bestselling author of more than fifty works of published fiction and is forever at work on yet another book. Lambda Literary has called him: "A writer that doesn't disappoint…"

Rick lives in Palm Springs, CA, with his beloved husband and their Boston terrier.

Website: www.rickrreed.com
Blog: www.rickrreedreality.blogspot.com

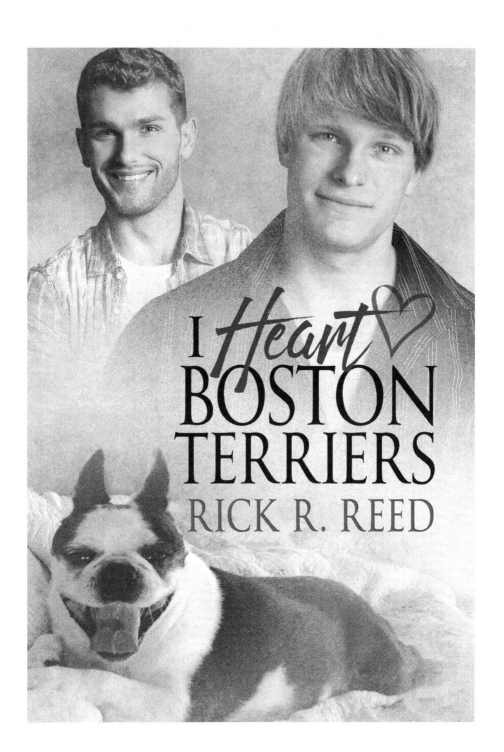

When Aaron finds Mavis, an emaciated and shy Boston terrier, at a pet adoption fair, his heart goes out to her—completely.

When Christian, manning the adoption fair for the Humane Society that autumn Saturday, finds Aaron, his heart goes out to him—completely.

This is a story about embracing love, whether it's for someone who walks on four legs or on two. Mavis's journey back to wholeness and finding her forever home parallels the story of two men discovering each other at the perfect moment—a moment that defies logic, propriety, and common sense. But when did love ever follow a rational course?

www.dreamspinnerpress.com

Three great stories.
One great love.

M4M

RICK R. REED

Finding and keeping love can be a challenge in the modern world of blogging, social media, and online dating, as one man will learn in this trilogy.

VGL Male Seeks Same

Poor Ethan Schwartz. At forty-two, he's alone, his bed is empty, and his HDTV is overworked. He's tried bars and other places where gay men are supposed to find each other, but it never works out. Maybe he should get a cat?

But his life is about to change…

NEG UB2

Poor Ethan. He's received the most shocking news a gay man can get—he's HIV positive. Until today his life was perfect, with a job he loves and Brian, who could be "the one." The one to complete him and fill his lonely life with laughter, hot sex, and romance.

But Ethan's in for another shock. Could Brian have infected him?

STATUS UPDATES

Alone again, Ethan wonders if life is worth living, even with a cat. When an old nemesis sends a Facebook friend request, Ethan is suspicious but intrigued. It seems this old acquaintance has turned his life around, and the changes might hold the key to Ethan getting a new lease on life… and love.

www.dreamspinnerpress.com

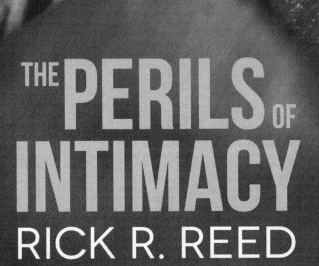

THE PERILS OF
INTIMACY
RICK R. REED

Jimmy and Marc make an adorable couple. Jimmy's kindness and clean-cut cuteness radiate out of him like light. Marc, although a bit older, complements Jimmy with his humor and his openness to love.

But between them, a dark secret lurks, one with the power to destroy.

See, when Marc believes he's meeting Jimmy for the first time in the diner where he works, he's wrong.

Marc has no recollection of their original encounter because the wholesome Jimmy of today couldn't be more different than he was two years ago. Back then, Jimmy sported multiple piercings, long bleached dreadlocks, and facial hair. He was painfully skinny—and a meth addict. The drug transformed him into a different person—a lying, conniving thief who robbed Mark blind during their one-night stand.

Marc doesn't associate the memory of a hookup gone horribly wrong with this fresh-faced, smiling twentysomething…. but Jimmy knows. As they begin a dance of love and attraction, will Jimmy be brave enough to reveal the truth? And if he does, will Marc be able to forgive him? Can he see Jimmy for the man he is now and not the addict he was? The answers will depend on whether true love holds enough light to shine through the darkness of past mistakes.

www.dreamspinnerpress.com